P9-CQR-191

THE RULES
OF WOLFE

Other Works
By James Carlos Blake

Novels
Country of the Bad Wolfes
The Killings of Stanley Ketchel
Handsome Harry
Under the Skin
A World of Thieves
Wildwood Boys
Red Grass River
In the Rogue Blood
The Friends of Pancho Villa
The Pistoleer

Collection
Borderlands

THE RULES
OF WOLFE

A BORDER NOIR

JAMES CARLOS BLAKE

The Mysterious Press
New York

Published simultaneously in Canada
Printed in the United States of America

FIRST EDITION

ISBN-13: 978-0-8021-2129-5

The Mysterious Press
an imprint of Grove/Atlantic, Inc.
841 Broadway
New York, NY 10003

Distributed by Publishers Group West

www.groveatlantic.com

13 14 15 16   10 9 8 7 6 5 4 3 2 1

In memory of

JUAN CANO BLAKE

You're going to have things to repent, boy. . . . That's one of the best things there is. You can always decide whether to repent them or not. But the thing is to have them.

—Ernest Hemingway, "The Last Good Country"

. . . unknowing youth, savage with health and armed to the teeth with time.

—Philip Roth, *Exit Ghost*

There is nothing either good or bad, but thinking makes it so.

—William Shakespeare, *Hamlet*

Life *is* trouble. Only death is not. To be alive is to undo your belt and *look* for trouble.

—Nikos Kazantzakis, *Zorba the Greek*

PROLOGUE

Rudy and Frank

Eddie Gato pleaded with us to take him on that run last winter but we said no. We'd been having the same argument with him for months. So had others in the family. He said we didn't have to let anybody else know—we could keep it between us. Frank told him that's not how we do things, not among ourselves, and if he didn't know that by now he still had things to learn.

Frank's my big brother. Eddie's our cousin and was all of nineteen years old.

"I've got everything it takes for this business," Eddie said, "and you guys know *that*."

He did have what it takes, no question about it, and I understood his frustration. But that wasn't the point. For the umpteenth time, I told him if he really wanted to work with us all he had to do was hold to the rule.

"That's another three *years*," Eddie said.

"That's how it works," Frank said, stroking his mustache the way he does when he's tired of arguing.

"Fuck the rule," Eddie said, and headed for the door, muttering something under his breath that sounded very much like "And both you too."

I said, "What was that?" But he kept going and didn't quite slam the door behind him.

Frank was right. The kid had things to learn.

We're a large family, we Wolfes. About half of us live in Cameron County, Texas, and most of the rest in Mexico City. Our Mexico City kin own a couple of investment firms and are partners in one of the country's largest banks. They're also among the capital's social elite, but because several of them have "Jaguaro" as their first or second name, they get a lot of ribbing from their friends about being connected to the shadowy organization called Los Jaguaros, reputed to be a major supplier of arms to some of the criminal cartels. The Mexican Wolfes accept this friendly teasing with good humor and the often expressed wish that their own business might someday be as profitable as the Jaguaros' is said to be.

The truth is, they *are* Los Jaguaros, and we Texas Wolfes not only provide much of their supply, we now and then deliver it to their buyers. It was their guns Frank and I were carrying on that January run Eddie had begged to go on.

The load was three cases of HK-nine pistols and two of M-4 carbines. The buyer was a Tuxpan outfit called Los Cuernos, a small bunch reputed to be in league with the Gulf cartel. It was the first time the Jaguaros had sold to Los Cuernos, and they stressed that point to us in warning to be extra careful. But we always are, whether we're delivering to somebody for the first time or the tenth. We know our business.

The transfer was set for midnight at coordinates a half mile offshore and around twelve miles north of Tampico. The Cuernos had been instructed to get there before us, in a shrimp boat with its nets deployed and three green lights strung vertically from the bow stem. We were in a small trawler rig of false Mexican registry. It had a modified hull for shallow draft and greater speed, and a pair of Hemi engines that could pull your head back when you hit the throttles.

I was at the wheel and Frank was scanning forward with the big 180×70s, looking for the green lights as we drew near the rendezvous spot. A cool offshore breeze carried the tangy smells of the estuaries. The sky encrusted with stars. An amber crescent moon low over the black mainland. The shrimper should have been in sight by then but the only vessel we could see was a tanker on the horizon.

We didn't like the feel of things, and I brought us to a stop a half mile shy of the transfer point. We each had a Browning nine in our waistband, and the wheelhouse locker held a pair of Mossberg 12-gauge pumps holding buckshot loads. With the engines idling we bobbed on the easy swells while Frank kept panning southward with the big glasses.

Then came the faint growl of an engine cranking up near the dark shoreline. And then the unmistakable rumble of it heading our way.

"Speedboat," Frank said. "It's a rip."

He switched off the running lights and I spun the wheel to starboard and gunned the Hemis. The acceleration leaned us rearward as the prow rose and we sped toward the barrier of rocky islands forming the outer rim of a lagoon. Frank checked the GPS and shouted a bearing for the nearest inlet. They were running without lights too and we still couldn't see them against the southward coast, but we knew they were trying to cut us off. They could've done it easy if the transfer point had been farther out or we'd made the mistake of getting closer to them before stopping. But then, if we'd done that, they would've nailed us out there. They were cowboys. Come fast and hard and shooting, take you out quick.

I had to slow down for the inlet, and my gut tightened at the roar of them closing on us. They were near enough now for us to see it was one of those open military speedsters but we couldn't tell how many guys were in it.

As I steered into the passage, they cut back on their engine and opened up with automatic rifles, the rounds smacking against the wheelhouse, popping through its glass. Then we were in the lagoon and out of their view, and the question now was whether they knew the place as well as we did.

The lagoon is full of shadowy palm hammocks, but the main channel's open to the sky and I could see well enough to hold to it. We snaked around the hammocks and went past two branching narrower channels before I turned into the next one. I cut off the engines and we bumped to a halt against a mangrove root in the darkness of the overhanging palms.

We figured that if they were familiar with the lagoon they'd play it smart, post a guy at the inlet we came through and patrol the other cuts along the outer bank where we might slip out. We had a plan for that.

But they came in after us. Rumbling slowly up the main channel. Cowboys. Afraid of nothing.

Frank took an angle-head flashlight out of the locker and clipped it to his belt, then handed me a flare gun and one of the Mossbergs. We could've laughed out loud and they wouldn't have heard us over their engine. We hustled out of the boat, crabs scuttling over our boots, some crunching underfoot, and took positions about twenty feet apart on higher ground from which we could see the main channel. I crouched beside a palm that curved sideways and gave me a clear view of the overhead sky.

We heard the boat getting closer. Then its dark form appeared around the channel bend.

When it came abreast of me, not ten yards away, I pointed the flare gun straight up and fired, the discharge muffled by the loudness of the motor.

The flare was set with a quick fuse and burst into a white incandescence about forty feet up, starkly illuminating the five of them, instinctively gaping up at the blinding light—and we started blasting, holding down our triggers after our first shot and pumping the slides as fast as we could in a rapid-fire volley. At such close range in an open boat, they had no chance at all, the buckshot tearing them apart, blowing away portions of them, removing most of the head of the guy at the wheel—who fell against the throttle so that the speedboat roared and veered into the opposite bank and rose straight up and almost completely out of the water before keeling over and crashing back into the channel with a terrific splash and crackling of steam.

They didn't get off a round. It was over before the oscillating parachute flare descended into a palm, gave a few more sputters, and died. And the darkness closed around us again.

Frank turned on the flashlight, holding it out to the side in one hand, his pistol in the other. His beam found each of them in turn, all in awkward sprawls and none moving or making a sound. I set the Mossberg aside and went down the bank and took out the Browning and held it over my head as I waded across the chest-high channel, then slogged out and slipped the pistol back into my pants. Frank held the light on the body nearest to me and I started searching pockets.

The third guy I tried had the money. A wad of American currency that on later count would total exactly what they were supposed to pay us. So why the cross? Their boss put them up to it? They take it on themselves to try to impress him by stealing the load? They sell *him* out? Who the hell knows? It didn't matter to us. This was a Mexican bunch, the Jaguaros' concern. We'd tell them what happened and they'd take it from there.

Then a voice croaked, "Mátame . . . por amor de Dios."

Frank's light flicked over to a guy on his back at the bottom of the bank slope, his legs in the water. One of the two I hadn't searched. Most of his side had been ripped away and the flashlight exposed a wreckage of ribs and viscera. Unbelievable what a body can survive even for a little while. He wasn't much more than a boy, seventeen, eighteen. A boy who'd been all set to kill us.

"Por favor . . . los jaibos. Me van . . . a comer."

He was right. You could hear the rustling and clickings of the crabs on the move in the dark. Converging on the fresh bounty. They'd start eating him while he was still alive.

I took out the Browning and cocked it and held the muzzle a few inches from his forehead. His eyes rolled up to regard it. And I fired.

I would've done it in any case. When you make a deal you stick to it. Rock-hard rule. You don't renege, you don't sell out. You hold up your end and expect the other party to do the same. If the other party doesn't, you're entitled to deal with every man of it as you see fit in order to set things right.

No—you're more than entitled. You're obligated. Or the rule would mean nothing.

⌒∞⌒

As always after a job that takes us anywhere near Tampico, we spent the next few days there. A pleasant laid-back town, excellent for recouping one's mellow. We dined well on the local cuisine, danced with lots of girls to the tierra caliente music in the plazas, did some cantina crawling. All in all enjoyed ourselves plenty.

At some point it occurred to us that this was the first time we'd ever had any real trouble on a Tampico run. And that Eddie Gato of course would've loved it.

Then we got back home and heard all about the family fight and that Eddie was long gone.

SONORA

FRIDAY

1

Eddie

Eddie Gato Wolfe watches the plume of dust rise from the distant shimmer of ground heat and begin to come his way like some badland apparition. He cannot account for his ominous impression of it. He is not given to apprehensive fancies and anyway knows that the dust is from a motor caravan bringing the Boss's people. Even so, you should never disregard a foreboding of threat—a presentiment, intuition, hunch, call it what you will. It's a rule. But then his family has many rules, and although some of them are more deeply rooted in him than he knows, there is one he has refused to abide by. That is why he is here on this late summer afternoon, in this desert watchtower of Rancho del Sol, at such far remove from home.

And then as abruptly as it came to him, the spectral notion passes. The dust now looks only like dust as it carries over the sunburned stony terrain of scrub brush and cactus and skeletal trees. He chides himself for his momentary illusion and lowers the binoculars and calls down to the courtyard, Here they come!

Flores, the security chief, gives orders and his men leave off flirting with the maids and hustle to their posts. The servants make for their stations. The security men are armed with AKs, the compound guards with M-16s. In the watchtower Eddie Gato mans a .50-caliber machine gun loaded with armor-piercing rounds.

For a little over two months the only inhabitants of Rancho del Sol have been Eddie Gato and the three other resident guards, plus an old married couple that does the cooking and laundry and sundry other chores, and a gardener of indeterminate age who keeps to himself. Then four days ago the ranch received notice from Culiacán that a party of guests would be arriving on Friday. The next morning a crew of maids and other workers came from the village of Loma Baja to begin getting the place ready. Eleven miles from the rancho but a part of its property, Loma Baja is flanked by the only local parcel of ground suitable for the airstrip the Boss put there for his small jet plane, and the only bus in the village was supplied by the Boss to transport workers to the rancho. Once a community of goatherds, Loma Baja now exists for no purpose but to provide occasional labor for the rancho and to maintain the landing field and the garage alongside it that houses the Boss's Cadillac Escalade.

On Wednesday, the dapper Flores and his security team showed up, plus a communications crew with its load of equipment. They had all flown from Culiacán to Ciudad Obregón and then driven to the rancho in six dark-windowed SUVs of various makes. Flores posted pairs of armed guards at roadside points fifteen and seven miles west of Loma Baja, and another two guards on the crude road from the village to the compound, where he at once set up a security perimeter. Then yesterday came the trucks with their large cargoes of food and spirits, plus a chef and his kitchen staff.

And now, under the swelling billows of dust, here come the guests.

Flores has informed the staff that the Boss himself has been detained by last-minute business and will not come until midday tomorrow, when he and his brother, El Segundo—the Company's second in command—arrive in Loma Baja in the jet.

Eddie Gato is the youngest of the four rancho guards, having turned twenty in May, and he is one of the two newest, the other being twenty-two-year-old Neto Rincón. Both of them have been here four months. Javier Monte, also twenty-two, has been here ten months, and Jorge Santos, the twenty-seven-year-old guard captain, more than six years.

There is really no need for guards against thieves. The region has few inhabitants and they all know whose rancho this is and nobody would dare to steal from it even if it were left unattended and all its doors and windows open wide. But it is imperative to guard against infiltrators who may attempt to plant surveillance devices or explosives. The military. The police. Business competitors. Whoever.

The four guards work a regular rotation of eight-hour shifts in the watchtower so that every fourth day one of them has a full day off. They have ample diversion in their off-duty hours. The compound has a swimming pool, billiard tables, a library, satellite television. There are video games and a vast collection of music CDs and of DVDs ranging from the latest Hollywood movies to the best pornography on the market. There is a small gymnasium.

There is a target range behind the house. The kitchen is always amply stocked and the old woman is a good cook. To satisfy their sexual urges they can go into Loma Baja and avail themselves of its handful of homely whores.

There are, however, stringent restrictions. The guards are forbidden to possess a passport, and any man found to be hiding one will be dealt with summarily. There is no telephone line to the rancho, and although there is a cell tower in the form of a flagpole displaying the national flag, guards are not permitted to have cellular phones and are prohibited from using the phones supplied to the old couple for contact with the Company, each of which is destroyed after a single call. Drug use is certainly forbidden, and the guards may not possess liquor on the property. The large bar lounge in the main house is kept locked when the Boss is away, and on his order the sole cantina in Loma Baja was years ago razed and the village told to stay dry. The guards may drink only on their day off and someplace other than the rancho and Loma Baja, and the old couple is under strict directive to report any man they suspect of being drunk or having booze on the property. On his free day, every guard in his turn usually chooses to go to Ciudad Obregón in one of the compound Jeeps. The city is seventy miles away in a straight line but almost twice that on the odometer because of the serpentine route from the compound to the state highway, a drive of more than three hours. The Hotel Rey in Obregón is available to the guards at no charge. In addition to a fine cantina, the hotel has a resident cadre of whores better-looking than those of Loma Baja—though in Eddie Gato's estimation not by much.

Eddie and Neto were informed of the rules before they accepted the job, and when they arrived, they and their baggage were searched and the guard captain Jorge Santos advised them to take the rules very seriously. A guard under the influence of

drugs or alcohol was an intolerable threat to security. The two guys
they were replacing had been dismissed because the old couple
had smelled liquor on them and made a phone call. The next day
four security men arrived from Obregón and searched the guards'
quarters and found a bottle under a mattress. The guards admitted
they'd sometimes take a drink in the room but swore neither of
them had ever been drunk on the rancho or in the village. The
man in charge only shrugged and he and another man took the
guards away. The other two security men stayed behind to fill in
for them until permanent replacements were sent. But because
the Boss believed that ranch guards should be willing volunteers
and would not have anyone assigned there who did not want
the job, it was nearly three weeks before Eddie and Neto were
selected as the replacements.

Neto said he thought the two guards deserved to lose their
jobs but it galled him that the old couple had snitched. He said
the guards should have told them they'd break their neck if they
ever ratted on them.

Jorge Santos said it would be foolish to threaten the old
ones. Like us, they must do as told, he said. And anyway, who do
you think they are more afraid of, us or the Boss?

He told Eddie and Neto a story about one of the Boss's
nieces and a Company lawyer who was also an old friend. The
niece and the lawyer went on a date one night to a notorious
nightclub and both got very drunk. While they were dancing
she stripped to her underwear as the crowd cheered her on and
she ended up sucking the lawyer's cock on the dance floor in
front of everyone. When word of the incident reached the Boss
the next day, he was embarrassed and extremely displeased. The
lawyer was having lunch with some friends when he excused
himself to go to the men's room and that was the last anyone saw

of him. It was rumored that he had been slowly towed behind a boat in the Sea of Cortéz until the sharks were finished with him. Others said his punishment was in truth not so severe, that he'd only had his dick cut off and was sent to a small Company office in the Yucatán for the rest of his life. As for the girl, it was said she had been placed in a ratty whorehouse in Los Mochis and anybody could have her for ten pesos. She was there for several months and became infected with an awful disease and then was removed to a convent hospital somewhere where she has since spent her days cleaning up shit and vomit.

My point, Jorge said, is this. If the Boss will punish one of his friends that way for displeasing him, if he'll punish a *niece* that way, how do you think he would punish the old couple? Punish *you*?

Eddie Gato asked what became of the fired guards. Jorge said he had heard they were taken to Flores, who told them that because they liked to drink he was going to treat them to all the liquor they could hold. He had them stripped naked and drowned in barrels of rum. The barrels were then sealed with clear glass tops so you could see the men's upturned faces, their bulging eyes and bared teeth. The barrels were said to be in the courtyard of the Boss's Culiacán offices where everyone who comes and goes can have a good look. A sign on the barrels says "Drink Responsibly."

It is easy to understand why there are so few willing to be a rancho guard. Almost the only ones who volunteer for the job are young recruits ready to do anything—live in the desert, forgo liquor and phone communication, make do with unattractive whores—just to be part of the Company. But the Boss understands how hard it can be for a man to live in such isolate conditions for very long, and he permits reassignment to any guard who wants it after a year at the rancho. A guard who likes the job can keep it as long as he wishes, but it seems to Eddie that only a man of reclusive nature and minimal appetites could ever choose to stay here longer than the requisite year.

Like the other guards, Eddie is not a heavy drinker, so the booze restriction is no burden. But unlike the others, he receives no pleasure at all from the village whores and very little from those of the Hotel Rey. Their lack of allure has limited his satisfaction to that of scratching an itch. He keenly misses the sort of girls he has enjoyed since he was thirteen. None of them less than very pretty and all of them sweetly clean. He misses the fun of sexual banter, of seducing and being seduced. But this job was the only ready entry into the sort of life he desires and he took it with the certainty that he could bear its privations until he earned a transfer to a better post. A smuggling crew is his ambition. If he can't have that at first, well, the job of an enforcer or a bodyguard or collector will suit him too. Even chauffeur to a chief will suffice, if that is the only position open. Any such duty would not only be more exciting than this one but also get him closer to a smuggling branch of the Company. And of course would offer him more interesting cities than Obregón. Larger cities, with their greater numbers of pretty women.

Still, before he can get a transfer he must endure eight more months at the rancho, and the boredom of the job already weighs on him. He no longer even wears his watch, having no desire to remind himself how slowly time is passing.

The Boss

"Rancho" is too thin a term for this retreat at the foot of the western slope of the Sierra Madre. It is a renovated hacienda, an expansive property whose walled compound contains several courtyards and a sprawling main house of two stories with dozens of small suites. The estate's most exceptional feature is the cold-water stream running down to it from the mountains, so that even in this lower reach of the Sonoran Desert the courtyard trees and gardens are lush and the swimming pool is always full. The summer days are of course very hot, but under the looming sierra the rancho nights are often cool even during the dog days.

The Boss—whom the news media have made widely known as La Navaja but to his people is always and simply the Boss—loves the seclusion here. Loves the clear dry air of such contrast to the mugginess of Culiacán. Loves the black night's trove of stars and its howls of wolves. He has been heard to rue that his business keeps him from visiting the rancho more often than every few months and only for three or four days at a time. But for all his professed love of the place, his intimates know he could never be at home anywhere other than Culiacán, where he was born and has lived all his life and whose every street and alleyway he is familiar with. Where he gained early fame as the foremost assassin in the state of Sinaloa.

It is a secure haven, this rancho, impossible for anyone to approach, even in the dark, without distant detection. Should he receive warning of an imminent attack, the Boss is certain he can get to the village airfield ahead of the raiders and into the sky and gone. In the event he was somehow cut off from the airstrip, he and his brother would resort to a covert ground route to make their getaway. El Segundo had found it on their last visit when he and a favored girl went out in a Jeep one morning to hunt quail. He came across it behind a low escarpment south of the compound where nobody ever had cause to go except to hunt and he was the only one who ever did. It had once been a donkey track out of the mountains and was not much wider than the Jeep. Curious to see where it led, he followed the rugged route through scrubland and outcrops. It took well over an hour to go twenty-plus miles—the girl bored and unable to nap in her seat for the Jeep's constant jouncing. The trail finally connected with a dirt road, an old mining run, long unused and badly weathered. But he could drive a little faster on it and it lay mostly straight and an hour later he was merging onto the federal highway heading north to Ciudad Obregón and thirty minutes after that was there.

Eddie

In a raise of dust, the motor caravan comes wheeling through the outsized open gates and into the main courtyard. A black SUV in the lead, followed by a white Lincoln and a half dozen other luxury cars, another black SUV bringing up the rear. All vehicle glass bulletproofed and tinted to obscurity. The rock and rap and narco-corrido music booming within the cars is audible even to Eddie Gato up in the tower.

They park one behind the other in the shade of the palm trees around the circular fountain centered on a statue of a mermaid pouring water from a conch shell. The engines shut off and the music stops and the passengers alight amid much laughter. A few favored chiefs emerge from the Lincoln, underbosses of various sectors of the Company, the men dressed as if for golfing. Eddie easily spots El Tiburón, the Company's number three man, who keeps his hair cut short to better exhibit the scarred and earless right side of his head. Lesser captains have come in two of the other cars.

The rest of the cars carry only women, young and attractive without exception, their light summer dresses exposing much skin. Servants begin unloading luggage from the car trunks and one of the SUVs.

Eddie scans the guests in vain search of a certain one, and he feels a keen disappointment.

But then there she is. The last to exit the cars. Big sunglasses. Little yellow dress showing lean brown legs. Gleaming black braid to the small of her back.

Miranda.

2

Eddie and Miranda

This is the second party held at the rancho since Eddie Gato has been here, and he has been looking forward to it, notwithstanding that it is only for the invited guests. Even in their off-duty hours the rancho guards and security men are excluded from the fun.

The last party was in late May and spanned four days. Delivery trucks coming and going, the air thick with the aromas of roasting meats. The evenings boisterous with music and gaiety and shrieks from the windows of the upper floor where most of the bedroom suites are. There were periodic shooting contests in the patio behind the bar lounge. The indoor lights and courtyard lamps blazed through the nights.

It had been Eddie Gato's first look at the Boss, little more than a glimpse as the man and his entourage passed by him in one of the narrow galleries that ran the length of the building walls facing the courtyard. The Boss was tall for a mestizo and walked with an athletic litheness, his dark eyes taking in everything, including Eddie when their glances met for an instant. The man was said to be in his forties but Eddie thought he looked younger.

He'd heard that the Boss's brother had come too, but if Eddie saw him he did so without knowing who he was.

The Miranda girl had also been among the guests, though Eddie did not notice her until the third day, when for the first time since the party began he had the 8 AM to 4 PM shift in the tower. Neto had told him of the treat he had in store. The tower offered a clear view of the swimming pool courtyard, where some of the girls would sunbathe topless in the morning.

He had been in the tower nearly an hour when a group of them appeared in the pool courtyard, all of them in short robes and big hats and sunglasses. The sun had cleared the mountains and the air was already warm. The compound was in a brief period of quiet and you could hear the crooning of doves. At poolside the girls took off their robes and draped them over the lounge chairs and from their bags withdrew lotions and cigarettes and magazines and MP3 players with earphone attachments. They wore thong bikinis and they all but one took off their tops. They applied lotion to their legs and bellies and breasts and by turns to each other's backs and buttocks. Some lay faceup and some facedown and Eddie kept looking from one to another to another and wished he had more eyes.

The girls seemed oblivious of him. From time to time one looked his way but it was as though he were invisible, and his strenuous smiles were to no effect. And he knew better than to use the binoculars. The day before, one of the girls had glanced up at the tower to see Neto glassing them and she gave him the finger and yelled for him to go fuck his hand. The others laughed. Neto backed away from their line of sight for a while before easing up to the parapet again to peek some more but without the glasses. They evidently did not mind being admired but drew the line at binoculars. From this distance Eddie couldn't hear them talking but at times caught low ripples of their laughter.

The sun was well up and the heat still rising when they started to gather their things and head back indoors. The music had once again cranked up in the house and it carried over the compound on outdoor speakers. The last of the girls to leave had kept herself somewhat apart from the others and their conversations. She was the only one who had not removed her top, and so at first received the least of Eddie's attention, though he'd noticed a little pair of indistinct red tattoos on her back, one on each shoulder blade. Now he was wondering what her breasts looked like uncovered. They weren't large but seemed well formed. She put on her robe and left it unbelted and put on her hat and slung her bag on her shoulder. Then adjusted her sunglasses and looked up at the sky. Then turned her gaze toward him.

His reaction was impulsive. He snatched off his hat so she could clearly see his face and he formed his hand into a pistol and pointed his index finger at her and flicked his thumb as he silently mouthed, *Pow*. She grinned whitely in the shadow of her hat brim and slapped a hand to her breast as if shot. Then turned and sauntered away.

Eddie leaned over the parapet to keep her in sight all the way to the end of the courtyard. She was almost to the house when she paused at a row of shrubs in bloom with large yellow flowers. She fingered a flower and leaned down to smell it. The gardener came around the corner with his wheelbarrow of tools and nodded a greeting as he maneuvered past her. She spoke and he stopped, and she spoke again and gestured at the flowers. They conversed for a moment and he tipped his hat and she went into the gallery and out of Eddie's sight.

Neto had told him to expect a second entertainment around mid-afternoon when some of the girls would return for a dip in the pool. And some did, though fewer than in the morning, and absent the one he'd flirted with. There were a handful of men with them this time, guys who had slept off their hangovers and were ready to resume the fun.

This time the girls got completely naked. Their crotches were shaved bare or pubic hair neatly trimmed to fuzzy patches, a cosmetic option Eddie Gato had not seen in the flesh since Jackie Marie's little auburn arrowhead. But the men kept their swim briefs on even when they joined the girls in the pool for splashing horseplay.

Neto showed up for his shift a half hour early in hope that some of the girls would still be poolside, and he was delighted by the antics taking place. "Madre bendita," he sighed. Why can't *one* girl in the village—or even at the Hotel Rey—look like any of those down there? Were there many this morning?

More than now, Eddie said. I wonder when they sleep.

The old woman said they don't drink very much, not like the men. They don't get hungover. And they know how to take naps. Like cats, she said.

The frolickers were in the pool only a short time before getting back out, the girls teasing some of the men for their obvious hard-ons and yipping as the men plucked at their breasts and bottoms. They all put on their robes and hurried off into the house to continue their good time upstairs.

Despite his youth, Eddie Gato has great confidence with women and believes he knows a thing or two about them. He sets great store on humor's value as a lubricant to carnal cavort. Show him a woman who laughs at a playful come-on and he'll show you one who is readily amenable to sexual adventure. Which was why, after her reaction to his pantomimed shooting of her at the previous party, the girl with the red tattoos had remained in his mind. The party girls were the best-looking women he had seen in many months and he was heady with the conviction that he could have his way with Miss Tattoos.

The problem was the lack of time to work his way with her. The Boss was hosting a big dinner for all his guests that evening and the party was due to break up the next day. But there would be another party in another two or three months. Eddie figured that if he moved fast he could at least prepare the groundwork with her for the next time.

That evening he went to the gardener's quarters. The man was plainly nervous at this visit from a guard, and Eddie had to assure him that he wasn't in any trouble, that he only wanted to know about the girl who had spoken to him in the courtyard. What'd she say to you? Eddie asked. The gardener told him she wanted to know what the flowers were named. She had never seen such flowers and thought they were very beautiful. She was delighted to know they were called delicias. She said it was a perfect name for them.

At noon the next day, as servants were carrying suitcases to the cars and while the Boss and his men had a parting drink together in the bar lounge, Eddie Gato stood in a dim recess near the bottom of the stairway the girls would use to come down from their wing of suites. The M–16 slung on a shoulder would identify him as a guard to any security man who might take note of him.

Then the girls were descending the stairs in a chattering flock and heading off along the gallery toward the main courtyard. He was hoping that she would again trail behind the rest of them. And she did, coming down the steps in no hurry at all, a little swing to her hips as if in time to some tune in her head. Hair in a ponytail and again the big sunglasses. A green strap dress bared her brown shoulders but covered the tattoos on her back. A canvas tote bag dangled from her shoulder.

He stepped out from the wall, one hand behind him, and said, "Buenos días, señorita."

She turned in a slow whirl like a dance step. Then saw she'd been hailed by a guard and her mouth tightened in irritation. "Y tu qué quieres?" she said.

He pushed back his hat. Remember me? he said. He pointed his index finger at her and clicked his thumb.

Ah yes, of course, she said. "El asesino en la torre." She showed a small smile. I see you have a rifle this time. Do you intend to shoot me more seriously?

Up close her face was even more striking than he'd thought, even with the sunglasses masking her eyes. Her lips were full and without paint and he imagined himself gently biting the lower one.

Well . . . what is it? You have a message for me or what?

A message, yes, he said. The message is that I feel very guilty for shooting you and I beg your forgiveness. I wish to give you a token of apology.

Her face stiffened.

He brought his hand out from behind his back to present a posy of yellow flowers. I saw them in a courtyard, he said, and for some reason they made me think of you. They're called delicias.

What the hell are you doing, kid?

His ears warmed. He didn't care for being called kid by a girl who didn't look any older than he was. As I said, I am apologizing for shooting you.

Her head tilted as something behind him caught her notice, and he turned and saw a pair of security men walking toward the courtyard gate. But the men did not look Eddie's way and then were gone.

He extended the flowers to her. I promise not to shoot you again.

You are very foolish.

How sad that you think my apology foolish. And my promise.

He stepped closer, the flowers now almost touching her breasts. She sighed in exasperation as if at an importunate child, then plucked one of the flowers from the bunch and put it in her tote. Thank you.

As she started to turn away, he said, One thing more.

"Ahora qué?"

What is your name?

She stared at him.

You have a name, no?

She pulled her glasses down a little to give him a searching look over them, her eyes darkly bright. Then slipped the shades back up and said, "Miranda."

"Yo soy Eduardo."

"Adiós, Eduardo."

She walked off with lean hips swaying. And then without slowing made another graceful twirl—a full-circle spin—to glance at him once more, and then her back was to him again and he watched her all the way to the gate.

The whirl-around was the clincher. When they take a look back they're interested. And when they make such an obvious show of it, well, they're ready for anything.

Next time, Miranda baby, he thought.

During the following weeks Eddie had often thought of her. His plan was to approach her again and say the right things and make the right moves and get her to slip away from the party at the first opportunity when he was off duty. They would meet someplace—his room, the pool bathhouse, he had various trysting spots in mind—and he would damn well make up for what he'd been missing these past months.

But what if she wasn't with the party next time? Jorge Santos and Javier had said they'd seen some of the same girls at different parties, but they saw most girls only once and there were new ones every time. If she didn't come, he would have to start from scratch with some other girl and might again be thwarted by the lack of time.

He anyway preferred the Miranda one. The more he thought about her—her fine legs and bottom, that sassy mouth, the playful peek over the sunglasses—the more he couldn't wait to get his hands on her. They were all pretty, these party girls, some even prettier than she was, but she was different from the rest. She held herself apart, among them but not of them. The best thing about her, in his view. A girl without friends was always easier to deal with than one with a close circle of pals, and could more easily slip away for a short while without attracting anyone's notice. He intended to work on a different girl at each of the parties to come, but first he wanted this one. And the more he wanted her, the more he fretted he might not even see her again.

But here she is, the last of them to exit the cars. Miranda. On this sultry Friday near the end of July. Sunglassed and cinnamon-skinned. In a little yellow dress and her black hair in a plait.

The men precede the women into the house and she again lags behind. Eddie wishes she would look up. But she doesn't.

Neto relieves him at a quarter to four and is displeased to see that none of the girls are at the pool to refresh themselves after their hot trip.

3

Eddie and Miranda

That evening Eddie stands in the same dark recess near the same stairway as before, M-16 again slung on shoulder, waiting for Miranda to come down to supper. The sun has set behind the mountains and the courtyard lamps have come on. The lounge music thumping from the courtyard speakers will grow louder yet as the night deepens.

He learned the party routines the last time. He knows the girls are excluded from taking supper in the main dining room with the men except at the big dinner on the last night of a party. On the preceding nights, the girls eat in the smaller of the house's two kitchens, tended by the old cook, while the men dine in the main room on meals prepared in the main kitchen by a chef from Culiacán. After supper the girls will put on their party dresses and join the men in the lounge with its dance floor and live band, and the raucous hilarity will carry through the compound until dawn.

It has occurred to him that she might not come down alone. Might this time be with some girl she has befriended since the last party. If that's the case, he will approach her anyway and ask if he can have a private word. She will say yes or no, and if no, well, too bad for him. But he's sure she'll be alone.

And here they come. He watches from the darkness as they descend, dressed in jeans, shorts, T-shirts, sandals, chatting and tittering. She isn't among them and he isn't surprised. But time passes and she still does not appear. He wishes he'd worn his watch. He wonders if maybe she doesn't eat supper. The old cook said some of them don't.

When she still hasn't come down after what he judges to be at least another fifteen minutes, he knows she isn't going to. The other girls will shortly be back to dress for the party. There's nothing he can think to do but try accosting her in the morning near the entrance to the pool courtyard. A riskier tactic for being in open daylight and with other girls nearby, but if it's all that he can do it's what he'll do.

He starts across the courtyard toward the gate leading to the guards' quarters, then looks up at the gallery fronting the suites where the girls are lodged and sees a girl leaning on the rail at the near end of the gallery—sees her face clearly enough in the glow of the gallery's lantern lights to recognize her as Miranda. In a dark robe and smoking a cigarette. Studying the starry sky.

He stops and looks about, sees no one else in the courtyard. He walks over until he is almost directly below her. She remains unaware of him, her attention still on the sky.

"Oye," he says.

She looks down and he extends his arm toward her and once again shoots her with his thumb and forefinger.

Even in the low light, he sees the vague whiteness of her grin, and she puts a hand to her breast.

She scans the deserted courtyard and looks back down at him for a few long seconds during which he feels like some commodity under appraisal. Then she beckons him with a waggle of fingers without raising her hand from the rail.

He casually walks to the shadowy stairway—thinking, Yes, yes, yes—and then takes the stairs three at a time. She is standing by the second door down from the landing. As he heads toward her she goes inside, leaving the door ajar.

He enters a small dark parlor lit by a single candle atop a low table next to a sofa. From a shadowed doorway across the room she says, "Cierra la puerta."

He shuts the front door and follows her into the bedroom, congratulating himself on the ease of it all.

The bedroom too is lit by a single candle, and in the low orange light she draws back the bedcovers and shrugs off the robe and eases naked into the bed as if into a pleasant pool of water.

Eddie Gato's experience with sexual windfall has taught him the wisdom of keeping his mouth shut at moments like this. He props the rifle against the wall and shuts the door and swiftly undresses. Thinking, Fish in a barrel.

They are just completing their first coupling when they hear some of the girls passing by on the gallery. He drops onto his side, pulling her with him, and they lie that way a few minutes, their gasps slowing, before he detaches from her. She is facing him, the candle behind her so that she is in silhouette. She runs a fingertip over his lips and he lightly bites it and she laughs low in her throat. Before long they join again, this time her atop. And this time they are less urgent about it, restraining themselves until they ache and then finishing in a flurry of grunting flexions. She collapses on him, and then rolls off with a sigh.

They lie on their backs for a time, again catching their breath, keeping to their own thoughts. Then she sits up with her back against the headboard and pulls the sheet up over her breasts and tucks it under her arms. She lights a cigarette and offers the pack to him.

"No, gracias," he says. The first words to pass between them since she told him to shut the door. Only now does he notice a bruise under her left eye. He gestures at it and asks how she got it.

Carelessness, she says.

Again they hear the other girls out on the gallery, their voices and laughter louder this time. Excited. On their way to the men in the lounge.

Hell, he says.

What?

He gestures toward the gallery. You have to go.

No I don't.

Those guys are waiting for you.

Not for me.

She takes a drag of her cigarette and exhales the smoke at him and smiles as he fans it from his face.

He feels a stir of apprehension. I don't get it, he says. How come you. . . . And now remembers the Boss isn't at the rancho and won't be until tomorrow.

He sits up. Jesus Christ, you're *his* girl!

Whose girl?

The Boss's.

She laughs and says, Is that what you think? Her expression turns sly. What if I am? I hope you won't wet my bed in your fright.

Oh man, you crazy bitch.

He starts to get out of the bed but she grabs his arm. Whoa, kid, calm yourself, I'm teasing. I'm not the Boss's woman, I swear. She grins. You ought to see your face.

He cannot read her eyes. Has no idea if she's telling the truth. Then why don't you have to be down there with the others?

What does it matter to you? Look, I told you I don't have to go and I told you I'm not the Boss's woman. And nobody's going to come to fetch me—another thing you don't have to worry about. You don't want to believe me, fine. If you want to go, go. I never would have thought you are such a rabbit.

That stings him.

She lets the sheet fall to her waist and grinds the cigarette out in a bedside ashtray and then busies herself lighting another.

He doesn't believe her. There's no reason she'd be exempt from the party except she's the Boss's girl. Then again . . . the man won't be here until around noon, Flores himself said so. Why not enjoy her some more while she's available? And why, he wonders, given the severe threat to his ass if discovered, is he feeling so . . . *pleased* with himself?

Well hell. The *Boss's* girl! His cock stirs.

She blows a smoke ring at it and smiles. I think he is more daring than you.

What about you?

You think there is no danger to me in this? she says. I am not the Boss's woman, but we are not supposed to fool with any of you guys. Rancho guards, security men, none of you.

Yet here I am.

Yes, yes, I know. It's just . . . they have all these fucking *rules.* Sometimes I just—

Whatever she was going to say, she catches herself. Then says, "Me caes bien, chacho." You're fun. Stay fun, all right?

Quit calling me kid. I told you, my name's Eduardo.

I'm so sorry, she says with mock rue. I did not mean to offend your manly dignity. Then nods at his erection and says, I think maybe he's had enough talk.

He makes himself twitch and says, I thinks he agrees.

She grins and takes up a small clock from the bedside table and winds it. The clock has hands that glow in the dark and she says its alarm is loud enough to wake the dead. She sets the ringer for three o'clock.

At that hour, she says, everybody will be drunk and fucking and nobody will see you slip out.

She places the clock beside her on the stand and then slides down onto her back and stretches with exaggerated languor, arching her breasts upward.

And laughs as he growls and pounces on her.

They converse in the interludes between lovemaking. The music from the bar lounge is now audible to them even at this distance and in this rear room.

He has discovered that the red tattoos on her shoulder blades are of little wings broken at their joints. He asks why she got them and she says she lost a bet and it's a long story and maybe she'll tell it to him some other time.

For her part, she's curious about his blue eyes. Is he a gringo?

No, he lies, but some of his ancestors were. Most members of his family are Caucasians of Anglo and Spanish blood, though there are a few mestizos in there.

Her curiosity now the more piqued. "Como te apellidas?" she asks.

"Porter," he says. It is the surname by which he is known here but is in fact his mother's maiden name.

Can you speak English?

"Claro que sí," he says, and intones, "My nem ees Eh-war Porrter."

She laughs and asks what he said about his name and he tells her.

Where are you from?

The border. And thinks, Porter from the border. I'm a poet.

She says she doesn't believe him. She knows people from the border, not only from Sonora but Chihuahua too, and his accent is different from theirs.

Because he's from the other end of the border, he tells her, from Matamoros, near the mouth of the Rio Bravo.

"Ah, pues," she says. And asks what brought him so far from home, how he came to work for the Company?

Her questions becoming too many for comfort. To deflect them he says, How did you?

She says it is another long story.

Mine too, he says.

She laughs and rolls onto him.

SATURDAY

4

Eddie and Miranda

He wakes to darkness and a sense of threat.

The candle has burned out. The clock reads 2:25.

Rock music booming through the compound. The girl sleeps on her side with her back to him. He sits up and sees a bright line of light along the lower edge of the bedroom door.

Boss!

He bolts out of bed and over to the wall alongside the door, heart jumping. The M–16 is on the other side of the doorway. He is about to spring over and grab it when the door opens toward it and blocks it from him.

In the high shaft of light from the outer room, a man's shadow extends from the threshold to the bed.

The girl stirs, raises her head, squints into the light. "Chacho?"

"Quién?" says the man.

A wall switch clicks and the room comes ablaze with overhead light as a man in a cream suit enters.

The girl's eyes reflexively cut to Eddie at the man's right—and as the man starts to turn to see what she's looking at, Eddie lunges and clamps an arm around his neck from behind.

They stagger across the room, crashing into furniture, the man bucking and flexing to try to break free of the choke hold. He is taller than Eddie and very strong but Eddie Gato is very strong too and has a solid grip on the wrist of the forearm across the man's throat.

One of the man's hands scrabbles into his coat and the girl cries, "Pistola!"

The gun now in the man's hand and he angles it behind him and Eddie twists away from the muzzle as the gun fires and he feels a burning in his side. The pistol blasts again as he wrenches the man around and slams him headfirst into the wall without losing his hold on him and the gun clatters to the floor.

They stumble and fall down, locked together like crazed lovers. The man now making guttural sounds, thrashing and kicking wildly, clawing with both hands at Eddie's throttling arm as Eddie constricts the forearm with all his strength. It seems the man will never cease struggling. And then he goes slack and there is a stink of shit. But if you're fighting for your life hand to hand and have to kill somebody, you better be damn sure he's dead before you let up, and even though Eddie can feel that he's dead, he maintains his hold full force for another ten eternal seconds during which he hears only the music from outside and his own gasps and expects security men to come bursting in at any second and kill him.

It is painful effort to unlock his hand from his wrist, his arm from around the man's neck. Heaving for breath, Eddie gets to his feet and picks up the pistol, a Glock 15. He extracts the magazine and its weight tells him it is nearly full, then he snaps it back in place. He looks into the front room and sees the door is shut. The music outside is thunderous. Could be nobody heard the shots. Must be. Or they'd be here.

His side is burning and he feels a fleeting impulse to vomit but fights it down. He has never killed anyone before, though he has come close to it. He inhales through his teeth as he probes the raw patch of powder-burned flesh with his fingertips, searching for a bullet hole but not finding one.

He now has his first clear look at the dead man's face—tongue extruding, mustache thick with red nasal discharge, bulging eyes scarlet. It takes him a moment to comprehend that this man is not the Boss.

The girl is zipping up her jeans, pulling on a T-shirt, big-eyed but moving with purpose. She takes up an open switchblade from the bedside table and folds it closed and puts it in her pocket. Eddie has no idea where the knife came from. Under her pillow? As she stuffs T-shirts and underwear into her tote bag, she asks Eddie if he's hurt.

It rankles him that she seems less frightened than he is, but his anger helps to suppress his fear.

Who the hell's this guy?

She takes a wad of pesos from the dresser drawer and puts it in her jeans. You don't know? Enrique.

Who's Enrique?

"El chingado Segundo," she says. The bastard wasn't supposed to be here till much later. Him and his prick brother.

She lofts Eddie's pants to him.

Segundo? You're *Segundo's* woman?

She looks at the dead man. Not anymore.

Oh Jesus Christ . . .

Take it easy, kid. We—

Take it easy? They'll kill me twenty times.

Me too, she says. But they have to catch us first.

She tends to his wound in the bathroom with swift dexterity. It's on his flank, directly below his rib cage, a raw seared gash of about three inches. As she cleans it with a wadded cotton sock doused with hydrogen peroxide, he grunts and flinches, and she chides him for a baby. He's got the Glock in his hand and keeps cutting looks at the bedroom door, though it's not likely anyone will come to disturb the number two man while he's taking his pleasure with his woman.

She folds the other sock and soaks it with peroxide and has him hold it against the wound while she twirls a large light scarf into a band and then wraps it snugly around his waist to hold the folded sock in place and fastens it with a safety pin. Eddie puts on his shirt and leaves it untucked to cover the Glock in his waistband.

They go back into the bedroom to search Segundo, expelling hard breaths at the stench of his stained pants. Only now does Eddie notice the money belt the man is wearing. It does not feel very thick as he takes it off him to find that it holds a layer of American hundred-dollar bills. He thumbs through a portion of them and approximates a total of maybe seventeen or eighteen thousand. He puts the belt on under his shirt, fitting it above his makeshift bandage. In Segundo's jacket they find a cell phone, a packet of Mexican currency in 200- and 500-peso notes, a thin wallet with some American credit cards. Eddie pockets the cash, tosses aside the phone and cards.

All the while, they are talking fast about what to do.

Eddie thinks they can make it out of the compound easily enough in a Jeep with her hidden under a tarp behind the seat. The security men all know he's a ranch guard and he'll tell the guy at the gate he's going to the village to get laid. But he doubts he can talk his way past the guard posts between the village and the Obregón road.

She tells him they don't have to go by that route. She knows another one. It's a bumpy little trail but drivable if they take it carefully. But when she says it's in the opposite direction from the village, Eddie shakes his head.

The guard in the tower will see the way we're heading and wonder what's going on and give the security guys a call. Unless . . .

What?

Unless we're in the Boss's car. It never stops at the gate. With its dark glass the guards won't know who's in it. They'll assume it's the Boss, or maybe Segundo, like always.

The *Boss's* car, she says.

We can do it, he says. The car park is way off in the corner of the compound, out of sight of everything. The flunky drivers aren't going to question a guard who says Segundo told him to use the Boss's car for . . . I don't know, some errand. I don't have to explain anything to them. But there may be a security guy there. If there is, I'll tell him, ah . . . Segundo ordered me to fetch a briefcase he forgot on the plane. And to be damn quick about it.

Yes! That's very good, *yes*.

But how to explain you?

Me? Segundo sent me with you because . . . because I've been on the plane. I know where he keeps the case.

I don't know, Eddie says. Might work. If it doesn't—

It *will* work, she says. "Ya lo verás."

He grins despite himself. I'm real glad to hear it.

But then? she says. Where do we go?

Out of the country damn quick as we can. There's no hiding from these guys anywhere in Mexico. We go to Ciudad Obregón and get on a plane to the United States.

Her face pinches. I can't fly out of the country. I have no passport.

Eddie says neither does he—though in truth he does, some six hundred miles away at a place called Patria Chica—but he tells her they don't need passports, Segundo's money will get them across. He knows a charter pilot in Obregón with his own plane. For a few grand in American dollars he'll file a phony flight plan and take them to some cow pasture in Arizona or New Mexico. He slings the M-16 on his shoulder.

She grins and picks up her bag. That is a very fine plan.

At the front door she says, Wait. Let me see if there's anyone around. She hands him the bag and opens the door just enough to slip out.

As soon as she's gone he is seized by the certainty she's not coming back. She's decided her best chance is to go straight to the security team and tell them what happened. After all, she didn't kill Segundo. Yes, she fucked a guard, but that was all she did, and so—

"All clear," she says at the door.

Eddie's driving without headlights, the SUV rocking and pitching over the donkey trail, the stony landscape eerily illumined by a lean crescent moon scarcely clear of the mountains. The M-16 is propped between the console and her seat, the Glock between his legs.

It's frustrating to have to drive so slowly in an SUV with a high-horsepower V-8. Eddie repeatedly and unconsciously speeds up until the tires start to lose purchase on the curves, and he each time marvels when the Electronic Stability Control senses the skid sooner than he does and counteracts it by working the brakes in ways impossible to him. He feels like all he's doing is steering while the Escalade does the driving. He's reminded of the common grievances some in his family have against computers—the loss of control to machinery, the surrender of privacy and personal freedom, and so on and so forth—even though almost all of them use computers for one purpose or another, even most of the oldsters, and some in the family are aces with them. He thinks of his cousins Rudy and Frank and their beloved Mustangs and Barracudas with stick-shift transmissions and he can imagine what they think of the Escalade and its ESC. But he's damned glad to have the device. And that the gas tank is full.

There had been a security man at the car park and he nodded when Eddie explained his task for Segundo. The man's attention was mostly on Miranda, who made eyes at him while the Escalade was brought from the garage. He told her she could get arrested for looking so good even with that black eye, and she laughed and said she guessed it was a good thing for her he wasn't a cop. He asked how she got the eye and she said, Wouldn't you like to know? His only remark to Eddie was about carrying a rifle simply to get a briefcase at the airfield. Eddie said, Yeah well, orders, you know how it is. The man nodded and said he sure the fuck did.

It's Eddie's guess that they've got at least until sunrise before anybody has reason to look for Segundo and goes to Miranda's room. By then—if her recollection is accurate about how long it took her and Segundo to get to Ciudad Obregón that day in the Jeep—they should be arriving at the Obregón airport. If they're really lucky, however, Segundo won't be found until much later in the morning, by which time they'll be in the States. They could use a little luck with Eddie's pilot pal too. Evaristo. He lives only a few minutes from the airport, so even if he's not at his hangar and they have to call him at home he can get there fairly fast. Here's hoping he's not off on some job. If he is, well, they'll find another charter, that's all there is to it. There are plenty of private pilots ready to cross the border for the right price.

She finds some CDs in the console and slips a disc of contemporary corridos into the player and sets the volume low. Then lights a cigarette and directs the smoke out her partially open window.

They've been driving about half an hour and have exchanged fewer than a dozen words when she says, I'm glad he's dead.

He cuts a look at her but she keeps her gaze out the window.

A minute passes. Without turning from the window she tells him she was kidnapped off the streets of Mazatlán five months ago. She and her boyfriend Gabo were walking to the movies when a car pulled up beside them and a pair of men sprang out and one of them grabbed her. There were pistol shots that made her ears ring and she saw Gabo huddled on his knees as the men dragged her into the car. She was able to get out her knife and tried to cut them but they got it away, nearly breaking her thumb, then cuffed her hands behind her and told her to quit struggling or they'd knock her cold and wrap her in rope. As they sped away she looked back through the window and saw Gabo lying in the street with the awkwardness of the dead. People peeking from doorways and behind parked cars. She kept asking where they were taking her but they wouldn't answer. She knew that gangsters kidnapped rich people and sometimes some who were not so rich and demanded ransom from their families. She told them they had a big fucking surprise coming if they thought they would get ransom for her. Her only family was a drunken mother who didn't have fifty pesos to her name and even if she had any money she wouldn't use it to ransom her. You stupid bastards snatched an empty purse, she told them. She was so scared she couldn't stop talking and she was afraid they would hurt her to shut her up but they ignored her as if they were deaf. They took her far out of town to a house with a view of the sea. Segundo was there, though she didn't yet know who he was. He politely introduced himself as Enrique—she would later come to know that he was called Rico by his brother and close friends, Segundo by everyone else. He said he was the brother of La Navaja and asked if she had ever heard of that man. Of course she had. Like everyone, she had heard a great deal about the Sinaloa criminal organization and its leader. Had heard of their gun battles with other gangs and the police and even the army. Had heard of the horrific things they did. Heads left in bags at the doors of police stations. Bodies hung from overpasses. Charred corpses along country roads. Atrocities of every sort that had become so commonplace they were no longer shocking, only something to take precautions against, like the flu. And here was the brother of the chief of that organization of murderers. She was scared, naturally, but scared mostly in that strange way like at a movie about monsters or ghosts. Scared but also kind of excited, she can't explain it. One of the men handed him the switchblade he'd taken from her, and Segundo snicked it open and smiled and then closed it and gave it to her and she put it in her pocket. He told her he'd seen her near the market a few days before and thought she was very beautiful. He said he wanted her for his girlfriend. He said she would have her own apartment with a big television in a nice colonia in Culiacán. He would take her to wonderful parties. She would dine on the best food and drink. She would have pretty dresses, jewelry. She would have a life most women can only dream of. He said he could see she was afraid, maybe too frightened to refuse him, but he promised he would not harm her if she turned him down. He would be disappointed, yes, but he would send her back to her miserable life if that was what she chose. His exact words—"tu vida miserable." He said he knew how hard it must be for her to believe this was happening and she probably needed some time to think about it, and so she should do that while he made a phone call in the patio.

She lights another cigarette. On the CD player a norteño band sings of a bold contrabandista idolized by the common folk for his bravery and violent defiance of the law.

Imagine my life, she says. Then tells Eddie she was born and raised in Mazatlán in a loud portside barrio that always stank of fish and rage and meanness. A neighborhood of derelict apartments where every night you heard cursings, shriekings, wailings. As a child she many times saw men brawl in the streets and once was witness to a fight with knives that left both men dead on the sidewalk like mounds of bloody rags. She saw a man beat his wife to death with a hammer in an apartment hallway. She saw a woman flung from a rooftop and her head burst on the street like a melon. But her father was a big man, strong, a good fighter, and other men were afraid of him, you could see it in their faces. Her father made her feel protected, her and her one-year-elder sister Felicia and their mother, who was very pretty and always getting looks from men. He worked on a fishing boat and often spoke of getting a house of their own in a better part of the city, but he loved to gamble and was not good at it and they could never afford to move out of that awful place. She was almost fourteen when he drowned at sea. Then life became truly hard. Her mother had no money, no family or friends she could ask for help. She worked at a cannery for a while and earned barely enough to support them. Then there was an accident with a machine and she lost the thumb and part of the first finger of her right hand and nearly died from the infection before she got better. They were going hungry by then, they were close to being put out on the street. So her mother naturally became a whore, an old story everywhere and especially in that neighborhood so full of whores where the seamen came for their fun. But as a whore she could pay the rent and feed the three of them. She brought men to her room almost every night. All the men drank and so she drank with them and became a drunkard. Over time the drinking spoiled her looks and fewer men came home with her and she made less money. By that point she was almost a stranger to her and Felicia, who were now learning for themselves about men and sex and the power of being pretty. When Felicia was seventeen she got pregnant by a forty-year-old man who owned a café in Villa Unión, and rather than have an abortion she gulled him into marriage. Being wife to a café owner was her sister's notion of a good life. She herself continued to go to school for a while longer, mostly because it was a clean and safe place to pass the day, and it was there that she learned about contraception. She had liked sex from her first time at fifteen but had been unbelievably lucky not to get pregnant before learning how to prevent it. She had seen what happened to so many young girls who got pregnant, married or not. Had seen how fast they got fat and bitter, how fast they got old. When she took up with Gabo, who was an errand runner for a waterfront boss, the only thing she knew about her future was that she did not want it to be like her mother's or her sister's. She did not love Gabo, but he was good-looking and fun and tough. He made her feel safe, as her father had, and he taught her a few things about protecting herself, like how to use the knife he gave her for her birthday. All of which was sadly funny when you consider what happened when Segundo's men drove up in the car.

So, she says to Eddie. Imagine yourself a woman and in my place. What choice would you have made?

The same one you did, I guess.

You guess?

I'm sure I would've.

Segundo was happy to hear her choice. Then took her into a bedroom and fucked her.

He gave her all he promised. The apartment with the big TV, the nice dresses. He took her to fancy parties and night-clubs. But although he and his brother owned several houses in Culiacán and in other cities, he never took her to any of them for the simple reason that he had a different girlfriend at each of them—a fact she learned from some of the women at the parties, catty bitches who told her Segundo went through young girls even faster than his brother and she better be ready for the day he got bored with her and kicked her back into the street. She felt very foolish for not having understood that's how it would be, that of course he would have other girls, of course he would one day get bored with her. She told herself it didn't matter, since she was not in love with him and wasn't jealous. What did she care what he did when he was not with her? Why not enjoy the luxury while she could? But she very soon had to admit it did matter. Because it forced her to face the fact that she wasn't a girlfriend, she was a whore, one more whore in a world with no lack of them, as much of a whore as her mother, except better dressed and fed and housed and protected. No, more of a whore, because her mother had no alternative but to become one, while she had chosen to. It was an undeniable truth. One that every day became harder for her to bear. She'd been with Segundo two months when she ran away. She got on a bus to Mazatlán, but before it was ten miles out of town a big car with two men in it forced it to pull over, and one of the men came aboard and got her and they drove her back to Culiacán. Segundo seemed more amused than angry by her attempt at escape. She told him she'd changed her mind, she didn't want to be his girlfriend, and asked him to please send her back to Mazatlán as he had said he would do. He said no. He had given her a choice and she had made it and now must live by it. But why not let her go, she asked him. He'd soon be tired of her and kick her out anyway. He said that was very possible and when that happened she could leave but not before. He had a tattooist put the little broken wings on her back. A reminder, he told her, that she could not fly away from him. More effective than the tattoos were the informants she now knew were keeping watch on her and would report to him any attempt she made to leave. A couple of weeks later he took her to a party at Rancho del Sol. It was the farthest she had ever been from home, not only in miles but in feeling. The vastness of the desert frightened her. Everything looked too far away, even the cloudless sky. There was nowhere you could hide in such emptiness. She hated the other women, who were out-and-out whores and who hated her in turn for looking down on them. It was four days of drinking and fucking except for one time when he took her to hunt quail but they spent most of the day driving out here in the scrub. She was glad to get back to Culiacán. During the next two months he came to see her at the apartment more often than before. It was as though her desire to be free of him had made him want her more. But he also seemed very ready to hurt her if she should fail to satisfy him. She had heard stories of what he had done to women who had displeased him, and she did not hesitate to grant whatever favors he asked and do so with enthusiasm. She was convinced he could smell her fear and that it increased his pleasure, a realization that made her almost as angry as she was afraid, but she was careful to conceal it. It wasn't so much a matter of who did he think he was, to take such enjoyment in making her afraid, as who did he think *she* was? But of course she already knew the answer to that question, and every time she thought of it she wanted to both weep and hit something. Then a few days ago he told her to pack a bag, they were going to another party at Rancho del Sol. Without thinking, she said, Shit, and next thing she knew she was on the floor with a numb eye socket and an eye blurred with tears. Excuse me, he said, I don't think I heard you clearly. Did you say you couldn't wait to go? She was able to nod and he smiled and said that's what he thought. He said it would be fun, like last time. Maybe they would go on another quail hunt. But on the morning of departure she was driven to the airport by a lackey who told her that Segundo and the Boss had been delayed and did not plan to join the rest of the party until the next day. She was glad to hear it. It meant one night of freedom at that damned ranch.

But apparently, she says, there was a change in his plans.

Apparently, Eddie says.

And a minute later he says, How old are you?

Nineteen.

They arrive at the dirt road and pick up speed and in another hour they spot the distant lights of traffic moving along the federal highway. The eastern horizon now red as a raw wound.

5

The Boss

The Boss enters the malodorous room, accompanied by El Ti-burón. Already present are Flores and his main security aide, Chato. They step aside as the Boss goes to his brother's body and stands over it. He is a master of inexpressiveness, a trait that has long served his reputation as a man of cool blood whose decisions have the solid finality of a gravestone. His face gives no hint of his sorrow or his rage—or his embarrassment at his brother's fouled trousers. He's known countless men who shat themselves in fear or agony at the moment of death and he never before felt anything about it except occasional disgust.

Looks like he caught her fooling with a guy, Flores says. One of the ranch guards. There was a fight, obviously, and . . . He gestures at the body. We found two casings, he says, nine-millimeter. One hole in that wall, one in that one. There's a towel with blood on it, but not much. I'd say Rico tried to shoot him while they were fighting but couldn't do it but anyway managed to bloody his nose or mouth or something. They took his pistol and cash, left the credit cards and phone. Seems the guy's not completely stupid.

Who is he? says the Boss.

Eduardo Porter. According to Santos, he's been with—

Santos?

The guard captain.

Go on.

Porter's been with us since March. He was hired by Morales. As far as Santos knows, it's the kid's first job with the Company. Been reliable, he says.

Tiburón snorts and says, Till now.

The Boss ignores him. How old is he?

Twenty.

Where's he from?

Tampico, Santos says.

I want to see everything we have on him.

It's on the way, Flores says. Photo too.

The Boss squats beside his brother. They had finished their business in Culiacán sooner than expected and decided to fly to Loma Baja tonight instead of wait until morning. Decisions sometimes have extraneous consequence, usually too insignificant for remark, but sometimes . . . sometimes the extraneous consequence is something like this. He fingers Rico's discolored neck and feels no break in it. Strangulation. They had been at the rancho only a few minutes and were having their first drink when Rico said he was horny as a goat and was going to go get a fast fuck from . . . the Boss has trouble recalling her name. The one from Mazatlán that Rico picked up three-four months ago. Marisol? Miralinda? . . . Miranda. Good-looking but with mustang eyes, like so many crazy ones. They can be great fun in bed but they aren't worth their loony irritations. He'd told Rico so a dozen times. But that's how he liked them.

He gently pushes Rico's tongue back into his mouth and closes his jaws and with two fingers draws the lids down over the bulbous red eyes. "Pañuelo," he says, reaching back without looking. Flores takes a folded handkerchief from his breast pocket and hands it to him and the Boss wipes the bloody snot and saliva from Rico's face.

He'd said he'd be right back, just a quickie. He still hadn't returned when Flores said the communications net with Hermosillo couldn't be completed until the tech crew had the new cell codes Segundo had brought from Culiacán. The codes were in a courier case he'd left with the Boss but the case was locked and Rico had the key. The Boss called Rico's cell but he didn't answer. Having too much fun with the Mazatlana, he thought. He gave the case to Flores and told him to get the key from Rico, then thought no more about it until a runner from Flores was shouting into his ear to be heard above the music, shouting Flores's message that he should come to the girl's room right away.

The Boss stands up and asks Flores, What do we know?

Prior to the Boss's arrival, Flores made some calls and has learned that an hour and a half ago Porter and the girl left the compound in the Boss's Escalade. The kid told the security man at the car park he and the girl had been ordered by Segundo to use the SUV to go to the plane and get a briefcase from it and Segundo meant right the fuck now. The security man knew Porter was a guard but thought of checking with Segundo anyway, but then was afraid he'd get his ass chewed for delaying their errand.

The men at the gate of course thought it was you in the car and let it pass, Flores says. So did the guard in the tower. He thought it curious you would drive off into the desert but who is he to question what the chief does?

The Boss sighs and rubs his eyes. The security man who spoke to him at the car park, you know him?

Yes, chief. Busteros. Been with us about four years. Good man.

No he's not. If he was, the kid wouldn't have got the car. Set him free.

It is the Boss's standard phrase for ordering someone's execution. Flores blinks at the severity of the punishment. Yes, chief.

The tower guard too, the Boss says. We cannot grant leniency for security failures. A reminder to the others.

The guard captain was in the tower, Flores says. Santos.

The Boss stares at him.

Done, my chief, Flores says.

The Boss turns to Tiburón. What do you think?

I think the kid's got stone balls, Tiburón says. He knew he'd never get by the checkpoints and the only way he could go was into the scrub. But even an SUV can't handle that country except at a crawl. And that's in daylight. They're in the dark. If they've got any brains they're scared shitless and they'll probably push it too hard and bust a wheel or roll over or something. Then they're on foot, if they can still walk. Even if they don't break down, odds are they'll be out there at sunup, roaming around like lost dogs. We can get a helicopter here and it'll find them damn quick . . . wherever they might be.

The Boss doesn't miss Tiburón's insinuation. If the Escalade had a tracker in it they would know exactly where they were and could easily cut them off at the highway. Almost all of the Company's vehicles carry such a device, but he did not permit one to be put in the Escalade for fear that enemies might intercept its signal.

If they don't break down, the Boss says, they'll be at the highway by first light. There's a trail out there, an old mining road or something. Rico told me. He said it's rough but it got him to the highway. The Mazatlán cunt was with him when he found it.

Tiburón rolls his eyes at Flores, who looks away.

Have a chopper search the scrub at first light anyway, the Boss says, in case they do break down. But if they make it into the highway traffic, the chopper won't be any help.

As Tiburón punches numbers on a cell phone and starts speaking into it in low voice, the Boss says to Flores, Get me a road map.

Right here, chief, Flores says, and gestures at Chato, who produces a map from his coat. Flores shoves aside the jumbled sheets and spreads the map on the bed. The Boss bends down and studies it.

Tiburón places his hand over the cell mouthpiece and looks at the Boss in wait of further instruction.

They'll come out somewhere in here, the Boss says, sliding a fingertip over a portion of the federal highway between Ciudad Obregón and a toll station about twenty-five miles south of the city.

They can't hide anywhere this side of the border without us finding him, Flores says. If he tries to lay low to let things cool, he'll make the odds worse for himself. The question is whether he's smart enough to know that. Flores puts his finger on the airport symbol a few miles south of the city and says, Odds are he's heading here. Or some private airfield. He can't fly out of the country without a passport, but he'll probably try to fly as far from here as he can.

Get his picture to our people in Obregón, the Boss says. I want lookouts on the airport entrance road, men everywhere in the terminal, at every ticket counter and boarding gate. I want the word out to every charter flight company in Sinaloa and Sonora, every airfield, no matter how small. I want men at the train stations, the bus stations, every car rental place.

In case the kid sticks to the road we should put men at the toll plazas north and south of town, Flores says. And get men cruising the stretch of highway that runs through the city.

Do it, the Boss says.

Tiburón relays the orders into the phone to a captain of Luna Negra, the Company's main band of enforcers.

The Boss stares at his brother on the floor. His anger seethes under his blank aspect.

What more, chief? Tiburón says.

Put the word out, the Boss says. Anybody who helps him in any way at all will be made into dog food. Their families too. He pauses to consider how very much he would like to have the kid alive, but knows that when you try to take one alive you give him a better chance at escape. I want his head, he says. The man who delivers it will be well rewarded.

Very good, chief. And the girl?

Fuck her to death and throw her in a garbage pit.

Tiburón nods and speaks softly into the phone.

Just before sunrise the Boss's jet lifts off the rude airstrip at Loma Baja, bearing him and his brother's body to Culiacán, the only other passenger a bodyguard in the cockpit with the pilot. There is a funeral to be arranged, and as always, a host of urgent concerns await the Boss's attention. Tiburón will oversee the search for Porter from a Company office in Ciudad Obregón and keep the Boss informed of developments. The ranch guests have also departed, transported to the Obregón airport in the motorcade that brought them, from there to disperse to their own regions and the operations of their respective corps and undergangs. Every man of them carrying copies of Eduardo Porter's picture.

In the plane, the Boss opens a manila envelope containing a single sheet of information about Porter and a three-by-five-inch color photograph of him taken on the day he was hired. The data are mostly physical details. Five feet ten inches tall. One hundred sixty-five pounds. Light complexion, black hair, blue eyes. The face is brown but the Boss can tell it's a darkness of sun, not racial lineage. A face cocky with youth. A horizontal white scar under the left eye. He recollects having seen him at the party before this one. They passed in a gallery. The eyes bluer than in the picture. And quick. Quick and intelligent. The record shows that Porter was enlisted in Culiacán by Elizondo Morales, who does much of the Company's lower-level hiring.

It is a flight of less than an hour and a half, and the Boss spends most of it thinking of his brothers. Less than twelve hours ago he and Rico had been on this plane and headed for the rancho, drinking and laughing and ready for fun. They somehow got on the subject of their brothers, and Rico told one of their favorite stories about Marco, the eldest, about the time when he was seventeen and was caught in bed with both daughters of the barrio butcher. He managed to escape through a window, running naked through the morning traffic, dodging cars and pedestrians on the sidewalks, the butcher chasing him with a huge knife for almost three blocks before giving out. There were dozens of witnesses and one of them took a picture and mailed it to him. It showed him in mid-stride, grinning hugely, his dick and balls outslung, bystanders gawking. Marco liked the picture and wished he knew who'd sent it so he could pay him. The four sisterless brothers had been orphaned a few years earlier and had since then been living with their widowed Aunt Juanita, who was something of a bohemian spirit. She loved the photo so much she framed it and hung it on the living room wall. Marco had to keep a sharp eye out for the butcher after that, and had to fuck the daughters elsewhere than in their own house.

The Boss had enjoyed that story many times before and did so again on Rico's retelling. And now he recalls that six years later, when all four brothers were working for a city gang chief, a van carrying five drunken teenagers swerved across the median on the state highway and hit Marco's truck head-on at seventy miles an hour, slaughtering everyone in both vehicles including a girl riding with Marco. The bloody evidence strongly suggested she had been sucking his cock at the time. The Boss was nineteen then, Rico seventeen, their other brother Pedro twenty-one, and that there were no survivors on whom to take vengeance was the greatest frustration any of them had yet known.

It was a different matter some five years afterward when Pedro was shot dead by a trio of gunmen belonging to a rival gang. He and Rico found out who Pedro's killers were and disposed of them one by one. They cut the throats of the first two and left their bodies hanging in public by the feet, one from a tree in a park plaza and the other from a lamppost in a soccer stadium parking lot. The third man—who was said to have spit on Pedro after they killed him—they burned alive. Then deposited his charred remains in a garbage bag in front of the central police station to ensure his forensic identification and that his name be made known in the news. The Boss had razored both ears from all three men and to each corpse appended a note saying, This is what happens to whoever harms my people. And signed it La Navaja. The severed ears became his signature, and his notoriety grew with the number of bodies found earless. The Company was at that time still known as the Alliance of Blood and called itself a syndicate. He became its main assassin and Rico his partner. He won the admiration of many of its men and gradually gained the allegiance of some of the strongest underbosses. At the conclusion of a brutal internecine war for control of the organization, he emerged as el jefe máximo. The supreme chieftain. The Boss. The Company was soon afterward one of the two most powerful criminal societies in the country.

Today the major news agencies on both sides of the border less often call them organizations or syndicates and more often call them cartels. Like most of the other bosses, he likes the term for the same reason the news media do. "Cartel" has an impressive ring. It suggests a powerful association of international capacity and outsized ambitions. Like OPEC.

But he also knows that, like most of what is reported in the media, the term is erroneous. A cartel is a group of businesses that deal in the same goods and conspire to regulate the availability and price of those goods, and he cannot envision that sort of cooperation ever obtaining between Mexican criminal outfits. As much as he likes the term "cartel," and even the public nickname "Las Sinas," he still prefers that his people call themselves the Company. But even that name is really no more accurate than "cartel." Despite their great size and power, the Boss knows that all of these groups are truly nothing more than gangs.

Naturally, other men have tried to take his place. Always there is someone watching for a chance to do it. The latest of them a sly young tough called El Chubasco, the chief of the Company's enforcement gang in Los Mochis. He is reported to have made clandestine overtures to some of the other undergangs, even to have made contact with one of Las Sinas' Peruvian cocaine suppliers. The Boss knows he must tend to that fucker very soon. Deal with him as with the other overly ambitious young Turks.

It is a constant struggle for the Boss to retain his command of the Company, but over the years he has done it well, with Rico as his segundo and with a cadre of good captains like Tiburón and Flores, men reliable and proficient and—most important of all—trustworthy. To a degree, anyway.

He has no wife or children and has never wanted either. In this treacherous whore of a world he has never put full faith in anyone but his brothers. And now the last of them is dead. Wrapped in a blanket in the aisle of this aircraft bearing him to a Culiacán graveyard. Rico. Enrique.

Alone in the cabin, the Boss weeps for the first time since childhood. Weeps for his little brother. For all his dead brothers. For himself. For the lonely isolation he must henceforth endure to the end of his life.

And weeps the more furiously for his deep shame at such reprehensible self-pity.

6

Eddie and Miranda

The sun is clear of the hills when Eddie eases out of the flow of traffic on the federal highway and onto a frontage road and then into a large service plaza. He pulls up to a gasoline pump at one of the dozen islands and sits there with the engine idling as he scans the parking lot and the vehicles at the other pumps. His burn wound now stinging only a little under the scarf bandage.

As they were bumping along the trail in the dark it had occurred to him that the Escalade is carrying a tracker. He'd cursed himself for a dope for not having thought of that before. But then what difference would it have made if he had? They could not have gotten away except in the Escalade, and all the Company's other vehicles were certain to be rigged with trackers too. He knows something of such devices—they are among the commodities in which his family traffics. He reflects on the ironic possibility that the unit in the Escalade was shipped into Mexico by his own kin. It would be so well hidden he'd be wasting precious time in searching for it.

The bright side, he tells himself, is that nobody intercepted them when they got to the highway. Which means that Segundo hasn't been found yet, and may not be for a while longer, and that would be ideal. Or it could mean he's only just been found and they're now in the process of getting a fix on the Escalade. Or they already have a fix and are heading this way at this very minute.

It's only another few miles to the turnoff to the Obregón airport, and although the Escalade is low on fuel they easily have enough to get them there. But it's a rule that you can never know how a plan will go, so it's best to be prepared in case it goes bad. Right now, the only preparation Eddie can think of is a full tank of gas.

Miranda too is peering all around. What are we looking for? she says.

Anything that doesn't seem right. Anybody who looks suspicious.

Hey man, everybody out there looks suspicious.

Yeah, he says. You know how to pump gas?

Oh hell no, it's way too complicated.

He ignores her sarcasm and shuts off the engine. Then slips the pistol under his shirt and says for her to fill the tank while he calls Evaristo.

Dear God, I pray I am able do this, she says as she gets out.

The plaza building is divided into a restaurant and a convenience store. There is a bank of telephone booths along the rear wall of the store, and after he gives the girl at the register a deposit to activate the gas pump, he finds a booth with a directory and looks up the number for Evaristo Sotomayor's charter aircraft company and is relieved to find a home number for him too. He'd been afraid he might have only a cell. Evaristo is a longtime friend from school days in Brownsville. He learned to fly a plane before he was legally old enough to drive a car, and he'd been out of high school only a year when he got his Mexican commercial license in Matamoros and then went to work at a charter business in Ciudad Obregón that was co-owned by a cousin. Five months later the cousin was killed in a crash landing and Evaristo became the co-owner. He still has kin in Matamoros and has visited a few times and on each return got together with Eddie for a beer or two. But they haven't seen each other now in almost a year. He's the only person not in the Company whom Eddie knows anywhere in Mexico except for Mexico City and Tamaulipas state.

He calls the office first and the woman who answers tells him Evaristo isn't there. No, he isn't out on a flight, and she doesn't know if he's at home. Eddie thanks her, then tries the home number. An answering machine tells him to leave a message. Damn, what if he's not home? The machine beeps and he says, "Oye, Risto," and then pauses, unsure how to proceed, not wanting to record anything the wrong people might hear. Better to decide what to say and then call back. He's about to hang up when the receiver clicks and Evaristo's voice says, "Bueno?"

"Risto. Eddie Wolfe here. Long time, mano."

"*Eddie?* . . . Oh, fuck, if I'd known it was you . . . whoa . . . you on a cell?"

"Landline. Why? What's going on?" Damn, Eddie thinks, if *he* knows . . .

"What's going on? The word's out on you all over hell is what's going on. Every charter in town's been warned. I don't know what you did—and don't tell me, don't, I do *not* want to know—but the word's out, mano. Anybody helps you is fucked. Completamente chingado! Christ, I'm sweating gasoline just talking—"

"Just over the line, Risto, all I'm asking. Ten grand, American."

"Fuck no! You're outta your goddamn mind dicking around with those people! Lo siento, Eddie, but no way, man. Forget it."

"Fifteen grand, I got it right—"

The line's dead.

Son of a bitch. He keeps the receiver to his ear, telling himself to stay cool, think a minute. Think.

Something's not right.

They found Segundo and put the word out on you, threatened anybody who helps you. Why bother with that if they've got you on a tracker and know where you are? Why didn't they nail you at the highway? Could be they didn't find Segundo soon enough. But they've got people all over this town and could have a dozen guys on top of you this minute.

So where are they?

He hangs up the phone and ambles to the front window and sees that the gas dispenser is back in the cradle of the pump next to the Escalade. Behind the tinted glass she's probably tapping her foot and wondering what's taking him so long.

He goes to the cashier and buys a bag of shelled peanuts and gets his change for the gasoline and makes a casual inspection of the people in the store. Nobody looks suspect, though that's no assurance. He goes outside and stands on the walkway and runs his gaze over the other vehicles as he munches peanuts.

They wouldn't sit here and watch you, he thinks. They wouldn't wait to do it somewhere less public. They'd pop you here and now, fuck the witnesses.

But they haven't done it.

Because . . . they're not here.

Because . . . they don't know you're here.

Because . . . there's no tracker in the Escalade. Or . . . there is, but it's not working.

But no question whatsoever that everybody's got the Escalade's description and plate number.

Switch the plates or get another set of wheels? Plates is easier and there are a lot of black SUVs on the road. But not that many Escalades. And what if there *is* a tracker and it starts working again?

Best switch to another vehicle lickity-goddamn-split.

But not here. Parking lot's way too open to view and he anyway lacks the door-lock and hotwire tools. Do it in town.

It occurs to him that their major identifying traits are the blue of his eyes and her bruised one. Make sure she keeps those shades on.

He goes back inside and buys a pair of sunglasses for himself and a state road map, some plastic-wrapped pastries, and two takeout cups of coffee. Then notices the prepaid cell phones on the shelf beside the register, and without dwelling on a reason for it he buys two of them.

When he gets back to the Escalade he opens the driver's door, saying, I've got some bad news and some—

She's not there.

He sets the purchases on the seat and touches the pistol under his shirt and looks around the lot and sees no sign of her.

Her zipped-up tote bag is still on the seat.

He returns to the store and surveys the place but doesn't see her. Then enters the restaurant through the indoor entrance and looks around. Not there either.

He doubles back into the store. When did they grab her? Where would—?

He spots her coming out of the women's restroom. She doesn't notice him as she heads for the door.

God damn it! Why couldn't she wait till . . .

Easy does it, bubba, he tells himself. Be cool. She has to get your permission to take a piss? Good to be alert, my man, but not so fucking jumpy.

He lets out a long breath and follows her out to the Escalade.

❧

They meld into the heavy traffic bearing toward the city.

We can forget the airport, Eddie says. They'll have people all over it. Same for the trains, buses, everything. It'll be like that at every airfield and depot from here to the border. We can't even stay on this highway. They'll have guys at every toll station. Don't stand a chance at a toll station.

They can do that? Miranda says.

Yes.

They can have people *everywhere*?

Just about. And we can't know where they don't. He gives her a quick look. Hey, listen. We know what they can do. They don't know what *we* can do.

Right, she says. Her smile frail.

He hands her the map and tells her to mark all the toll stations north of Obregón. She opens it on her lap and starts circling the stations with a ballpoint from the console. She sees how close they are to the Sea of Cortéz and that there is a ferry at Guaymas. She says maybe they should cross over to Baja California.

He's already considered that and says it's a bad idea. The Company will have people at every port and marina. Even if we could cross, he says, we'd be on a peninsula. Fewer ways out. They'll cut off the north end and down at the mouth of the Gulf. Forget Baja. It'd be stupid.

Excuse me, she says, it was only a suggestion. And I'm not stupid.

I know that, he says.

A few seconds pass. You're right, though, she says. Forget Baja.

East? The Sierra Madres are in the way. He came to Sinaloa through those mountains, and the guys he was with said the

Sierras are just as rough from one end to the other. The few roads that completely cross them are crooked as snakes and very slow going. Rockfall obstructions everywhere and sometimes blocking a road entirely. There are curves that run along the very edges of the cliffs. The slopes are littered with rusted and burned-up hulks of cars, trucks, buses. There aren't many stretches without little white crosses marking the sites of fatal accidents. The real stopper, though, is that the Company has marijuana and poppy fields and processing labs all over those ranges through a chain of seven states and keeps a close watch on those roads.

We get spotted up there, Eddie says, we'd have nowhere to even try to run. Forget cutting through the Sierras.

He asks how far they are from the border, and she places a paper matchstick on the map's mileage scale and then uses the match to calculate the distance. A hair over three hundred miles.

"As the crow flies. Too bad we ain't crows."

"Cómo?" she says with a frown at his use of English, and he repeats himself in Spanish.

She studies the map, the expanding desert north of Ciudad Obregón. There is no metropolis ahead of them but Hermosillo, the state capital. The only other towns of size between them and the border—and very much smaller than the capital—are Guaymas, a hundred miles south of Hermosillo, and Caborca, 150 miles to its north. On the border itself is Nogales, ten times larger than the town of the same name on the U.S. side. That's it for actual towns. The rest of Sonora is open desert encompassing widely scattered pueblos and villages, traversed by few paved roads other than the federal highway but by a wide web of dirt roads so little traveled they do not even have identifying numbers.

Eddie knows the Sinas will have lookouts at the federal highway's major intersections and exits, but they can't cover those backcountry tracks. As he sees it, the trick is to make it through Guaymas and into the desert. If they can get on those desert trails, they can make it to the border.

To where on the border? she asks.

Yeah, he says, that's the question.

She again consults the map. Nogales? The highway from Caborca connects with a highway going to Nogales. But no, she says, there's a toll station and no easy route around it. Forget that highway. There's another good road that goes up that way, but not directly into Nogales. There are two branching roads to it.

She holds the map up so he can take quick looks at it as he drives.

No, he says, there's no exit off either one. If they watch those, they'll have us. Forget Nogales.

He taps his finger on two places, one in smaller print than the other. There and there. Our only choices.

She peers closely and tells him the smaller one is called Sasabe and looks like no more than a village. The other is Sonoyta, a small town. From Caborca they can go to either place. Sonoyta's a little farther but the road to it is paved. The only way to Sasabe is a dirt road.

We'll decide in Caborca, he says.

The Company will have people watching for them everywhere along the border, but even though he has never been to this part of the country Eddie knows a few things about border towns and the smuggling of people. Hordes of migrants who want to cross to the United States—chickens, they're called by the traffickers who take them over—make their way to those towns every week. And in all those places are agents who can arrange for their crossing, the so-called coyotes, though the term is as often applied to the guides who lead them across. That's how it will be in Sasabe or Sonoyta, whichever they decide on. Flocks of migrants and plenty of coyotes ready to serve them.

We can hide among all those strangers, Eddie tells her, while we look for some guide who'll be happy to take two more customers into his group. Then over the line we go.

Very good, she says with a nod. As if some thorny problem has been fully resolved.

But he knows they're getting way ahead of themselves. They are only at the south periphery of Ciudad Obregón and it's a long way to the border.

It's a long way to the other side of Ciudad Obregón.

⁓

At the outskirts of town Eddie spies a hardware store in a small plaza and makes a quick turn into the lot. He finds a parking spot near the store and backs into it.

Hope you know how to drive, he says.

For Christ's sake, kid, I wasn't living with the Indians before I met you.

He tells her to get in the driver's seat and keep the engine running and be ready to get them the hell out of there fast if it comes to that.

He returns with a plastic shopping bag containing screwdrivers of different sizes and two sets of electrical wires with spring clamps at either end. They are all the tools he needs to avail himself of almost any motor vehicle. She clambers back into the passenger seat and he turns off the distraction of the music. And they drive into Obregón.

7

Eddie and Miranda

The highway serves as a north-south thoroughfare through the city, and as on every Saturday market day Obregón's traffic is thick and slow. Through a sequence of odd timing, they don't come to their first red traffic light until they're midway into town, but they catch every red light thereafter.

Eddie curses at each of these stops, where the Escalade is immobile and easier for the surrounding world to scrutinize. With hundreds of eyes on the lookout for this vehicle, it feels to him as conspicuous as a circus wagon with flashing lights. He keeps checking all the mirrors, though he has no idea how he would recognize Sinas men except by intuition. He takes little comfort from Miranda's belief that the bastards will have a hard time spotting them in this heavy traffic. All the other cars are like camouflage, she points out, and theirs is not the only black SUV among them.

He's keeping an eye out for a good place to snatch a vehicle, but Saturday morning on the city's largest thoroughfare is not an ideal time or place to steal a car. Every parking lot they see is too open to view, too full of shoppers coming and going. He doesn't want to leave the protective cover of heavy traffic to search the side streets for a car, but they're almost to the city limits and the last of the traffic lights, where he will have to double back.

But now they come abreast of a shopping mall with the sort of lot he's been searching for. It goes all the way around the big mall building, and its parking rows are lined with shade trees. He checks the rearview mirror and sees a station wagon crammed with three adults and a pack of kids, and behind it a bus. In the adjoining lane, a taxi, and a smoking Chrysler of 1960s vintage. Nothing to alarm.

He turns into the lot and goes around to the side of the mall where the trees are heaviest and their trunks present the most obstruction to the view of passersby. He drives slowly between two rows of cars, studying the array of vehicles, and fixes on a late-model Dodge van that has tinted windows and whose locks and ignition system he knows how to deal with.

That one, he says. It'll do fine.

I like it, she says. We can sleep in it.

He stops short of the van, leaving himself room to back it out of the parking space. He rummages in the bag for a screwdriver and a set of clamp wires and then waits while a man and woman and two small children get into a gray sedan parked farther down the row. A minute later the car drives off, and he takes another look in the rearview before getting out. And sees a large red pickup truck with smoked windows come around the far end of the row.

It advances slowly and halts about ten yards behind them.

Miranda turns around to see what's caught his attention. Oh shit.

The idling truck remains motionless.

If it's them, she says, what are they waiting for?

Eddie is wondering the same thing. Then understands there's another one coming around to cut them off.

He guns the Escalade forward and the red truck leaps after them—and up ahead a white sedan comes wheeling around from the far end of the row.

Eddie floors the accelerator and rams the left front of the sedan in a smash of metal and glass and knocks the car completely around and into a row of parked cars. The Escalade caroms to the right and scrapes against two or three cars before Eddie makes a tight left turn with tires shrieking.

The red truck swerves into view behind them.

A coming car veers out of his way and Eddie speeds past the next five rows and makes a squealing turn into a wide lane leading to an exit.

A woman pushing a shopping cart across the lane freezes at the sight of the Escalade barreling toward her and Eddie veers and misses her but smacks the steel cart flying. It ricochets off a parked car and twirls into the air with its contents strewing and it drops behind the Escalade and hits the red truck's windshield and glances off.

Eddie touches the brakes and exits onto a side street and speeds up again. The truck staying in his rearview, its windshield cobwebbed on the driver's side, the driver hunched down to see out through a small clear segment.

They're on a residential street running parallel to the highway and four or five blocks east of it. As he speeds down the street Eddie leans on the horn to warn away a group of girls playing jump rope and they dart off into a yard. A few blocks ahead is a yield sign where the street merges into a divided four-lane road.

He has a clear view of that road's eastbound traffic coming from his left and tries to gauge its speed as he begins to slow down. There is a muted clatter from behind them and a hard rapping against the back of the Escalade and Miranda cries "Chingados!" and hunches down in her seat. Eddie cuts his eyes to the mirror and sees pale starbursts with dark centers on the back window.

They are almost to the cross avenue now and he can see the merging lane curving off to the right past the yield sign, but he's going too fast to hold in that merging lane without slewing out into traffic. Then he sees a gap in the flow of traffic in the nearest lane and his foot jumps back and forth from the accelerator to the brake as he tries to time his approach.

He makes a sharp skidding turn that carries him past the merging lane and into the gap in front of a green car that brakes hard to keep from hitting him and the green car is rammed by the car behind it—and the car behind that one is smashed broadside by the red pickup skidding past the merging lane.

There ensues a chain reaction of explosive crashings and screeching tires and spinning vehicles. In the rearview Eddie sees a car veer over the median and partly into the westbound lane and strike a station wagon almost head-on and then go whirling back into the eastbound lanes to collide with a minivan. The station wagon slews sideways and is hit by the semitrailer behind it and knocked onto its side and skids to a halt with its front end on the median. The semi is able to stay in its lane as it stops.

Traffic comes to a standstill behind them. Both of the eastbound lanes are completely blocked by the wreckage. The near westbound lane is obstructed, as well, and only the westbound outer lane remains clear, though it has slowed to little better than walking speed.

Miranda sits with one hand tight on the door handle, the other clutching the seat. Breathing through her mouth.

You all right? he says.

She looks at him and nods, eyes vibrant with fright and exhilaration. My God . . . we're still moving, she says.

Yeah we are, he says.

They need to reverse direction to get back to the highway. He turns left onto the wide median to try to get through the near westbound lane, the line of stalled vehicles closed up tight and making intermittent horn-blowing meldings into the slow passage of the outer westbound lane. Directly in Eddie's way is a panel truck and behind it is a taxi, both drivers looking away from him over their shoulders for an opening in the crawling line of traffic.

Eddie hands Miranda the Glock and tells her to keep her finger off the trigger and lower her window. When the panel truck is at last able to slip into the far lane and the taxi starts to close the gap, Eddie gooses the Escalade forward and crushes the cab's front fender. The taxi jerks to a halt and the driver's face whips toward him, scowling, mouth working. Eddie tells her to point the gun at him, and she does, and the driver gapes and raises his palms off the steering wheel. He stays in place as Eddie backs up a bit and then noses the Escalade off the median and ahead of the cab.

Eddie then leans on the horn and the oncoming driver in the outer lane looks over and sees Miranda pointing the gun at him and hits the brakes so sharply his car bobs. Eddie pulls in front of him, and the guy lets the taxi cut in too, perhaps to put a buffer between himself and the crazy people with the gun. The taxi does not crowd the Escalade as they move along in the creeping traffic.

They slowly come abreast of the destruction, a tangle of smashed and steaming vehicles amid shards of glass and black-and-green sheets of oil and radiator fluid. Sirens already sounding in the distance, though barely discernible through the ceaseless blare of car horns. People milling, some limping, some bloody-faced, many with cell phones to their ears. A woman sitting on the ground with her hands to her face. A man's head jutting from the jagged windshield of an old VW microbus looks like it's been scalped. A woman hangs head-down in an awkward twist from the open door of a car, skirt bunched at her hips, hair draping the ground.

Miranda is staring wide-eyed at the carnage, a hand to her mouth. We did this, she says.

You could look at it that way, he says. Since we could've chosen to stay in the parking lot and talk things over with those guys.

She looks at him. They would have killed us.

Yes. And put our heads in a bag.

Yes, she says, yes. They would have . . . done that.

They spot the red pickup that pursued them. It's on the median and partly in the westbound lanes, its windshield folded outward from the frame like a big cobweb gaping on the driver's side, the driver half out and facedown on the crumpled hood. There's no sign of the one who did the shooting.

"Dumbfucks," Eddie mutters.

Then says in Spanish, They should've shot our tires. Very basic rule.

8

Eddie and Miranda

They reach the highway and turn north onto it and in minutes are clear of the town. Eddie has to assume the guys in the red truck reported the Escalade's location, and with a mashed front fender and a bullet-pocked rear window it is now even easier to identify.

A few miles ahead is the little town of Esperanza, and then a few miles beyond that is a toll station, where the bastards can easily block them in. But the map shows road junctions with the highway at points past the toll station. He tells Miranda they'll switch vehicles in Esperanza and then take a side road to one of those junctions.

Yes, she says. He can see she's still quivering with adrenaline. He feels the tremor of his own.

They're almost to the first exit into Esperanza when he detects a black SUV three cars back in the outer lane. Dodge Durango. He knows it's them without knowing how he knows.

Damn it, he says.

She turns in her seat and looks back through the ruined rear window. She says, The black thing like ours?

Maybe. Keep an eye on it.

He moves over into the exit lane, just ahead of a pink Ford sedan with a woman at the wheel and a young girl beside her.

They're coming, she says. Three cars back.

He exits onto a frontage road and then turns off on a poorly paved two-way street of light traffic. The pink Ford stays behind them, but the next car turns the other way and the Durango closes up behind the Ford.

They are at the south end of town, and two miles farther on are past the town and into farmland irrigated by the Yaqui River. They cross a bridge over a canal and come to a red light at an intersection. To the right the road curves back into Esperanza, to the left it goes past a cluster of roadside businesses and a run-down residential area and then into a mix of farms and scrubland. Across the intersection the road remains wide but is of dirt and runs through an enormous patchwork of sugar fields.

An old Chevy pickup is in front of them. The left-turn signal is blinking on the Ford in back of them. The girl and woman are having an animated argument. The Durango looms behind the Ford, its windshield black as obsidian. If anyone steps out of the Durango, Eddie intends to ram the old pickup into the intersection and then work his way through the smashup or turn right toward Esperanza, whichever might seem easier.

Far behind the Durango, a police car turns onto the frontage road and comes their way, roof lights flashing. Eddie watches it in the rearview, Miranda in the side mirror.

The light turns green and the old truck lumbers across the intersection, black smoke issuing from its exhaust pipe, as traffic begins to cross from the opposite direction. Eddie stays in place, his eyes cutting back and forth from the green light to the rearview mirror. A line of vehicles is forming to the right and left on the crossroad. The woman in the Ford has turned her attention from the girl and is scowling at the Escalade. She gives Eddie a little beep of her horn and he puts on his left-turn blinker and eases the Escalade halfway into the intersection and halts there to wait for the only car still oncoming, though it is yet so far away Eddie could easily make the turn before it reaches the intersection. The car finally goes by but Eddie stays put, and the woman in the Ford gives him a longer honk of the horn. The cop car is coming very fast and Eddie sees now that it's state police, but as its siren closes to audible range it is drowned out by the onset of the Ford horn's steady squall.

The traffic light turns red and still he remains midway in the intersection, blocking the cars to his left, whose drivers now join the Ford in blowing their horns at him. The driver of the lead car to his right, a green Buick, motions angrily for him to get on across the intersection. Eddie looks at him but does not move. The man makes a gesture of exasperation and starts to cross in front of him—and Eddie stomps on the gas and the Escalade lunges across the intersection and the Buick brakes sharply to keep from hitting it.

Eddie sees the Durango pulling around the Ford, but its passage is now impeded by the cross traffic. And now the police car is there with its commanding lights and cutting ahead of the

Durango, the other traffic haphazardly trying to get out of the way so the cops can pass by.

And now here they both come, the cop car and the Durango behind it.

Looking through the rear window, Miranda says, I think the police are with them.

What a surprise, Eddie says.

He has a large lead on them as he speeds down the wide road through the sugar fields. He passes the old Chevy truck at almost seventy miles an hour, engulfing it in dust. He can't see it from here but he knows the highway is a few miles to their right and runs parallel to the road they're on. Miranda checks the map and reckons they're almost past the point where the highway toll station stands.

The canebrake to either side of the road is crosshatched with alleyways for farm vehicles, and Eddie's sure some of them connect to a highway junction road. The cops are neither gaining on them nor losing ground.

Eddie spies an alley entrance coming up on the right, then taps the brakes a few times and makes a hard turn onto it, skidding partly into the cane and mowing down a portion of the outermost rows, the stalks whacking against the Escalade, the tires losing purchase in the soft irrigated earth before regaining traction, and then he's on the alley and resuming speed, the dense cane like green walls a few feet to either side of them. The shadowed alley is well graded and much less dusty than the outer road and runs straight as a ruler toward a green vanishing point.

In the mirror, he sees the tan dust cloud of their pursuers advancing toward the lane's entrance, and then the police car comes into view as it makes a sliding turn. Then the Durango.

Get over here, Eddie says. He raises his ass and the Escalade weaves a little as she slides over the console and squeezes under him and takes the wheel and he scrambles back into the middle row of seats. He takes up the M-16 and chambers a round and tells her to reduce speed a little, let the cops get closer. The rifle has an automatic-fire option but the full magazine is all the ammunition he has, and thirty rounds can get eaten up very fast on automatic fire. He sets the selector on three-round burst.

The cop car is gaining on them, the Durango behind it as though it's being towed. When I say Now, he says, take your foot off the gas and leave it off till I say Go, then stomp it.

She nods, and he says, *You hear me?* and she says, Yes, *yes*.

He lowers the left-side window, admitting a loud rush of air.

The cops are within a dozen yards of them when one of them leans out of the passenger-side window with a pistol in his hand and starts shooting, the reports sounding like small balloon pops, the rounds thunking against the Escalade's rear glass.

Now! Eddie yells.

The Escalade decelerates and the cops close up faster and Eddie juts himself out the window and fires two three-rounders, all six bullets punching through the car's windshield on the driver's side. The car abruptly slows and the Durango fishtails as it brakes to keep from running into it and the cop car swerves into the cane and out of sight.

Go! Eddie shouts, ducking back inside, and the Escalade surges forward. He'd known the cops' glass wasn't bulletproof but doesn't know about the Durango's and can't afford to waste ammunition finding out.

Without the cop car in its way, the Durango starts to gain on them. Supercharged bastard, Eddie thinks.

Oh God, Miranda says, cutting glances at the rearview.

Just hold your speed, Eddie tells her. He intends to let them get a little closer and then shoot out their tires.

But they beat him to it. A man with a small machine gun leans out and fires a burst and the left rear side of the Escalade abruptly sags. Miranda curses and fights the steering wheel.

Into the cane! Eddie yells. Get in the cane!

She veers into the canebrake and it's like plunging into a shadowy green sea. The Escalade bores through the stalks in a great clattering, bouncing and swaying over the furrowed ground as Eddie yells to go left, go right, directing her in a zigzag course to stay out of the Durango's view.

Stop! he yells, and she brakes hard and the Escalade slews to a halt amid the high stalks in a raise of dark dust.

He pushes the right-side back door open against the hard press of cane and slides out with the M-16 and stays behind the open door for cover, facing back into the ragged swath they gouged through the field, ready to shoot.

They don't appear.

He tells her to cut the motor and she does and he hears the Durango's idling engine out on the alley. Then it too falls silent.

They're coming on foot, he whispers.

He reaches in for the Glock and tells her to come on. She crawls over the console and out the door and he takes her by the hand and leads her into the cane ahead, holding the rifle crosswise in front of him to ward the sharp-edged leaves from his face, feeling them cutting his knuckles. A few yards in, he squats and pulls her down beside him. The front of the Escalade is discernible through the packed stalks. They listen but hear only their own breath. The air is still and heavy and smells of dirt.

He instructs her in a whisper to lie on her stomach, facing toward the Escalade, then brandishes the Glock and asks if she knows how to use it. She shakes her head. He says, That's all right, it's an easy gun to shoot, there's no safety lever to work or hammer to cock. He hands it to her and tells her it'll fire with every pull of the trigger, but not to shoot unless she see somebody. If she shoots one and he falls and she can still see him, shoot him again, and if he still moves, shoot him again. There's at least two of them, he whispers, but there could be more.

I'll be over there, he says, gesturing ahead and a little to the left, so don't shoot in that direction. He instructs her to count to thirty and then give the stalks a little shake and listen hard while she counts to thirty again. If she doesn't hear anybody coming, shake them again and count again. Same thing over and over till she hears somebody coming or she hears his call for her.

She nods. Eyes wide. Start counting, he says.

He eases carefully through the cane to a spot abreast of the Escalade and maybe twelve feet from it and hunkers on one knee. He hears a swishing of stalks over where he left her, and he starts counting to thirty but is only at twenty-four when the stalks swish again. She's nervous and counting a little fast.

She has swished the stalks once again, and he is at the count of nineteen when he hears the crunch of someone treading on the flattened stalks in the nearest bend of the Escalade's trail into the field.

He breathes deeply and slowly through his mouth and holds the rifle ready.

But she evidently hasn't heard them yet and swishes stalks again and the footsteps stop.

Silence. Then raspy unintelligible whispers. Then rustlings. He's sure now that there are only two of them and they have split up and are advancing on either side of the Escalade.

There are no more swishings from where she is. She's heard them too.

The one coming around on Eddie's side is stepping slowly and carefully, but it is impossible to move through the cane in silence. A moment more and the shadowy form of a man appears a few feet in front of him and Eddie fires a three-rounder into his face and the man heaves rearward, triggering a reflex burst of automatic fire that rips through the stalks over Eddie's head and brings chunks of cane down on him.

From the other side of the Escalade a man shouts, *You get them?*

Eddie eases forward and sees the man he shot sprawled in a cane furrow. Boots, jeans, green muscle shirt. Eyes wide and lightless, a hole under one, two holes above it. The ground mucking red under his head. A MAC-10 machine pistol near his hand, a chromed Beretta in his waistband, a cell phone holstered on his belt.

The cane rustles loudly as the other one starts coming around the front of the Escalade in a hurry and Eddie hears the Glock fire twice and the man cries out and the pistol cracks twice more and there's a soft thud.

Eddie backtracks through the stalks until he's within a few feet of the front of the Escalade and sees a man in a Houston Astros baseball cap and a yellow guayabera shirt, its front gleaming with bright blood. The man sits against the front bumper, chin on chest, legs doubled under him, arms lax at his sides. A MAC beside him.

Eddie strains to hear whatever he can but there is only the croak of a nearby crow. Keeping his eyes on the man, he says, "Miranda."

"Chacho?" Her voice small.

There is no other sound. He's convinced now there were only the two of them.

I'm coming out, he says. Don't shoot *me*.

Keeping the M-16 pointed at the man's head, he steps over to him. On one inner forearm is a well-wrought tattoo of the Holy Virgin cradling an AK, and on the other, above the wrist, is a black circle the size of a nickel with short black rays extending from it. The sign of Luna Negra, the Company's elite cadre of gunmen. The man has two distinct wounds in his chest and his arm is bloody from another. Eddie puts his foot to the man's shoulder and pushes him over on his side, the cap tumbling off to reveal the wound in his neck where a bullet passed through it.

Miranda comes out of the stalks, holding the Glock out before her, mouth slack, eyes wide and focused on the dead man.

Eddie sidles out of her line of fire and slings the rifle on his shoulder, then shows her how to place her finger on the trigger guard to prevent an accidental discharge and gently pushes down her hand so the pistol points at the ground.

I was so scared, she says. She examines the crotch of her jeans. I thought I wet myself.

Doesn't look it, he says. Listen, you did real good. Hit him every shot.

You said shoot till he falls and doesn't move.

Yeah, you sure did that.

Her eyes again fix on the dead man. I don't . . .

What? he says.

What do you . . . I don't know . . . *feel*? She gives him a quick look as if she's afraid he's going to ask what she means.

I feel a lot luckier than these pricks.

She wipes at her nose and nods awkwardly. Yes, she says. Yes. Me too. Then something settles in her eyes and her mouth tightens—and she kicks the man's leg and mutters, *Pig*. And slips the Glock into her jeans.

Eddie smiles and thinks, Some girl. Grab our stuff, he says. We gotta move.

As she hurries off to the Escalade, he takes up the MAC and detects no smell on it of recent firing. He removes the magazine of .45-caliber cartridges and judges by its heft that it holds its thirty-round capacity or nearly so, then reinserts it. He's handled a few MACs and always liked the gun, though some guys he knows consider it practically an antique. They come with a retractable stock but this one lacks it. He pulls up the man's guayabera to get at his pockets and sees that, like the other Sina, he has a cell phone on his belt. The same model. He withdraws it from the holster and opens it and turns it on and taps a sequence of buttons he was taught by an aunt who knows about such things.

Shit, he says.

What? she says, returning with the tote bag.

It's got a tracker, he says. And begins pressing another combination of buttons.

What's that?

It lets somebody somewhere else know exactly where we are.

They *know* where we are? She looks all about in alarm.

He smiles, staring at the phone. No.

But you said—

It's turned off.

He looks at the dead man and then toward where the other one lay. I get it, he says. They didn't want their own guys to know where they were.

But why not? The more who help to chase—

Because there's a reward for us and they didn't want to share it. Except with the two cops. And the only reason they called them into it was to clear the way, give them cop cover.

How do you know there is a reward?

If you were the Boss wouldn't you offer one for whoever killed your brother?

He shuts off the phone and closes it and shoves it into her bag, then considers the phone holster on the man's belt. No need to let whoever finds him know for sure he had a phone. He removes the holster and adds it to her tote, then goes through the man's pockets and takes his money and the keys to the Durango.

He leads her at a clumsy trot over the crushed stalks back to the field alley. He emerges from the cane and sees the Durango ten yards to his left at the end of parallel brake ruts in the dirt. And then on his right sees a crouching uniformed cop not ten yards away, raising a pistol at him. Even as he's cocking and bringing up the MAC, Eddie thinks, He's got me.

But no. The cop's gun barrel bobs slightly and he looks confused in the instant before Eddie's burst hits him just above the eyes and sprays the top of his head onto the dirt behind him and he falls backward.

Eddie goes to him and picks up the pistol. A blued Taurus 9-millimeter with the safety lever still on. He wonders if the cop was unused to the gun or simply panicked and forgot.

Miranda comes up and makes a face at the sight of the man's destroyed head.

The one who shot at us, Eddie says. Car must've got stuck in the field. He should've walked off the other way.

He puts the Taurus and the MAC in her bag and then drags the body into the cane while she stands lookout in the alley. Then they hustle to the Durango and get going.

He can't believe nobody else has shown up. Which doesn't mean they're not on their way—even though there's no show of dust from the road on the other side of the fields.

Luck, luck, luck, Eddie thinks. Talent is a very good thing to have, but absolutely nothing beats good luck. There's a rule of some sort about it.

They come to a cross alley and turn west. A few miles farther, they exit the sugar field at a road leading to a junction with the highway.

She has kept silent ever since they got into the Durango, smoking one cigarette after another. He wonders if she's dwelling on how close she has come to getting killed in recent hours and is perhaps wishing there might be some way to make her peace with the Company.

As if she's heard his thoughts, she turns and says, All I want is to get to the other side.

Well, yeah, he says, a little puzzled. That's the whole idea.

No . . . I mean I don't expect anything from you once we get across. I just . . . I want you to know that.

He looks at her. Then back at the road. He knows that when a woman says she doesn't expect anything from you, you can bet the ranch she damn well does. No response is best if they let you get away with it.

I only hope you don't run out on me before we get across, she says.

It's not a remark that can be ignored. I wouldn't do that, he says.

It would not be so strange, she says. Men do that.

Yeah? Well . . . not me. And not your father. And not . . . what's-his-name. Gabo. Hell, neither man you've told me about has run out on you.

No. They both died.

He can't read her face. Well I promise you I'll do my best not to die. All right?

Thank you, she says. And half a minute later says, You did come a little close back there, you know.

Yeah, well . . . so did you.

She nods and looks out the window and then back at him. But here we still are, she says.

Damn right. As somebody I know once said, they have to catch us before they can kill us.

They exchange a grin. Then both look away and then back at each other. And erupt into laughter. Into huge convulsive guffaws. She stamps the dashboard with her feet. He pounds the steering wheel with his palm and nearly runs off the road—and they laugh even harder and it takes a while for them to gain control of themselves, cramped bellies aching.

At the highway junction is a small plaza comprising a gasoline station, garage, and café. He sends her into the café for a takeout bag of food.

While she's at it, he takes out his mini Swiss pocketknife and removes the back cover of the Sina phone. And there the tracker is, nestled in the array of circuit board components. On casual inspection it looks like any one of dozens of other parts, but on careful scrutiny he spies a miniscule pink dot near one end of it and then knows what kind of tracker it is and is impressed. Made for insertion in a cell phone, it's nothing but a directional signal with a distance readout. Nothing uncommon about it, except that according to his Aunt Laurel—who owns and manages Delta Instruments & Graphics and knows everything there is to know about these things—its signal is transmitted in a broken pattern.

Frequency fragmentation, she called it, something like that. Almost any receiver within range can pick up the signal fragments but they will seem to be coming from different directions. As she explained it, the only way to "descramble" the signal is by connecting a second receiver to the first one as a sort of ancillary booster and calibrating them to operate in tandem on the same screen. But because the tracker's signal is configured according to minute differentials in a given phone model's circuitry, the calibration varies not only from one brand of phone to another but also from model to model of each brand. Without knowing the calibration code for the receivers *and* both the brand and the model of the phone the tracker is attached to, it's impossible to tune in its signal. That's the device's big selling point. The thing had showed up on the black market a year or so ago but nobody knew who made it. The shipping points were from all over the world. Laurel thought it was some maverick nerd somewhere, but because the batch she bought—which came with a thick booklet of calibration codes—was from a longtime associate in Taiwan, at Delta Instruments they called it the Buddha. She'd paid a pretty penny for them, but they were in turn sold to Mexican buyers at a hundred-percent markup. The next time Laurel tried to buy some, however, her Chinese associate said he was unable to get any more. Rumor had it that Israeli agents had tracked down the maker and confiscated his entire supply, but it was only a rumor. Eddie grins at the thought that the tracker in this phone might have come from a Delta sale.

He puts the phone back together and returns it to her tote, then checks the map. Guaymas is less than fifty miles up the highway. The highway forks a few miles south of the city, one branch passing through the town, the other looping around it but passing through a toll station. Forget the loop.

Miranda returns with a whole grilled chicken, a half dozen cheese empanadas, some roasted ears of corn, a variety of small pastries, two big paper cups of coffee. The aromas are delectable.

But he has spotted a helicopter low in the sky and coming from the direction of Obregón. Maybe it's a commercial craft. Or maybe not.

He cranks up the Durango and wheels out of the plaza lot, an empanada in one hand, and turns onto a frontage road that a mile farther on merges into the northbound traffic of the federal highway.

9

The Boss

That morning the Boss receives a summoned Elizondo Morales in his office. The room is almost chilly with air-conditioning, yet Morales's face shines with sweat. He confirms for the Boss that he hired Porter back in March. The kid was brought to him by Alberto Desmayo, chief of the crew that collects arms purchases throughout the central zone. Desmayo had met Porter at Patria Chica, a large ranch in San Luis Potosí state belonging to the Little family.

The Boss knows who the Littles are, though he has never met any of them in person. A clan descended from an American who settled in Mexico long ago, hence the surname. Even as they prospered in beef cattle and thoroughbred horses, they have also trafficked in an assortment of illegal trades, mainly arms broker-ing, and mainly for a Mexico City group called Los Jaguaros. By way of the Littles, the Company has been buying guns from the Jaguaros since before he became the Boss. He has never met any of them, either.

Morales explains that Desmayo has been making the arms pickups from Patria Chica for three years and has come to know the Littles well. On his most recent trip there, they introduced Porter to him as a distant in-law from Tampico who'd had to leave there a few weeks before because of some trouble with the law. While they were loading the arms, the kid asked Desmayo if there was any chance of getting a job with the Sinas. The Littles seemed surprised that he was willing to leave them, but Porter said he wanted to do something more exciting than work with cows and horses and sometimes load guns on trucks. Desmayo told the kid the only Company jobs he'd heard of lately were for a couple of guards at a ranch the Company chiefs at times use for special parties. He warned him it was a shitty job, way the hell in the desert, no drinking or phones allowed, no women on the premises.

Morales interrupts himself to assure the Boss that he means no offense in his description of the ranch job but is only repeating what Desmayo told the kid. The Boss shows no expression and gestures for him to continue.

When Porter said he wanted the job anyway, Desmayo told him it was of course required that a guard be a good shot with a rifle, and he would have to prove it before he was hired. So the kid got a rifle from a truck and showed how well he could shoot. Put on a hell of a show, according to Desmayo, who agreed to take Porter back to Culiacán with him and recommend him for the job. The Littles tried to talk him out of going, but the kid was set on it.

So Desmayo brought him to me, Morales says, and I made him show *me* that he can shoot, and I have to say, he's a deadeye. He looked pretty strong and healthy, so I saw no reason not to hire him. I am truly very sorry to hear of what happened to El

Segundo, my chief. When I was informed of it this morning, I immediately sent a copy of Porter's file to Tiburón. Believe me, if I'd had the least suspicion that Porter—

The Boss raises a hand to silence him. He has been weighing in his mind whether Morales made an error in hiring the kid. It is Morales's good fortune that he has decided he did not. He has determined that Morales could not possibly have known Porter would be trouble. He thanks Morales for his report and tells him to go back to work. And nearly sighs at the great relief on Morales's face. How can a man bear to live in such fear of another?

He considers having the transport chief, the Desmayo fellow, brought to him for a talk. Then decides against that too. The kid had worked for the Littles, which was recommendation enough for Desmayo to in turn recommend him to Morales. Nothing questionable about it. And the Littles would never have let the kid come here if they'd known he was a crazy bastard capable of jeopardizing their ties with the Company. Money always comes first with them. It's in their gringo blood. Desmayo could not know anything about Porter except for what the Littles told him. Could not know anything he should have told Morales but did not.

So does the Boss decide.

Shortly past noon he receives a call from Tiburón, who with customary straightforwardness reports that Porter was twice spotted driving north and was both times pursued and both times escaped. In the first instance, two Company men were killed in a multi-vehicle smashup in Ciudad Obregón. In the second, two Company men and two state cops in the pay of the Company chased him into a sugarcane field north of town where all four were later found dead. Witnesses to the beginning of the second chase said a police car was after a black SUV and then another black SUV sped after the cops, but none of the witnesses could identify the make of either of the civilian vehicles. A police helicopter was dispatched and spotted the cop car and one of the SUVs in the cane field and directed a squadron of cops to the scene. The SUV was the Boss's Escalade—whose registration is in the name of an orphan child who died five years ago in Mexico City. The police interpretation is that the cops got caught in a fight between rival gangs. They think the two cops tried to call for help but their radio malfunctioned. They have identified the dead guys in the cane field as ex-convicts with extensive records but are unaware that they were in the Company's employ. They know nothing about the ones who got away other than they were in a black SUV.

All this information, Tiburón tells him, derives from police reports that were copied to the Company's underboss in Ciudad Obregón as soon as they were filed at police headquarters. Copies are en route to the Boss. The Obregón underboss apprised Tiburón that the two Sinas in the cane field had been driving a Dodge Durango, and so Porter obviously fled in it, though by now he may have switched to another vehicle.

Tiburón has also spoken with the head of the Little family, who expressed dismay on learning of Porter's murder of Enrique and asked that his condolences be conveyed to the Boss. He assured Tiburón that nobody at Patria Chica had heard from Porter or expected to hear from him, but if the kid should make contact they would let the Sinas know right away. The Little boss said their kinship to the kid was too remote for it to warrant any disturbance of their long association with the Company.

In short, Tiburón says, the Littles see it as Porter's fuckup and Porter's problem. The kid's on his own.

The Boss smiles tightly in appreciation of his own prescience.

Tiburón has posted Company men at every airport and train depot and major bus station north of Guaymas and between the seacoast and the Sierras, and the word has gone out to every private airfield. But, he tells the Boss, he believes Porter has anticipated all of that and will stick to the road and try for the border. All of the Company's lookouts on the coast and along the mountain roads have been alerted and there are men at every toll station. But if Porter's as smart as he seems to be, Tiburón is sure he will avoid those riskier courses and will head for the backcountry roads. If he gets into them, there's not much chance of intercepting him before he reaches the frontier. On the other hand, he'll have to take it a lot slower on those trails and probably won't reach the border till late tomorrow. The only real question is where. The kid was with the Company long enough to know how easily they can cover the main highway exits and toll stations, the ports of entry. He must know how stupid it would be to try for California on the only road through the Altar Desert. He's probably figured out the only choice he's got is to cross somewhere between Nogales and Sonoyta. That still gives him a door some 125 miles wide, but it's the worst part of the desert and he'll have to cross it on foot. Maybe he's crazy enough to try it on his own, but his only real chance is with a guide. His picture has gone out to all the known coyotes in Sasabe and Sonoyta. The Company is of course not the only organization smuggling drugs and migrants in that region—the Baja outfit and its undergangs persist in their encroachments, and God alone knows how many independents are still at it despite the dozen or more of them killed in warning this past year—but word of the fat reward for him has been spread all along the line, and Tiburón has ordered lookouts assigned to every hotel, motel, and private residence where coyotes are known to assemble their chickens in readiness to take them across.

If the kid looks for a guide in either place, Tiburón says, we'll have him.

The Boss agrees with Tiburón's assessment of Porter's intentions and approves of the actions he has taken to try to intercept him. But the assessment is full of "ifs" and it's clear enough that despite Tiburón's efforts to nail the kid at the frontier, the fucker may still get away.

Keep me posted, the Boss says. His tone a cool veneer over his anger.

He deliberates briefly after the report from Tiburón and then taps a number into his phone.

A recorded voice says, "Digame."

The dealership has a new truck in stock, says the Boss. Very good price. Give him a call. And presses the "off" button.

Not a minute later his phone rings and he says "Bueno" and a man asks, What is it?

Are you free to accept it immediately?

I am as always free to do as I please. Tell me what it is and I'll tell you if I want it.

They have done business with each other a few times before, the Boss and this man—whose name is Humberto Xinalma, although most have heard of him only as El Martillo. A large man of great strength, he is a former member of a band of Mexican Special Forces deserters known as Los Zetas, an organization of enforcers for the Gulf cartel—though the Zetas have recently formed their own drug operation as well as begun vending their enforcement services to other organizations besides the

Gulf people. More than a year ago, however, El Martillo went into business for himself and has fared well as an independent contractor. It is said that he could have been an excellent police detective, that he misses no detail, that he can know your next move before you do. He works with a partner named José Sarasate, known as El Pico, tall and lean and clean-shaven, with an almond-shaped head, and he too is a former Zeta. They are natives of Nogales and thoroughly familiar with the desert, and both can speak English. On their most recent assignment for the Boss, they put a stop to the snooping of a pair of nettlesome newspaper reporters from Aguascalientes, leaving the heads on the front seat of their editor's car.

After the Boss gives him a summary of the situation with Porter, Martillo says, You did not say how he killed your brother.

Strangled. From behind.

He's that good? This kid?

He's been that lucky.

He offers Martillo the usual fee if he kills him and can prove he did. Should the proof consist of Porter's head, he gets a bonus of twenty-five percent. Should he deliver Porter to him alive, his fee will be doubled. Should someone else get Porter first, Martillo may keep one-third of the advance.

If necessary, do I go over the line to complete the job? Martillo asks.

The Boss understands it's riskier over there and he agrees to Martillo's price if he has to cross the border to get him. I don't care if you have to chase him to fucking Chicago, he says.

Understood, Martillo says. You say he's now around Guaymas?

That's the latest information.

One moment, Martillo says. And a few seconds later says, I'll take it. Payment by the usual arrangement.

Of course, the Boss says.

Send the information to Mamá García's, Martillo says, referring to a backstreet diner in Hermosillo, one of many Sonora venues he uses as message centers.

It's on the way, the Boss says. Will you give me periodic reports?

He already knows the answer, and Martillo knows he knows, and says nothing.

Others do, Boss says.

Am I others? Martillo says.

The Boss checks his irritation. All right, I'll hear from you when I do.

Correct, Martillo says.

10

Alberto Desmayo

Alberto Desmayo is having a late-morning coffee at a restaurant near the Plazuela Rosales and ogling a happy group of chattering teenage girls in miniskirts at a nearby table when Mono Vásquez comes rushing in and sits down beside him. In a breathless whisper Mono gives him the news of Porter's killing of El Segundo the night before and his escape with Segundo's bitch. The story has been racing through the Company. Vásquez is a member of Desmayo's arms pickup crew and well remembers the Porter kid and the shooting exhibition he put on at Patria Chica.

They say the Boss had Morales brought to the office and chewed his ass for hiring the fucker, Vásquez whispers. The guys were taking bets if Morales would come out alive but he was lucky. Anyway, the word is, they got Porter cut off every way but by car. They say he's headed north and gonna try crossing the frontier on foot. Fucker's gotta be crazy. The Boss has promised a fat reward to the guy who brings him the kid's head. Man, wouldn't I like to collect that!

Why don't you try?

Give me the time off with pay and I will.

Go fuck yourself, Desmayo says. He stands up and brushes crumbs from his shirtfront. While you're doing that, I'll be fucking a little cutie I got waiting for me across town.

He ambles out of the restaurant. And as soon as he's out of Vásquez's sight he hurries to his car and then speeds for home. He has worked for the Company for almost four years and he well knows how unforgiving the Boss can be toward underlings who make serious mistakes. He cannot be sure the Boss will regard his recommendation of Porter to Morales as a serious mistake but neither can he be sure that he won't. Better to disappear in his own way than in the Boss's.

An hour later—with all the money from his closed-out bank accounts and only a pair of suitcases, accompanied by his young wife and baby daughter—he is on a train bound for Tenango, Guatemala, where his brother-in-law owns a lumber mill and will be glad to have him as an affluent partner.

If they had not had to wait at the station for twenty minutes for their train to arrive, Desmayo would not have made the telephone call. But standing in the waiting room and seeing a station phone booth so nearby and available, he felt a tug of obligation. The Littles had held to their side of the arrangement and made the deposits into his bank every week. They did not deserve to go uninformed. He went into the booth and made the call and quickly told the person at the other end all that he had heard, but did not give the man a chance to ask any questions before wishing them luck and hanging up.

11

Eddie and Miranda

Eddie parks the Durango under a shade tree on a side street and gets out. She slides behind the wheel and watches him walk to a used car lot a block away. In his pocket is the Mexican currency they took from Segundo. A half hour later he drives out in a battered 1989 Ford F-150 pickup of pale green with a rusty white camper top. Its odometer shows 156,000 miles, but its V-6 engine is sound, its air conditioner functional, and its backcountry tires show ample tread. A fifteen-year-old vehicle of good disguise, beat-up and homely but tough as a tractor.

She follows him to a shopping plaza parking lot where they abandon the Durango. He asks directions to the nearest secondhand clothing store and they go there and buy faded pants and shirts, field shoes, a small army backpack of waterproof canvas. She assures him her tote is waterproof and she doesn't need a hardier bag. They next go to a shopping mall and buy a Guaymas map and supplies to clean and freshly bandage his wound, buy beach shorts, T-shirts, sneakers, bandannas, straw hats, snazzy black-and-orange Hermosillo Naranjeros baseball caps, a guayabera shirt for him and sandals for her. While he waits in line to pay at the register, she seeks out a large comb and a pair of barber scissors and, to keep these items a secret from him, pays for them at another counter.

They sip Cokes at the mall food court and he studies the Guaymas map, and then goes to a telephone stand and leafs through the chain-attached directory. He had at first thought to get clear of the city as soon as they could and then sleep in the truck somewhere out in open country. But now he thinks it is safer to rest a few hours in one of the old seaside motels a few miles west of the city. He doubts the Sinas will even try to distribute their descriptions to every single hotel and motel in town, but even if they should, if he keeps his blue eyes and facial scar covered and she hides her shiner, there will be nothing about their appearance to make them stand out from any other of the many young couples enjoying a weekend at the beach.

He pulls into the gravel driveway of Vista del Mar, a weathered assemblage of single-story units on a two-lane road fronting a beach of gravel and dark sand. He does not take off his sunglasses in the office, where he registers as Juan Castelos and wife, of Hermosillo. He then parks the truck in front of their room and detaches the M-16 into its two basic parts so it will fit in the backpack without jutting out and puts the MAC in there too. He locks the truck and wedges a matchbook cover into the bottom seam of the driver's door.

The room has a strong odor of disinfectant that does not entirely suppress the smells of wood rot and mold and of the numberless other people who have passed through here. There's a window air conditioner but when she turns it on it produces such a clatter he tells her to switch it off and open the window to admit the sea breeze and let them hear what goes on outside.

He takes off his shirt and the money belt and she removes the rolled scarf from his waist and sees that the wound has begun to scab. The wadded sock is stuck to it, and he winces when she snatches it off. She cleans the burn with peroxide and coats it lightly with salve and bandages it with gauze pads and adhesive tape.

He empties the money belt and counts the American currency, which amounts to twenty-two thousand dollars. Holy Mary, she says. We're *rich*. He smiles at her notion of rich and replaces the cash in the belt.

He feels they're safe here but still thinks they should take turns sleeping and keeping watch. He volunteers for the first turn and sits in a plastic chair by the window, the MAC on his lap, while she naps, stripped to her panties against the heat.

Their truck is in clear view from the windows but his gaze keeps returning to her, and despite his fatigue he is roused repeatedly. When he wakes her after two hours, he has taken off his clothes. She smiles at his readiness and draws him down to her. It is a swift and urgent mating, and on its completion she says, Jesus, I know some people around here who can really use a shower.

They cram themselves into the tiny stall, the MAC within reach in the sink. They soap each other to a lather and fuck standing up and climax with water cascading on their heads, her face against his neck.

I don't know what it is, she says in low gasps. It's like I'm . . . *starving*. Do I sound crazy?

Yeah. But I know what you mean.

She looks up at him, blinking against the spattering water.

It's good to be alive, he says.

She grins and kisses him.

His bandage is soaked and has begun to peel away, and after they dry themselves she applies a fresh one. Then she puts on a T-shirt and shorts and sneakers and takes over at the lookout chair, armed with the Glock. He puts the MAC under the other pillow and flops naked on the bed and is asleep in seconds.

She lets him sleep for an hour longer than she slept. When she wakes him the swollen red sun is almost down to the sea.

And he sees that she has scissored her hair to a ragged crop that bares her ears and nape.

She sits on the edge of the bed and turns her head from one side to the other. Surprise, she says.

Sure is.

You don't like it.

I don't know. Give me a chance to wake up. He reaches up and runs a hand over her head. Then grins. I like it.

Really?

Makes you look like a nice sweet girl.

She hits him in the chest. I *am* a nice sweet girl, you dick-head. Tomorrow I'll tie down my tits. We'll be a couple of guys in a truck.

He pulls her down on top of him and runs his hand through her hair again. So you're a guy, huh? Oh God, I must be turning queer.

She laughs and gently bites his lip.

Wearing shorts and T-shirts, sneakers and baseball caps, they walk with their arms around each other past the garish lights of the roadside motels and a few loud cantinas to a small eatery about a half mile down the beach. The Taurus and the money belt are under his guayabera, the Glock is in her little shoulder tote. Eddie's made a tally of their ammunition and found that the M-16 still holds twenty-one rounds, the MAC eleven, the Glock nine. The Taurus is fully loaded with seventeen, plus one in the chamber. Always know how many bullets you've got left. Stone rule. He has shown her how to handle the Taurus and told her of the cop's fatal mistake, and she has practiced working the safety lever with the thumb of her shooting hand.

The thatch-roofed dining area is open-air, without walls on three sides, lighted by low-watt yellow bulbs strung along the ceiling. Ranchero music issues from scratchy speakers on the wall. There are few patrons at this early evening hour.

They sit at a dim corner table next to the railing that faces the beach road and the black Gulf beyond. The horizon is barely defined between the black sky and blacker sea, the darkness pierced only by the stars and the lights of scattered fishing boats. Since boyhood Eddie has been ever aware of the lunar phases and he knows a new moon is but a night away and tonight's thin crescent won't appear until shortly before dawn. He tells her so and she says she knows it. Her father was a fisherman, she reminds him. The moon was always of importance.

The seafood stew they order comes in large steaming bowls and is thick with shrimp, oysters, crab, white chunks of fish, seasoned with tomatoes and garlic and peppers. They mop sweat from their faces as they eat. Then both have a second bowl with another stack of tortillas hot from the griddle and another round of icy bottles of Bohemia.

They converse just loud enough to hear each other over the music. His plan had been to rest up until full dark, then drive through the night and make it to the Arizona border before sunrise. But he has changed his mind. The roads through the desert will probably be tough enough to negotiate in daylight, never mind in the dark. They would risk getting lost. And on the wild chance that they get spotted by a Sinas lookout roving around out there, they would be less apt to raise suspicion if they're poking along in their heap of a truck in broad daylight than if they're only a pair of headlights in the dead of night. Better to stay in the motel till morning before moving on. If nothing goes wrong, if they don't break down or get lost, they'll still make it to the border before dark.

Nothing will go wrong, she says. It is a good plan.

Glad to hear it, he says. But then everything sounds like a good plan to you.

Because any plan is better than no plan.

They buy two more Bohemias to take with them. As they stroll along the beach she takes off her cap and folds it into her back pocket and ruffles her cropped hair, then slips off her sneakers and carries them in one hand and runs splashing into the foamy sheets rushing up from the breakers.

It feels so wonderful! she says. She kicks water at him and spins in a circle like a happy child.

He has an urge to take off his shoes too, but you don't want to be barefoot if you might at any moment have to run or fight.

She comes and stands beside him and they stare out at the dark water. He says it is the first time in months that he has been to the seaside. He loves the sea and has missed it very much.

Ah yes, she says, the other gulf.

She says she has always lived near the sea and cannot imagine being away from it for very long. In childhood she often used to fish with a hand line in a brackish inlet of Mazatlán, and one afternoon she caught a fish three feet long with a long snout full of sharp teeth. Someone told her it was a gar, a trash fish and poisonous to eat, so she threw it aside, thinking she would later cut it up for bait, but she forgot about it. The next morning when she went back to do more fishing the gar was still lying next to the seawall. She kicked it into the water and watched it slowly sink. Then it suddenly twitched and stopped sinking. Then waggled its tail and swam away. She was astonished. How could any fish have lived out of water for so long? It must have held very tight to the last breath it took, she says. Think of the *will* that required.

She had not thought of that gar in years until the first time she went to Rancho del Sol. I had never before been so far from the sea, she says, and I felt a little bit like I was holding my breath until I could get back to where I belonged. But of course I am not so tough as that fish. I could never live on one breath for so long.

Alligator gars, we call them, he says. Plenty of them where I come from. They're survivors from way the hell back before there were people on the earth, and they sure look it. Saw one over five feet long in the river one time, swimming along the surface like they do. One of the guys in the boat shot it in the head with a twenty-two and it just turned aside and swam off.

He shot it? What for?

Because he's an asshole. I took the pistol from him and threw him in the water and popped a couple of rounds pretty close to his head to make him piss his pants. I was really tempted to put one between his eyes. I tossed the gun in the river and told him to swim out and walk home.

I wish the fish had come back and bit his balls. But . . . you were tempted to *shoot* him? For a fish?

For being an asshole.

Ah, yes, of course, how stupid of me. We should always shoot the assholes.

Be a better world if we did.

Christ, kid, there wouldn't be a hundred people left if you shot all the assholes.

He smiles.

But of course you and I would be among the survivors.

Hell yes, he says. And laughs with her.

They sip their beer in silence for a minute before she asks if he ever killed anybody before Segundo. Their backs are to the lights across the road, their faces in shadow.

No, he says. Almost. But no.

What happened?

Bastard tried to hurt me.

How?

A knife.

So you hurt him?

Yeah. Defending myself.

And you almost killed him?

Yeah.

But you stopped.

Well, I was . . . yeah.

You seem very good at . . . defending yourself. How did you learn to do it so well?

He shrugs. Guess I paid attention when I was growing up.

I don't understand.

Never mind. I'm just blabbing. Come on.

They toss the empties into a trash barrel and head for the motel. When they are abreast of it from across the road, they pause in the shadow of a palm tree and he scans the area. He tells her to wait there and crosses over to the motel lot and goes to the truck and finds the matchbook cover still in the door. Then takes another look all around before beckoning her.

They couple again, the room dark but for the amber cast of a streetlight through the open window, their grunts mixing with the low booms of the breakers. Amid their thrashings the Glock slides out from under a pillow and he moves it away. The MAC is on the bedside lamp table, bolt open and ready, safety off.

Afterward they flip a coin and she wins and chooses the first two-hour watch. She turns on the little lamp and rummages in her canvas tote for a fresh pack of cigarettes and takes out a cell phone and says she's been wondering why he bought it. Two of them. Plus the Sina guy's. Why all the phones?

Thought it a good idea to have a phone or two handy in case we need to call somebody.

Like who?

I don't know. Maybe somebody who can help us out. He smiles. You know anybody we can call for help?

No, she says, not smiling. Nobody. Do you?

He has been mulling that question off and on all day. He does not tell her that there are people who very possibly could help him and would probably do so without hesitation and no questions asked—at least not until later. That's why he bought the phones. He did not think about it when he did it, but he knows that's why. In case he should decide to call them. More than one phone because when you're being sought by Las Sinas you do not use the same phone twice. If he called and got a recording he would need a second phone to leave the number of, and even that would be risky.

But he has not been able to bring himself to make the call.

You do not tell people to go fuck themselves and then later when you're in trouble ask them to help you.

He had not heard it said as a rule but was sure it must be.

No, he tells her. Nobody.

TEXAS

SATURDAY

12

Catalina

It is early afternoon when the little phone silently vibrates in Catalina's skirt pocket. A gift from her great-great-granddaughter, the phone still looks to her like a makeup compact when closed and like some kind of silly toy when open. By her definition, a true telephone is one that has a wire leading into the wall and then running out to a high pole outside. There is such a phone in her house and it is listed under her name in the local directory, but many years have passed since she last answered the phone herself and began leaving that chore to her maids, none of whom knows how to speak English. Everyone Catalina knows is bilingual or speaks only Spanish, and so a caller who doesn't know Spanish is sure to be a stranger, and strangers who call on the telephone never have anything to say that she wishes to hear. If a caller cannot speak Spanish, the maids are under orders to say, "No hablo inglés," and hang up.

The wireless phone is but one more in the blur of technological inventions Catalina has witnessed in recent decades, and at first she had regarded it as a needless innovation and disdained to learn anything about the instrument. But then she decided she was willfully abetting her own ignorance, and one's ignorance is of benefit only to one's enemies. She has long known that truth, but with regard to the cell phone, she had been slow to remember it. And the reason for that slow realization was hard to deny. You're getting old, she had told herself, that's all there is to it. Then thought, *Getting?* Dear God, woman, have you ever been *other* than old?

She has since come to appreciate the many useful aspects of the little phone, and it is her practice to keep its ringer turned off in favor of a silent vibration in order to conceal from anyone within earshot the fact of an incoming call. She is a woman of many secrets, large and small, and of mysterious sources of information, and everyone in the family knows it. To one degree or another they are all a little in awe of her.

On this early Saturday afternoon she is in her reading chair on the back porch when the phone quivers in her pocket. She sees on the phone's screen that the call is from Patria Chica. She presses a button and says, "Bueno."

The caller is her very much younger cousin Stilwell, the present head of the family into which she was born. She and Stillwell are descended from the same great-grandfather but have never met in person, though they have known each other through the mail and the telephone for almost fifty years.

They exchange brief amenities and then she listens carefully while he speaks without pause for a full minute. He concludes with a caveat that he is simply passing on to her the information he has received and he cannot attest to its full accuracy. The only thing he absolutely knows for sure is that Edward is without a passport, having left his at Patria Chica because it is in his true name.

"Can you assist him?" she says, speaking in English in case a maid is within hearing.

"No. We have nobody on the other side of those Sierras. It's all theirs and they have people everywhere. It can hurt us pretty plenty if we even try to find him. Lo siento mucho, señora."

She says she understands. He says he will let her know if he should hear anything more, but doubts very much that he will. She thanks him and they end the call.

She ponders. Then refers to the little phone's directory, selects a number, and presses it. She listens for a moment, then says, "Es tu tía vieja. Call me at once." She tries another number and gets another recording and leaves the same message.

Then calls another number.

A gruff male voice answers, "Doghouse."

"I wish to speak to Frank or Rudy."

"Hey there, Mamacita! Nice to hear from you. Been a while. I'm doing fine, thanks for asking. How about yourself?"

"Cease the foolishness, Charles."

"Yes, mam."

In answer to her questions, he tells her Frank and Rudy left town on a business matter last night but are due back today, he's not sure exactly when. Yes, they took prepaid cells with them as they always do when at work, but no, they didn't notify him of a number, probably because they would be away so briefly.

She knows he's lying about not having their number. He simply doesn't want her to interrupt them while they're on an assignment for him, not unless she tells him why she must talk to them and he deems it sufficient reason to permit her do it. She will not submit to that. Charles Fortune's arrogance has always chafed her and she suspects he knows it, but she will not give him the satisfaction of hearing her say so.

"Have them call me the minute they return," she tells him. "Make sure of it, Charles."

"Yes mam. Can I ask what it's about?"

"Yes, you may," she says, and cuts off the connection.

Then makes a call to Harry McElroy Wolfe. Then one to El Paso.

13

Rudy and Frank

Frank and I had been looking for Brian Goetzman for over a week when we found out he was holed up in a cabin in the Hays County hills. The tip came from a guy in Laredo who owed us big and was glad of the chance to square things.

Goetzman was a driver for a Dallas engineering supply company that also traffics in black market high-tech military instruments. Twelve days ago he had been dispatched with a shipment of rifle scopes and night vision binoculars for delivery to Republic Arms, one of our family's firms, but he never arrived. Two days later his company minivan was found empty at a rest stop on I-35 a little north of San Antonio.

The Dallas guys agreed with us that it looked like an inside job. Goetzman had been with them less than three months and they were as pissed off as we were. They went to his apartment in Garland and found it an abandoned mess, absent all clothes and ·personal possessions. They sent us a photo and description. Big dude.

Six-three, 215. Brown hair to his nape, Marine Corps insignia tattoo on his inner forearm. Lengthy arrest record but few convictions and only two incarcerations exceeding sixty days—a six-month stay in the Travis County jail for assault, and eleven months at a Fort Bend farm for burglary. It was the Dallas company's experience that ex-cons generally made dependable hirelings, but every so often they'd get one like Goetzman.

We put the word out and started the hunt for him, but after eight days with no luck we were ready to believe he had skipped the state or was dead, or both.

Then late last night the Laredo guy called and verified that Goetzman had been in on the theft and told us where he was. He said Goetzman had been bought off by a San Antonio cholo gang who then smuggled the shipment across the river with the big idea of selling it to the Zetas, the enforcers for the Gulf cartel. The tipster said he didn't think anybody in the gang had ever met a Zeta. In Nuevo Laredo they made a deal with a local gang called Cien Demonios to broker the sale for them. The next day all nine of the cholos were found laid out along the shoulder of a road outside of town, each of them shot in the head and every man of them with his feet cut off—a Demonios signature treatment of intruders on their turf. Our guy said the Demonios worked for the Zetas and had turned the cargo over to them, so we could forget about getting it back.

How he knew all this is of no matter. We never ask that of informants. But their information had best be accurate. He gave us directions to where Goetzman was, but said he didn't know how long the man would stay there or whether he was alone.

We phoned our cousin Charlie Fortune and gave him the report. He told us to get a paper from Uncle Forrest and head for Hays County. He wanted us to recover whatever we could from

Goetzman and "impress upon that stupid sonofabitch the error of his ways." Over the years we've developed a lexical code with Charlie. "Impress upon" means bestow memorable pain but leave alive. We then phoned Uncle Forrest, apologized for disturbing him at such a late hour, and explained our urgency. He said he understood and would "secure the instrument without delay." That's how Uncle Forrest talks.

Forty minutes later we were zipping past Brownsville's north city limits.

On the dotted line we are Francis Fierro Wolfe and Rudolf Maxwell Wolfe. To family and close friends we're Frank and Rudy, sometimes Frankie Fierro and Rudy Max. It's no accident we're a large family, since we believe blood relatives make the most reliable partners, though now and then you'll get an exception to the rule. The family tree has grown so many branches, however, that we long ago quit specifying kinship by degree and number of times removed and so forth. We hold to the simple identifiers "cousin" or "uncle" or "aunt," regardless of the distance between us on the tree.

On our tax forms, Frank and I are "field agents" for Wolfe Associates, a Brownsville law firm whose top partners are our uncles, Harry Mack, Peck Bailey, and Forrest Otis. They are, respectively, among the best tort, criminal, and contract attorneys in Texas. They are the three elder males of the family and a kind of ruling triumvirate, Harry Mack the oldest at sixty-five and hence the present patriarch. Whenever some serious disagreement in the family can't be worked out between the disputants, the Three Uncles will hear both sides of it and then settle it with absolute finality by a vote among themselves.

We've been at the job since we got out of college nine and eight years ago—Frank's my elder by a year—and we couldn't ask for a better one. State-licensed investigators with carry permits. The Wolfe Associates job description calls for us to trace witnesses, serve subpoenas, do background checks, search criminal records, and so on. In reality our primary function is to resolve certain matters of Wolfe business that for whatever reason cannot be resolved through legal channels. The "fixers," some in the family like to call us. The matters we deal with only rarely concern any actual Wolfe Associates court case, but the firm always provides us with a subpoena attesting that the person named on it may be required to depose in some upcoming legal proceeding—and always assembles some quick file in ready support of the writ. A subpoena is a useful document to have in hand if, when we confront our guy, things take the sort of turn that attracts law enforcement agents. The only reason it took us forty minutes to leave town was having to stop at Uncle Forrest's to pick up the paper, and at a convenience store to buy a prepaid cell, whose number we called in to Charlie Fortune.

It was after midnight when we left Brownsville, and the sky was still dark when we sat down to breakfast about three hundred miles north at a diner off the interstate near San Marcos. We knew that some of the hill terrain could call for four-wheel drive, so we made the trip in a 4Runner. We would have preferred to surprise Goetzman in the dark, better still while he was asleep, but we weren't sufficiently familiar with the area and chose to wait until first light before we set off into the hills.

We took a farm road past the Blanco River and up into the scrub brush and cedar brakes. The sky was reddening along the hilltops, and every crest presented a vista. I've always loved early-morning light in all its geographic and seasonal varieties, and up in these hills was for us an uncommon way of seeing it. I remarked on it to Frank but he only gave a little nod in response. He thinks talking about such things takes something away from them. Hemingway man. Did his senior thesis on him. English majors, Frank and I. For a laugh I sometimes say, "We're English majors, Frank and me," but hardly anybody ever gets it. Grammar education ain't what it used to be. Me, I favored the Neoclassical poets. My own thesis was titled "The Role of the Interlocutor in Pope's Horatian Satires." Frank still asks now and then if Hollywood's called yet about the rights. Those university years now seem as far removed from our lives as the moon.

We found the side road we were looking for. More stony trail than road, narrow and winding and steadily uphill, but easy enough in four-wheel. We drove past a farm where a herd of goats came to the fence to watch us go by as if they didn't often see strangers. We topped the hill and the road curved a few more times before we came to a rusty mailbox atop a wooden post on which was hung a cow skull, just like the tipster said. The mailbox stood at the entrance of a fenced property with a closed gate but no lock. A dirt driveway went up through the cedars to a large cabin with a cherry-red pickup parked beside it.

I drove around the next bend and out of view of the cabin and then pulled over on the narrow shoulder and cut off the engine. Frank pulled a small bag of dog biscuits out from under the seat and put a handful in his pocket. We checked our pistols—HK nines with threaded muzzles—then tucked them under our shirts and walked back to the open gate and up the drive.

The sun hadn't yet cleared the hilltop trees, and the cabin was still in shadows. Its rear side was toward the road and had no door and neither of the two back windows showed any light. I was hoping Goetzman had made a big night of it and was still sleeping it off. I've never liked mixing it up early in the day. The smart thing would've been for him to have a watchdog, but of course you can't ever count on anybody doing the smart thing, for better or worse. Longtime rule.

The truck was a two-year-old Silverado in cherry condition. I took a look in the cab as I passed by and saw some CD cases of shitkicker music and an empty Pearl can on the seat. We drew our guns and Frank headed around the right side of the house while I took the left.

There was no door on my side but the cabin stood on a crest and had a grand view of the hills to the south, and the hillside sloped down sharply about ten yards to a wide slow creek whose opposite bank was lined with cottonwoods. A roofed porch ran the length of the house and there was a window to either side of the front door. Frank appeared at the other end of the porch and told me with hand signs that he had found a door on that side and for me to get set out here while he went in. I nodded and eased up onto the porch.

Just then the front door opened and a young woman in a dark blue A&M T-shirt that didn't completely cover her ass came out holding a cup of smoking coffee in both hands. She was somewhat hard-faced but very nicely put together. She blew on the coffee and looked off at the hills and then turned and saw me holding the gun on her and a finger to my lips.

Her mouth went slack and she dropped the cup. The hot coffee splattered on her feet and she yelped and broke toward the door at the same time that Goetzman came charging out in nothing but a pair of Jockeys and with a huge revolver in his hand and smacked into her with an ugly thud. The collision jarred him off-balance and he bonked his head on a support post and she was knocked rearward off the porch and went tumbling all the way down into the creek.

I yelled "Drop it!" and was *this* close to popping him in the heart when Frank came lunging out the door and swatted him across the face with his pistol. Goetzman spun half around and the revolver fell from his hand as he took a header onto the porch steps and then rolled down the slope too. The girl was standing in tit-high water alongside the bank when he crashed down on her.

I retrieved his gun—a blued Redhawk .44—and we eased down the slope as Goetzman stood up in the creek, coughing and snorting and bloody-faced. He saw us coming and turned and started slogging toward the opposite bank. Frank picked up a rock the size of a baseball and smacked him with it under the shoulder blade and Goetzman flinched and cried out and nearly went under again. At UT Austin, Frank twice struck out sixteen guys in a game. Had a heater that hopped a foot and a sinker that broke like it was rolling off a table. He was drafted by the Orioles in the second round but took a pass. A little better traction on that slope and he could've buried the rock in Goetzman's rear ribs.

"Get her up!" Frank said. "Move!"

The girl was struggling to stand up but kept falling and going under and seemed about to drown. Grimacing and bent sideways, Goetzman went to her and got hold of her hand but they were both having trouble with their footing and for a minute it looked like a tug-of-war as he tried to get her up and she almost pulled him down. She finally came upright, choking and hacking, hair plastered to her head, and she smacked him a good one in the face with her fist. He cursed and was about to punch her in return but Frank yelled for them to cut the shit and get out of there.

We let Goetzman haul himself out but I gave the girl a hoisting hand. I had thought she was bare-assed but now saw she wore a tan thong. It's a golden age in women's underwear. She hunched on all fours to heave up some more creek water, presenting me with a fine perspective of her lovely butt.

Both of them were pretty well scratched up, and the gash on Goetzman's cheek was oozing blood through his fingers. He sat cross-legged, muscular in that overtight way you can get from pumping iron as your sole exercise. Probably had a hell of a punch but lacked the speed and agility to land it against anybody who could fight. Still, he had almost half a foot and at least thirty pounds on either of us and I would've hated to let him get a good hold on me. The Corps insignia was the only tattoo on his arms but he had some of lesser quality on his chest and back. Jailhouse jobs expressing the usual banalities of the self-proclaimed badass.

"The fuck're you guys?" he said with as much bluster as a man can manage who's bleeding and dripping wet in his undershorts with a gun held on him. He had an easy face to read. He knew we weren't cops.

"You stole from some people we know," I said. "A serious lapse in judgment."

It's the way we usually work, Frank and I. He's the imperative, I'm the exposition. We share the punitive.

"Dallas guys, huh?" Goetzman said.

I let him believe it. "Oh shit, huh?"

He talked fast, saying it wasn't his idea, none of it, the "beaners" had come to *him*. "No offense," he said to Frank, and got the Stone Eye in return. Frank can be taken for a beaner easy enough with his big mustache and dusky complexion. In fact he looks a lot like our ancestor, Rodolfo Fierro, after whom we're both named. He was Pancho Villa's right-hand man in the Revolution, and his daughter by an American woman named Davis was our grandmother. Me, I look Anglo as they come, like most of the Wolfes this side of the river.

Goetzman said the cholo gang had threatened to kill him if he didn't turn over the load and blah–blah–blah. I said we could discuss it in the house, and we went back up there, me behind the girl to better consider the aesthetics of her behind. You can take it for a rule that if a woman has a good ass the rest of her will be nicely configured too, except for maybe the face. The face is always on its own.

We entered the cabin's main room and Frank told Goetzman to sit at the table and that if he moved from it without permission he would shoot him. He said it in a tone he's perfected over the years, one bespeaking bored indifference to whether he has to shoot a guy or not. I can do a fair imitation of it but I can't match his Stone Eye. It gives him the edge on me in the fearsomeness department.

The only phone in the house was a flip cell lying on the counter separating the main room from the kitchen. Frank put it in the microwave and pressed the "popcorn" button. I took the girl in the bedroom and told her to sit in the middle of the bed. There was a shirt hanging on a bedpost and she asked if she could put it on and I nodded. She turned her back only partway as she took off the wet tee, giving me a good gander at one hooter before she slipped the shirt on, then sat herself on the bed. Goetzman's wallet was on the dresser, together with a checkbook that showed a balance of a little over eighteen hundred. The wallet held 153 bucks, a Texas driver's license, three credit cards in three different names, and a photo of the girl lying nude on her side and facing the camera with a stiff smile. Not real artfully composed but I took a moment to appreciate it anyway, then winked at her. She

shrugged and turned up her palms. I told her to stay put and went
back in the main room.

One side of Goetzman's face was a bloated red-purple bruise
with a deep tear in it, but the bleeding had slowed to a trickle.
I told him the cargo he'd helped hijack was worth 125 grand.
In truth it was a hundred even, but why tell him, since that was
entirely beside the point, as was the fact we'd paid only fifty for
it. I said he had to reimburse us and asked how much cash he
could round up. He said not that much. The cholos had paid him
ten thousand but all of it had gone toward the truck he bought
the next day. He said there was five thousand in a sock in the top
drawer of a clothes chest in the bedroom and about two thou
more in his checking account and that was it. The cabin belonged
to a friend who was away in California and letting him use it.

I gave him a sad shake of the head and returned to the
bedroom and ransacked it and found no cash other than the five
grand in the sock. But I found a little metal case containing some
documents and current Florida and Georgia driver's licenses with
Goetzman's name and photograph. One of the papers was a deed
in Goetzman's name to an eighty-acre piney woods tract on the
Trinity River. Made me smile. Worth well more than $150,000.
Every once in a big while the recoup comes just that easily.

I went outside and searched the Silverado and found the
registration and title but no money. Then walked up the road and
got in the 4Runner and drove back to the cabin and parked it
out of sight of the road. I took a little briefcase from the backseat
and went back in the house. The briefcase held a miscellany of
blank legal forms and a silencer.

We didn't really need the silencer, not out in those boonies,
but the mere introduction of it can be very helpful in gaining a
guy's ready cooperation. Goetzman's eyes widened when he saw

me hand it to Frank, who took his time about screwing it onto the Heckler.

I showed Goetzman his property deed and saw in his face it hadn't even crossed his mind we might find it. He said he'd inherited the land from his grandmother a few months ago. Only good luck he'd ever had. His plan was to sell fifty acres and build a cabin on the rest, where, as he put it, "I can keep my distance from the fucken world."

I said I understood the impulse. Then placed the Silverado title and a blank property bill of sale in front of him and told him to sign the seller's line on both papers, and he did so without hesitation, saying the land alone was worth more than what he owed us. I said I hoped for his sake he was right, and we'd keep the difference as an irritation fee. I made sure the signatures matched the one on his license. When we got back home I would turn the papers over to people who are expert at the niceties of completing and registering official documents. Within a few days there would be a file on record in the county clerk's office of a series of legal actions regarding Brian Goetzman's outstanding debts to one or another Wolfe business and his settlement of them by way of property transfers.

Frank went to the kitchen and got a dishcloth and tossed it to Goetzman. Then told him to stick a leg out, whichever one he preferred.

"Aw shit, guys," Goetzman said, "I been cooperative, ain't I? You busted my face, you cleaned me out. You ain't gotta do *this*?"

"Brian," I said.

He sighed and rolled the dishcloth and stuck it between his jaws and bit down on it. Then gripped both sides of the chair seat and took a few deep breaths and extended his right leg, then quickly pulled it back and stuck out the left.

Frank was positioning himself as I went to the bedroom door to look in on the girl. She asked what was happening—and then there was a *thoonk*! sound and a scream and a heavy thump. The girl squealed and I pointed a finger at her and she put both hands over her mouth to stifle herself.

Goetzman was on the floor and wailing pretty loud even through the cloth between his teeth, writhing beside his toppled chair and clutching his leg above the knee. The knee looked like it had been pried open with a claw hammer. Frank knows how to shoot a knee so it's ruined for keeps but the guy doesn't have to lose the lower leg and get a prosthetic, not unless he chooses to. If he wants, he can settle for gimping on a stiff leg the rest of his life. A shot knee supposedly hurts worse than anything, but they say the same about belly wounds. All I know is you don't die from a shot knee. Goetzman had pissed himself and was streaming tears and snot, but all in all was being a good soldier. I've seen plenty of them pass out from a lot less pain.

Frank had picked up the casing and was using his buck knife to dig the round out of the wood floor. Way more precaution than called for, but that's Frank.

I set the chair upright and called for the girl to fetch a belt. She came out and saw the knee and looked like she might barf, but it was Goetzman who chucked when she helped me hoist him into the chair. We hopped aside quick enough to avoid getting any on us. When I was done wrapping the belt tight above his knee, Goetzman was breathing like he'd been chased a mile, but he wasn't bleeding anymore. Frank opened the door to admit some fresh air against the reek.

I told Goetzman this punishment was small compared to what would happen if he ever in his life trespassed against us or any of our associates again. I said we'd cut his arms off at the shoulder next time. He wouldn't be able to feed himself, wipe his ass, beat his dick. It's always an effort to maintain a menacing demeanor when I say such things. You only talk like that with smalltimers who can be scared out of even dreaming of crossing you again. With real players you don't make threats, you just get to it.

I said we'd call 911 for him as soon as we got back to paved road. He could tell the cops some guy broke in and shot him, then tossed the place. Some dealer, probably, who got him mixed up with somebody else. He could wing it any way he wanted, but none of it ever better splash on his former employers in Dallas. "We can find you again easy," I said.

He said he could handle it. Still snorting snot and wiping away tears he couldn't put a stop to. He looked at the big Redhawk in my waistband like he was losing a pal.

The girl asked if we could give her a ride to the San Marcos bus station. I looked at Frank and he shrugged, so I told her she had exactly two minutes to be ready. She dashed to the bedroom without a glance at Goetzman.

He said, "Hey Jenny, what the hell, man." Then looked at us and said, "I been *good* to her, no lie."

Frank said he took her for one of those who says, "Even if you get crippled, baby, I'll still love you. I'll *miss* you but I'll still love you."

Frank can be prone to the jocose once the work is done.

Goetzman said he didn't know why he gave a damn if she left, that she couldn't even give a decent blow job. "All the guys she's been with, you'd think she'da learned how to suck a dick."

"Maybe that's why they split from her," Frank said. "Her lack of aptitude."

"Shoulda stayed in the Corps, what I shoulda done."

I was inclined to say, "Woulda, coulda, shoulda," but I didn't. He'd had enough for one day.

We went out and Frank got in the Silverado and I got in the 4Runner and we were about to pull away when the Jenny girl came running out with a small suitcase. She had put on jeans and an orange Longhorns T-shirt. She paused for a second, looking from me to Frank and back again. Then got in with him.

A lot of them are like that. Choose the badder ass every time.

We dropped her off in San Marcos and at mid-morning stopped for coffee and pastry in a café in Three Rivers. We were tired after the sleepless night, so from the restaurant we drove over to nearby Choke Canyon Park and picked out a tree overlooking the lake and napped in the shade for a couple of hours. Then got rolling again and by mid-afternoon were back home.

14

Rudy and Frank

Wolfe Landing is near the tip of the lower Rio Grande region that the locals call a valley, though in fact it's a delta. The town stands roughly midway between Brownsville and the Gulf of Mexico, about a dozen miles from each, and a mile or so south of the Boca Chica Road. It covers sixty mostly raw acres in the middle of a 450-acre palm grove that abuts the meandering river for about half a mile. Once upon a time this reach of the Rio Grande was so thick with palms that the first Spaniards to land here called it Río de las Palmas. Now there's only one other palm grove left to speak of, a bit bigger than ours, upriver at the periphery of Brownsville and long since converted into a nature sanctuary and tourist attraction.

Frank once said it's an understatement to call it an over-statement to call Wolfe Landing a town, but it was duly chartered as one back in 1911, when it had all of eight inhabitants and one dirt street. It's now got a half dozen streets, all of them dirt but for tar-and-gravel Main Street, and, according to the latest census, fifty-one residents. At one time our family owned a tract of almost fifty square miles between Brownsville and the Gulf. The land was bordered on the south by the river and on the north by a creek that ran out to the Gulf along a route roughly paralleling the one the ship channel would follow when it was dredged in the 1920s and 1930s. We've always called that tract Tierra Wolfe, though you won't find the name on any map, past or present. We've sold off portions of it over time but still own more than half of the original expanse. It's primarily scrub and muck land and not worth much except as a buffer around Wolfe Landing. You can't see the Landing from the Boca Chica Road. You wouldn't even know it was there if it wasn't for a little sign on a narrow dirt turnoff that winds down toward the river and into the grove.

It is a shadowy place, the Landing, usually smelling strongly of the river and wet vegetation. Besides the palms, there are lots of hardwoods and a profusion of Spanish moss. You won't find many spots anywhere on the river nearly so lush. You enter the Landing on Main Street, which is flanked by palm thickets to the right and most of the town's main buildings on the left, the first of them being the town hall, containing two offices and a pair of jail cells. Then there's Riverside Garage, Get Screwed Hardware, Mario's Grocery, the Potluck Palace—which is a secondhand store and coin laundry—and the Republic Arms gun shop. You'll see a lot of dogs and cats on the loose, few of them belonging to anyone in particular. Past the Republic Arms and leading to the river is

Gator Lane, which ends at a dock next to Henry's Bait & Tackle
and the entrance to the parking lot of the Doghouse Cantina.

The Doghouse is owned and operated by our cousin Charlie
Fortune Wolfe, who also owns the Republic Arms but leaves its
routine management to his nephew, Jimmy Quick. In addition,
Charlie holds two civic positions—he's the police chief of a force
made up of himself and a deputy named Honario Milgracias, and
he's the mayor, now in his fifth consecutive term. He ran unopposed
the last time and won all but two votes, write-ins for Yosemite Sam
and Clint Eastwood, cast by a couple of guys he'd ejected from the
Doghouse the night before for being pains in the ass.

Beyond Gator Lane, Main Street branches north into a
narrow trail that winds through the Landing's residential area, a
scattering of three dozen or so cabins and house trailers, before
it dead-ends at Resaca Grande. "Resaca" is the local term for an
oxbow or bayou, and there are more of them along the lower Rio
Grande than can ever be accurately tallied. The only Wolfes who
live at the Landing are Frank and I, Charlie Fortune, and Jimmy
Quick. The rest of the family all reside in Brownsville except for
Uncle Harry Morgan and his wife, whose house is back up in
the dunes near the mouth of the river.

Frank and I moved out here shortly after our parents disap-
peared when we were sixteen and fifteen. They went sailing in
their sloop on a day of perfect weather and didn't come back. The
Coast Guard searched for three days but found no sign of them or
the boat. All our relatives invited us to move in with them, but we
chose to come to the Landing and live in a trailer. We didn't mind
the long drive to school every day. Charlie Fortune looked out
for us until we graduated, and he became more our big brother
than older cousin. Frank and I now live next door to each other
in similar cypress houses built solid as ships on eight-foot pilings,

high enough to be safe from flooding and to catch the sporadic breezes off the river. Charlie's got a piling house too, set in the deeper palms behind the Doghouse and overlooking Resaca Mala, aptly named for its gloomy dimness and because there are alligators in it. One of the present bunch is easily thirteen feet long. Whenever a dog or cat goes missing, there's not much mystery about what became of it.

Across the river from the Landing is Puerto Nuestros, a five-square-mile piece of Mexico the Wolfes have owned since the 1920s. It's a desolate piece of ground that was already shorn of most of its palms before we bought it, but it's still full of mesquite and high brush, what the local Mexicans call chaparral. The property's few inhabitants are all in Wolfe employ. On directly opposite sides of the river as they are, Puerto Nuestros and Wolfe Landing form an excellent venue for the oldest of the Wolfe businesses, which is smuggling.

Our forebears started smuggling almost as soon as they arrived on the border back around the turn of the last century. First booze, then guns too. Our family's been running guns since before the Revolution.

Which is another thing about Charlie Fortune—he's the chief of the family's smuggling enterprise and all its ancillary operations, the "shade trade," as we all call it, and he answers only to the Three Uncles. He's the one who gives me and Frank our field assignments, and even though he has a dependable cadre of runners for delivering contraband, when it comes to the riskiest deals, Frank and I are his preferred choice. Okay with us. We like doing runs even more than fieldwork.

Nowadays we Wolfes will smuggle almost anything except wetbacks and drugs if the price is right and the logistics are to our liking. We try to keep every transaction as simple as possible and the number of people involved to a minimum. Wetbacks involve too many people, too many tongues, processing stages, fingers in the money pie. Drugs involve all that too, plus the added hazard of having to deal with way too many volatile personalities of extreme inclinations. Lots of loonies in drugs.

We do smuggle people, but only solo individuals, though in special circumstances we will carry as many as three at a time. It's a select clientele, people who can afford the steep fee to be transported anywhere on the Gulf coast on either side of the border, or even to some farther destination if that's what they want and can pay for. We can earn more from carrying one such person than from crossing a couple of dozen wets. And if whoever we carry should be in need of identity papers, we can provide them too. Passport, birth certificate, driver's license, Social Security card, name it. You want it, we'll get it for you. One of our companies—Delta Instruments & Graphics—produces masterful forgeries. Or, if you're willing to pay top dollar, we can get you original-issue documents though our bureaucratic insiders, papers as legit as a dollar from the Mint. Together with guns and hi-tech gadgetry, a fully documented identity is one of our most lucrative articles of trade, and not just with fugitives. There are plenty of folk who aren't on the run but find it practical to have more than one identity, for the simple reason that everybody's hiding something and some are hiding a lot. Multiple identities are a kind of self-defense. Every one of us in the shade trade has at least one other identity readily available. If I wanted to, I could make Rudolf Maxwell Wolfe vanish from the earth tomorrow and assume a new life somewhere else under another name, with all the requisite documents to support a complete personal history since birth. The feds can't reinvent you better than we can.

15

Rudy and Frank

After we drop off the Silverado and its title at Riverside Garage—
the property bill of sale will go to our Aunt Katy Jane at South
Texas Realty, another family business—we wheel down to the
Doghouse to give Charlie our report and have a brew or two.
I've got a date in Port Isabel tonight with a girl I met last week.
Frank's got a girl coming over, Julie, who he's been seeing for
three months now, close to a longevity record for him.

It's not even four o'clock and the parking lot's already full.
During the workweek the cantina's patronage is mostly Landing residents who just walk over and you won't see but two
or three vehicles in the lot, but on weekends people come out
from Brownsville for the Friday supper special of all-you-can-eat
gumbo, and on Saturdays for the barbecue platter of pork or beef
ribs served with pintos and rice and flour tortillas. Besides the
best barbecue in Cameron County, the place offers booze and
beer and an excellent short-order menu beginning with breakfast.
There are pool tables, a dance floor, a replica Wurlitzer CD juke
with the most eclectic selection of music you've ever heard. The
only kinds of music Charlie Fortune won't permit in it are classical and rap. Classical because he considers it too good to use for
background noise, rap because he considers it an offense to the ear.

The place is loud with voices raised over Willie Nelson's
belting out of "On the Road Again." The ceiling fans are doing
a fair job of beating back the heat for now but won't do much
against the swelter of the packed house later tonight. Lila the
barmaid is chatting with a couple of guys down the bar and we
catch her eye and call for Shiner Bocks.

The aroma of grilling meat is wafting in from the fire pits out back where Charlie and his helper Moisés are at work. Lila brings the beer and we ask for a couple of plates of the supper special, but she says, "Too early, guys, you know that." The supper special hours are four-thirty to six-thirty and Charlie's a stickler about them. I tell her that the restriction doesn't apply to us because we're kin, but she only smiles and rolls her eyes. Franks asks her to tell Charlie we're here and she goes out the kitchen door for a minute and comes back and gives us a thumbs-up, then returns to the fellas down the bar with a little extra sway to her butt because she knows we're admiring it.

A minute later Charlie sticks his head out the kitchen door and sees us and beckons. He's wearing a sauce-smeared bib apron that says "Kiss the Cook" and he has a grill fork in one hand and a Negra Modelo in the other. We go around the bar and follow him into the kitchen, where Concha the cook and her young daughter Julia are tending the kettles of beans and rice and preparing big bowls of maize dough for the evening's supply of tortillas.

Charlie's the only Wolfe ever known to have achieved six feet in height. He's ten years older than Frank and stronger than both of us. He still works with free weights and does a few rounds a day on the heavy bag. His arms put me in mind of pythons. His buzz cut and the white scar through one eyebrow don't detract a bit from his formidable aspect.

"Well?" he says.

I tell him about the encounter with Goetzman and of the recompense that will more than cover our loss.

He nods, then looks at Frank. "Penalty?"

"A knee," Frank says.

"*One?*" Charlie says with a scowl. I'm about to explain why we thought one was enough, but then he grins and says, "Good job, gents."

It's sometimes hard to know when Charlie Fortune's putting you on.

We hear Moisés holler, "You mangy son of a bitch!"

Charlie's orange tomcat, the one-eyed Captain Kiddo, appears at the clear-plastic flap entrance at the bottom of the half-screened door, but the chunk of raw pork rib in his jaws is too big to fit through the entry. A rock ricochets off the door and Captain Kiddo flees with his prize.

Charlie goes to the door and yells at Moisés, "The pirate strikes again!"

"I'm gonna skin that bastard and put him on a spit!" Moisés bellows.

"You'll have to catch him first."

Frank remarks on how good the meat smells and says maybe he'll have a plate.

"Sure," Charlie says, and looks at his watch. "Only gotta wait another sixteen minutes."

"Christ sake," Frank mutters.

As we head for the door out to the bar, Charlie says, "Hey. What'd the vieja want?"

I ask what he means and he says he had Moisés stick a note on each of our front doors telling us to phone Aunt Cat. I tell him we haven't been home yet to see the notes, and he says she called the Doghouse in search of us about two hours ago. She wanted us to get back to her right away but wouldn't tell him what it was about, so naturally he didn't let her have the number of our prepaid. "But I don't want her nagging my ass, so call her, then let me know what she wanted."

Aunt Cat is my and Frank's great-grandaunt, the Wolfe grande dame. It isn't unheard of for her to telephone somebody in the family, but it happens maybe once in a blue moon. She mostly keeps to herself and gets by with the help of a pair of maids who'd sooner cut out their own tongues than betray her confidence. Besides them, the only one she confides in, so far as we know, is our cousin Jessie Juliet, who works as a reporter for the *Herald* but has literary ambitions and wants to write a book about her. The idea that Aunt Cat would agree to be interviewed about her life was laughable until Jess asked her if she would, and she said yes—on condition that none of the material be divulged until after her death. Jessie agreed, and I admire how well she's honored the old woman's trust. When she told us about their deal, Frank laughed and said, "Hell, kid, you been snookered. That old cat ain't ever gonna die."

Back at the bar we get another round of Shiners from Lila. We have no idea what Aunt Cat might want with us, but we know we'd better find out. Frank tosses a quarter and I call tails and that's what comes up. He says, "Damn it," and goes out to the 4Runner, where we left the cell.

A few minutes later he's back and says, "She wants us over there."

"When?

"Now."

"You ask why?"

"Musta slipped my mind. Why don't you call her back and ask?"

16

Rudy and Frank

She has lived in this small house on Levee Street since the Three Uncles were toddlers. Built by the first Wolfes to settle in the delta, it's made of stone and roofed in Spanish tile and has withstood every hurricane of the last hundred years with no more damage than a broken window or a lost tile or two. The small front lawn is neatly trimmed and bordered by flower beds and a chain-link fence. Frank parks the 4Runner in front and we pass through the gate and go up the walk.

We're admitted by the younger maid, Rosario, who says for us to please be seated, la doña will be with us in a moment. We no sooner settle ourselves on the sofa than she enters the room and we stand up again.

She's in a loose dress of a light blue that matches her eyes, her carriage erect, her silver hair cropped above dangling silver earrings, her only capitulation to vanity. Nobody we know has ever seen her with even a trace of makeup. She's a bit taller than most Wolfe women, a genetic advantage of her paternal lineage, a rugged Scotch-Irish family long since settled in Mexico. They're inclined to lankiness and are incongruously named Little. Her grandmother on her father's side was a Wolfe, and Aunt Cat's sole marriage was to one of her Wolfe cousins.

"Buenas tardes, Mamacita," I say, using the family's maternal address for her. It is also permissible to call her "señora" or Aunt Catalina in either language, but to directly address her as "Aunt Cat" or "tía Gata" would be excessively informal. Among ourselves, we generally refer to her as La Gata, and sometimes—if we're peeved at her for some reason and not under the same roof with her—as the "old woman" or "la vieja." Frank has pointed out, however, that it isn't really accurate to call her "la vieja," that to be precise we should speak of "la antigua" or "la prehistórica."

"Good afternoon, Rudolf, Francis," she says. "Please sit." Her voice a mild rasp but still strong. That she chooses to speak in English means she doesn't want the maids to be privy to our conversation. She eases herself into a chair on the other side of the low coffee table.

She looks to be in her seventies and in excellent health for her years, but the irrefutable fact is that the birthday we celebrated last New Year's Day at Uncle Harry Mack's house was her one hundred ninth. Harry McElroy may be the patriarch, but Aunt Catalina was already in her forties when he was born. Her only two children, both sons, are long dead, but her three grandchildren are alive and robust, and all four of her great-grandchildren are now adults.

"Phenomenal" is an insufficient descriptive of her. She wears glasses only to read or thread a needle. She uses a cane on her daily neighborhood stroll less as an aid to walking than to swat away overly frisky dogs. Her hearing's still good enough to keep us from even whispering about her when we're under the same roof. She cooks, works in her garden, submits to Jessie's interviews for hours at a time. Her known history is no less impressive. Her godfather was Porfirio Díaz, dictator of Mexico for thirtysomething years. Her American great-grandfather was said to be the chief of Díaz's secret police. She was sixteen in the early days of the Revolution when a train carrying her and her two siblings to the Texas border to live with the Wolfes was attacked by bandits who murdered her brother and abducted her sister. In some versions of the story the bandits raped Catalina, though nobody knows if that's true because nobody's ever mustered the nerve to ask her such a personal question. Maybe Jessie knows, but of course she won't say. A few months after crossing the border, she survived another bandit attack, this one at the Wolfe seaside home. The family's twin patriarchs died in that fight, but all the raiders were killed, and, as the story has it, Catalina herself killed one of them. With a knife. The most widely known fact about her—it made headlines in the 1930s—is that she shot her husband to death in front of more than a hundred witnesses at a party. Then spent thirteen years in prison for it. Of course Jessie Juliet wants to write about her. Every year since she turned a hundred the *Herald* has solicited an interview, and every year she has turned it down. Doctors from medical schools have asked if they might examine her, and university historians and anthropologists have requested meetings with her. All of them turned down too. Since the New Year's party, we'd seen her only once, back in April, at the funeral of an infant cousin of ours, who died at the age of three months. I suspect Frank and I weren't the only ones at the graveside who reflected on life's vastly unequal apportionments.

"You look well, señora," I say.

"As do you both," she says. "Though perhaps a bit thirsty."

She inclines her head toward the kitchen and without raising her voice says, "Rosario. Cerveza, por favor."

The girl brings in a tray holding three cold glasses of beer and places it on the little table and retreats. We wait for Aunt Cat to pick up her glass before we reach for ours and raise them to her. "Salud," I say.

Frank echoes the toast and he and I take a deep draft as she touches her glass to her lips, then sets it down. It's a superb pale ale, and I wonder of what label.

"I do not wish to be ungracious," she says, "but the situation is urgent and I must proceed directly to it."

"Yes, mam," I say. Wondering what the hell.

She tells us that Eddie Gato—"your cousin Edward," she says, referring to him as always by his formal name—is in serious trouble in Mexico. She's been informed that he angered some dangerous people in Sonora and they are in pursuit of him. If they catch him they intend to kill him. His only hope of escaping the country is to get to the border by motor vehicle and then cross it on foot, and the only part of the border he might hope to achieve is a segment along the edge of Arizona between Nogales and a place called Sonoyta. She's been told that although it is possible he could get to the border as soon as tonight, it is very doubtful that he will, considering the extreme caution he must exercise and the remote and roundabout roads he must use to avoid detection.

"More probable," she says, "is that he will not arrive at the border before sometime tomorrow. Should he get there at all."

She picks up her glass and raises it to her mouth and this time lets the ale touch her lips as we take another big slug of ours. She's giving us a minute to take in what she's told us.

I can see Frank's as knocked back as I am. We haven't seen Eddie in six months—nobody in the family has, so far as we know, not since the brouhaha about him and Jackie Marie—and I have to wonder what the hell he's done to get in such a serious jam. It's not entirely surprising, though, that this is about him. He's the only one in the family Aunt Cat's fonder of than she is of Jessie Juliet. Most of us believe there's nobody she's genuinely fond of *except* him and Jessie. As for why she's telling me and Frank all this, only one possibility comes to mind, and I don't like it.

Frank asks what Eddie was doing way over in Sonora. "We'd heard . . . I mean, there's always been talk he may have gone to . . . down to Mexico, but . . ." He lets it fall away. He'd almost said what many in the family have thought ever since Eddie took off—that he's been staying with Aunt Cat's people at Patria Chica, their place in San Luis Potosí. Nobody knows for certain if it's true, except for Aunt Cat herself, of course, and she's never said. The only one who's ever asked her if Eddie was really there was Aunt Laurel, one of her granddaughters, who said La Gata's "icy" response was "What makes you think *that*?" It put an end to the conversation, and despite several apologies for having asked such a presumptuous question, Aunt Laurel still got the silent treatment from her for almost two months.

"Why he was in Sonora is now irrelevant," Aunt Cat says. "The only pertinent point is that he is in danger there and is trying to get across the border to save himself."

"Yes, mam," Frank says. "But . . . do you have any idea why these people want to kill him?"

"I am told he killed someone of importance to them. I am told he did so in his own defense."

Oh swell, I think. And wonder how she can know all this except through her Patria Chica kin, however the hell *they* knew it.

"Do you know who they are," I ask, "these dangerous people?"

"A criminal organization of Sinaloa. So I am told."

Frank and I exchange a glance.

"I have summoned you because you are finders of persons. That is your trade. I am told you are very capable at it."

Oh hell, I think, here it comes.

"I want you to find him before those people do."

Frank cuts another look at me.

"Mamacita," I say, "we share your concern for Eddie—for Edward—but for *us* to go to Sonora, well, that's not . . . practical. Sonora's a long way from here. It would be better and faster if we arrange for someone who is already there to—"

"Forgive my interruption," she says. "I don't know anyone there. I know you."

Frank says, "We have kin in El Paso who—" but she cuts him off to say she has already spoken with them and they will help us. "But they are not finders of persons."

"With all proper respect, señora," I say, "we have duties here. We're employed by our uncles. We can't simply go away on some other . . . task. We need to speak with—"

"I have spoken with Harry McElroy and he has granted permission for you to go. It is all arranged. He will inform Charles that you will be away for a few days on a personal errand for him."

That's what she calls it. An errand.

She tells us she's not unaware of the difficulty of what she's asking. She's not unaware of the risks to us. She knows that the segment of border Eddie's heading for is over a hundred miles wide. Knows that it's a region of mean desert and alien to us. Knows that the men who are after him are killers. She understands all that. And she's sorry to say that her people in Mexico are unable to be of help to us. But, as she has said, our kin in El Paso will be able to assist us to some extent.

"You should also know," she adds, "that his seekers believe his name to be Eduardo Porter. And he may be accompanied by a woman. She was said to have fled with him but it is unknown if they're still together."

Of course a woman, I think. Eddie and his troublemaking dick. I'd bet a month's pay the whole thing has to do with her. It would explain why Aunt Cat's kin in Patria Chica are staying out of it. You don't risk harm to your people and your business for the sake of some distantly related kid's girl troubles.

"One other thing," she says. "The two of you and I and Harry McElroy are the only ones of the immediate family aware of this matter. I wish it to remain that way until . . . the matter is concluded."

"Yes mam," I say. And now I'm absolutely certain it was her idea for him to go to Mexico—to Patria Chica or Sonora or wherever the hell. It's why she wants this kept between us. If anything happens to him down there it'll be on her ancient head.

She rises and we hop to our feet. She tells us time is critical, to collect whatever we need and get to the airport as quickly as we can. "Harry McElroy has arranged an aircraft for you. The pilot will notify our people in El Paso when you are due to arrive."

She opens the drawer of the lamp table next to her chair and takes out a pair of cell phones and hands one to each of us. Prepaids. "Keep these with you," she says. "Should I receive more information regarding Edward, I must be able to convey it to you directly."

I almost smile despite my irritation with her. She'd been denied access to us by Charlie Fortune earlier today and wasn't going to let it happen again.

"I know it is not likely you will find him," she says. "But we must do what we can. All I ask is that you do your best. Please."

I've never before heard her say "please" in that way.

She turns her gaze to a wall clock. It's a quarter of six. "Váyanse," she says. And we go.

Back in the 4Runner, I say, "She sent him down there, you know. I'd bet the ranch on it. He wouldn't be in this fix if she hadn't."

"No," Frank says. "He'd probably be in some other one."

After zipping home for a shower and change of clothes, packing a small valise each, and picking out driver's licenses and passports to match, we head for the airport in Frank's '68 Mustang. His Frank Bullitt ride, he calls it. I had phoned Charlie Fortune to see if it was true that Harry Mack had cleared our absence with him. It was, though Uncle Harry hadn't told him what it was about. Charlie was irked at being left out of the proceedings and said he knew this had something to do with "the old lady" and wanted to know what. I said I couldn't tell him, not now, but I would when we got back.

"Goddamn right you will," Charlie said.

The security guard admits us into Spur Aviation Company's private lot, and twenty minutes after that we're in a twin-engine Beechcraft carrying only the pilot and the two of us, taking off and then banking toward the last red light of day, high over the tangled ribbon of the Rio Grande.

17

Rudy and Frank

Nobody in the family really knows why Aunt Cat has such particular affection for Eddie. His parents, Katy Jane and Roman Augusto—Catalina's only grandson—said it was obvious she took a special shine to him from the moment she first saw him. She'd asked Roman if they might name him Edward, which had been the name of her eldest son, Roman's uncle, and they did. Then went even further and middle-named him Gato in her honor. Every year on his birthday, from the time he was old enough to ride a bike, she's invited Eddie to her house for a special supper and to receive his present. Not even Jessie Juliet has ever received such special treatment. He's been to her house more often than anybody else in the family, but whatever they talk about, he's never said anything of it to us, or to anybody else, as far as I know.

But not even Aunt Cat could be of much help to him when he decided to buck the college rule. It happened last summer when he came home from his freshman year at Louisiana State and told his father he didn't want to go back to school—he wanted to work in our smuggling trade. The notion went against a family rule that any Wolfe who wants to work in the family shade trade must first get a baccalaureate degree. The rule was established by the family heads back in the 1930s. They believed a college education could help you make your way through life, regardless of how you chose to make your living. Most Wolfes of the last three generations have earned at least a BA.

But Eddie didn't think the rule should apply to him. He went to each of the Three Uncles in turn to ask for an exemption but they all said no and dismissed as immaterial his argument that a college degree was unnecessary to be a competent smuggler. They reminded him the rule wasn't intended to ensure shade trade skills but to give him an education and the choices it afforded. He talked to me and Frank about it too. He's ten years our junior and has always looked up to us, and he asked what we'd do if we were in his shoes. Frank said we *had* been in his shoes and what we did was go to college because that was the rule for working in the shade trade and there was no way around it.

It wasn't what he wanted to hear, but too bad. Rules that allow for arbitrary exemptions, or whose exemption can be bought, amount to a rigged game. Sad to say, that's largely the case with the rules of the system at large, and all you can do about it is try to work those rules to your advantage by hook or crook. We Wolfes are good at that kind of hooking and crooking—there are some half dozen lawyers in the family, after all—and we can play the rigged game as well as anybody. But we have our own rules too. And they don't grant exemptions.

Eddie can be a real hardhead, however, and just because he can't have his way doesn't mean he'll accept somebody else's. He insisted he wasn't going back to school, and he rented a ratty apartment near the ship channel and went to work for our uncle Harry Morgan. Captain Harry manages the Wolfe

Marine Company, which includes a pair of shrimp boats and a charter boat, fine vessels that bring in good catches—and of course serve well for smuggling contraband. Charlie Fortune sets up the runs and Captain Harry sees they get carried out. Naturally, Eddie tried to finagle Harry into letting him work some runs on the sly, but Harry told him nothing doing, not till he got his sheepskin. Eddie was irked but stayed on the job.

There's this to be said for Eddie—he's a damn quick study. Once you're in high school, the family rules allow you to spend your summers learning the ways and means of the shade trade and the commodities it deals with. To begin an apprenticeship, so to speak, though you aren't allowed take part in any actual operations, not before you get your degree. Eddie had spent his summers learning everything he could about the various modes of smuggling and about the commodities we carried. He'd be out on a shrimper with Harry Morgan and even while he was sitting cross-legged on the deck and heading shrimp he'd be asking Captain Harry all about the art of smuggling by sea. Charlie Fortune would sigh at seeing him come into the Doghouse, knowing another lengthy interrogation about smuggling logistics was about to commence. Eddie became such a distraction to the staff at Delta Instruments & Graphics with all his questions about the electronic devices we traffic in that Aunt Laurel, who manages the store, gave him a carton of handbooks to study and barred him from the premises. The only place he never wore out his welcome was the Republic Arms, where Jimmy Quick was always glad of his company and Eddie became expertly familiar with every kind of gun that passed through the store. He always did well enough in school, but if he had devoted as much time to his textbooks as he did to electronics and firearms manuals, he would've been class valedictorian.

Another thing—the kid can handle himself. Frank and I saw that for ourselves two summers ago, just before he left for LSU. We had taken him out for a few bon voyage beers, and when we came out of the bar we saw this guy at the far end of the parking lot pinning a woman against a truck and slapping her left and right. A couple of his buds were looking on with beers in hand and enjoying the show. Big honkers, all three. They saw us coming and one of them threw a bottle that just missed my head and the fight was on. I went at it with the bottle thrower and broke his nose, which hurts like a bitch and blurs your vision with tears you can't help. He hunched over with a hand to his face, waving the other and saying, "I quit, man." I almost laughed. Guy throws a bottle and thinks he can call it quits with a broken nose. I gave him one to the kidney that dropped him like he'd been shot and would have him pissing blood for a day or two. Frank had put his guy down by then as well, and kicked him in the ribs to make sure he stayed down a while. "How do you like it now, gentlemen?" he said. The woman was long gone.

Then we see Eddie's straddling his guy on the ground and holding him by the collar with one hand and punching him in the face with the other, drilling him hard again and again, even though the guy was making no effort to protect himself. We ran over and pulled him off and he almost took a swing at us. Then I saw that his cheek was bloody from a blade slash about an inch under the eye. No wonder he was fuming. The face of the guy he'd been pounding was a wreck and his arm was bent funny at the elbow. And I suddenly realized he was choking on his own blood. Eddie saw it at the same time and said, "Fucken guy," and bent down and yanked him over onto his side, loosing a gusher of blood from his mouth, plus a tooth or two. The guy's breathing was still gurgly but he wasn't drowning anymore. Frank spotted the knife on the ground and broke the blade off under his foot and lobbed the handle into a Dumpster.

As we drove Eddie to the home of one of our doctors—who would stitch him up in the kitchen and tell him he'd have a small but permanent scar—Frank told him that even though it's a basic rule that somebody who pulls a knife in a fistfight warrants no mercy, you don't want to kill the guy if you don't have to. This one had been down and out, but Eddie had kept punching him in such a frenzy he might've killed him before he knew it. "You gotta fight cool," Frank said. "Remember that."

"Got it," Eddie said. Despite the cut, he was feeling pretty good about himself, you could see it. And why not? There's hardly anybody in the family who doesn't know how to fight, and I mean the women too—we all start getting lessons when we're still in grammar school—but Eddie's a natural and learned faster and better than most. I mean, to take down a knifer bare-handed. Not bad.

Anyway, we thought he would sooner rather than later accept that he had to hold to the college rule, since the longer he put it off the longer it'd be before he could work with us. But then came the big to-do about him and his cousin Jackie Marie.

The news of it didn't exactly shock me and Frank. Jackie's always been a devilish sort, and from the time he was thirteen Eddie's often told us how she liked to pricktease him. She grew up best friends with his sisters Cassie and Carrie—they're all three or four years older than him—and spent many a night at their house, and whenever his parents were away she'd traipse around in her underwear or in just a towel after showering, giving him an eyeful and laughing at his gaga stares and efforts to hide his hard-ons. His sisters thought it was hilarious and sometimes joined in the teasing, doing stuff like leaving the bedroom door open so he could peek in and then all three of them mooning him or flashing him a tit before slamming the door shut and laughing their asses off.

Frank and I liked hearing his stories about it, and I admit I was envious. Jackie and both of his sisters have been knockouts since junior high, especially Jackie, one of those rare redheads with skin the color of caramel. Around the time Eddie went off to LSU, she got her degree in computer programming and went to work as the chief records keeper for Wolfe Marine and bought herself a house in a nice neighborhood. Then Eddie came home last summer and started working for Captain Harry, and in January the shit hit the family fan.

It happened while Frank and I were making the gun run down by Tampico that we'd refused to let Eddie come along on. The way we heard it, Jackie confided to Eddie's sisters that she was pregnant by him and had made an appointment to have an abortion the following week at a Corpus Christi clinic under a false ID. Eddie had agreed to take her. But his sisters were appalled. It was one thing to sexually tease a brother or a cousin but it was way beyond the pale to actually have sex with him. Jackie didn't see what the big deal was. She said sex was just sex, and if an accident happens you deal with it however you have to.

She trusted them to keep the secret, but the next day the sisters spilled the beans to their parents, Roman and Katy. That evening, when Eddie and Jackie got back to her house after a movie, they found four very upset people waiting for them—Roman and Katy and Jackie's mom Brenda, plus Aunt Laurel who is Brenda's sister. The only one not there you might have expected to be was Jackie's father, Mike Armstrong, who owns Armstrong Industries Corporation. He's been divorced from Brenda since Jackie was six but has always doted on his daughter and is so fiercely protective of her that they all agreed it would be best if he were kept in the dark about the situation until cooler heads determined what should be done about it. As it happened, however, Mike ran into Eddie's sister Carrie at a downtown café that same evening, and when he stopped to chat she broke down and told him everything. Like a shot he was off to Jackie's—where parental recriminations about who was to blame for what were flying back and forth so loudly that nobody heard him drive up.

They say he barged into the house looking insane and went straight for Eddie and grabbed him by the throat. Mike started out as a bricklayer and has the biggest hands I've ever seen, and just the thought of them around *my* neck makes me breathless. By all reports, the next few minutes were absolute bedlam. Mike had Eddie on the floor and was bent on throttling him, everybody yelling and trying to break them up. Feet and elbows were flying every which way and Aunt Brenda's nose got bloodied and Katy's lip was split and Jackie got a doozy of a shiner and Roman caught a wild kick in the balls and threw up on everybody. They say Eddie's face was *black* by the time he managed to gouge a thumb into Mike's eye and bash him in the face with his forehead, breaking Mike's nose and getting free of him. Then Eddie was kicking him and Mike was screaming he was blind and trying to protect his head with his hands and when Laurel tried to get between them Eddie shoved her crashing over a chair and kept on kicking. At which point Brenda pulled a .32 five-shooter from her purse and fired a round into the ceiling and everybody froze. She pointed the piece at Eddie and said if he kicked Mike one more time she'd shoot him. They say Eddie's face was still purple and his eyes were blood red and it took him a few tries before he was able to say, "All you . . . go fuck yourself." Then kicked Mike once more and hustled out to his car and left. Brenda was so stunned by that last kick she didn't even think to shoot.

Anyhow, none of us has seen Eddie since. He went directly to Aunt Cat's house—that we know, because Roman called her the next morning to ask if she'd seen him and she admitted he had been there and told her what happened and had decided to go away for a while until things settled down. Roman asked where he'd gone and she said she couldn't say, which isn't saying she didn't know, but added that Edward was a grown man and could take care of himself and would return when he chose to. It would have been fruitless for Roman to press her any further. She would've just clammed up altogether. The most popular supposition was that she'd sent Eddie to stay with her people in Mexico, the Littles, whom no one but her knows how to contact and who wouldn't tell us anything anyway without her permission.

Most of the family thought it was a good thing if Eddie was in Mexico. There was concern that the next time Mike Armstrong saw him he might do worse than try to strangle him. Mike had nearly lost the gouged eye, and the doctors told him some of the damage to his vision might be permanent. Hard feelings lingered as well between Eddie's parents and Jackie's mom—on Roman and Katy's part because of Brenda pointing a gun at their son, on Brenda's part because Eddie had nearly blinded Mike and seemed willing to kick him to death. And although Jackie was pissed off at all of them for butting into her personal life and damaging her furniture and ceiling, she and her mother arrived at an understanding and the following week went to Corpus together and Jackie had the abortion.

Then in April our baby cousin died and the whole family went to the funeral, and a funeral has a way of putting things in perspective. After the ceremony, I saw Roman and Katy and

Brenda and Laurel in a four-way hug. Then Mike Armstrong joined them and there were more hugs all around. Amazingly, Mike's vision was almost back to normal, and although he didn't apologize for trying to strangle Eddie, he did tell Roman he was glad no one had been seriously hurt and as far as he was concerned the matter was a bygone. Then they all went to dinner together.

It wasn't the first time a family tiff got a little out of hand and took a while to be set right.

Since then, everybody has continued to assume that Eddie's with Aunt Cat's people, though as I said, she's never corroborated that assumption to anyone.

Not until this afternoon, anyway, when she all but admitted it to me and Frank.

Now that Eddie isn't there anymore.

18

Catalina

She had made them promise to call every Monday to let her know how Edward was doing, and had told them not to allow him to take part in any criminal activity. Very well, they said. They did not ask why not, and she did not offer to explain that she did not want him to find in Mexico the occupation he was denied at home. He might then never return. Still, because the Wolfe family was well known in Mexico City, she agreed with the Littles' suggestion that Edward use a different name to avoid rousing speculation about the presence of a Wolfe at Patria Chica. He had chosen to be known as Eduardo Porter.

The Littles' early reports said he was well liked and seemingly content. But before he'd been there two months he was complaining of boredom and asking to go out on a bill collection or an arms delivery. They reminded him that Doña Catalina would not permit it, and he said there was no need for her to know. Such, they told her, was his willfulness. She granted their request to at least let him help load shipments of contraband for transport out of Patria Chica, as it might give him some small sense of the adventure he craved.

Then in March came the unscheduled call from cousin Stilwell to tell her Edward had gone to work for the organization called Las Sinas. He hastened to assure her the job had nothing to do with smuggling or any other dangerous undertaking. It was a guard post at some isolated ranch periodically used by Sinas chieftains for a brief recreation. Edward would be living there with only a handful of other guards and a few caretakers. He'd gotten the job by way of a Sinas crew that came to Patria Chica to pick up a shipment of arms. Stilwell could only assume that Edward took the job because he saw it as a possible means to the smuggler life he craved. But as the crew chief had described it, life at the ranch was so dull that Stilwell thought it very possible Edward would become even more bored there than he'd been at Patria Chica and soon enough return to the Littles, maybe even home to Texas. In any event, they could not have stopped him from leaving except by holding him prisoner. That, she agreed, would not have been the thing to do.

However, while Edward was gathering his belongings from the house, the Littles told the crew chief that the Porter kid was the boyfriend of one of their nieces and asked if there might be some way they could be kept informed of his well-being. The chief knew someone who worked in a minor administrative section of Sinas operations that included oversight of the Sonora retreat. They received periodic reports and requisitions from the place, but the only time a report might include mention of a guard was if the man was seriously hurt or too sick to work and a replacement for him was needed. The Littles said that was good enough. They offered to deposit a sum of money every week into a bank account in the name of the crew chief—money he might share with his administrative friend in whatever proportion he chose—in exchange for a weekly notice of whether there had been any communication from the ranch and, if so, whether it contained mention of Eduardo Porter. The chief said they had a deal.

Stilwell told her he was sorry they would be unable to report more specifically to her about Edward, but they would at least know if he should become ill or injured. It would be, Stilwell said, a case of no news being good news, as the gringos say.

Yes, she had said, so it would seem.

And so had it proved.

Until this afternoon.

TIERRA
DEL DIABLO

SUNDAY

19

Eddie and Miranda

The morning sun is flaring at the mountain ridge when they depart the motel. They wear their Naranjeros baseball caps and the work clothes from the secondhand store, shirts untucked. Before leaving she pinned two bandannas together and then wrapped them tight over her breasts to better disguise her femaleness from anyone who regards her from any distance beyond close up. Her shiner has faded to a pale yellow and Eddie's wound is healing well and almost painless under the cinch of the money belt. The MAC and Glock are between them on the seat and covered with a shirt. The Taurus is in his waistband, the M-16, detached in two, in his backpack.

They double back through town the way they came in, stopping at a grocery store for a plastic cooler and ice and soda pop and drinking water, then at a hardware store for a pair of five-gallon jerry cans and some jugs of radiator antifreeze—and

joke about the need for such a thing in order to drive through
a desert. At a fast-food place he buys a sack of takeout breakfast
tacos and two big paper cups of coffee, then at the edge of town
he pulls into a Pemex station and fills the truck's tank and the
jerry cans. Then they head north.

The Sunday morning traffic is light and there's no toll station
to evade on this portion of highway, but Eddie holds his speed
below the limit. They keep watch in the rearviews and get tense
each time they see some late-model truck or SUV with tinted
glass closing up behind them or coming from the other direction.
Then breathe easier when it passes by. She says some of them
must be Sinas. He says she's probably right. She says she feels like
a fish swimming through a sea of sharks.

Forty miles out of Guaymas he exits west onto a secondary road
that makes a wide sixty-mile northward curve to a junction on
the road between Hermosillo and the coast, and then he heads
farther westward, away from Hermosillo, in traffic thickening
with beachgoers. They pass through the ranching community
of Miguel Alemán and turn north again, passing by large cattle
ranches and farms. The good roads soon give way to rough ones
connecting smaller ranches lying farther apart from each other.
And then they are on a dirt road bearing into the open desert.

Take a good look behind you, he says. That's the last paved
road we'll see for a while.

She says her father once told her it was bad luck to look
back at the port as your boat set out to sea.

Yeah? Well, good thing we're not in a boat.

Once again resorting to a matchstick and the map scale, she calculates that Caborca lies roughly 150 miles ahead. From there it's sixty miles or so to the border.

A little more than two hundred miles is not so very far, she says.

He reminds her that those two hundred miles are on a straight line, while the roads ahead will be primitive and none of them at all straight. But that's all right. They don't want to get to the border before dark.

As they press deeper into the desert, the sky seems to get higher. The land becomes starker, paler, its vegetation coarser. The mountains ahead are slower to enlarge. The light now so bright Eddie squints behind his sunglasses. Small and large escarpments all around.

They come upon junctions with other rugged roads, unmarked on the map and leading who knows where. At each junction, Eddie opts for the way bearing most northward. The trails wind around clusters of peppercorn hills, snake between outcrops. The speedometer needle rises and falls, at times touching thirty-five, often bobbing below fifteen.

The heat swells and shimmers on the distant flats but he keeps the air conditioner at its lowest setting to avoid adding to the engine's strain. Each time she lowers her window a little to toss out a finished cigarette, the inrushing air is hotter yet.

They now and again pass by a village, none with a sign to identify it by name. Some are neat hamlets of whitewashed buildings, animal pens, a well or two, a tidy cornfield defying the surrounding barrenness. Others are but a litter of decrepit huts with no obvious means of sustenance. They see few vehicles in even the largest of these villages. See fewer still on the roads, and most of them so far off it is impossible to identify them as cars or trucks or something other. At times they see the dust of what might be a vehicle but proves to be a wayward whirlwind traversing the wasteland.

My God, Miranda says, even Rancho del Sol isn't as far from the world as this.

There's a lot more of this ahead of us. More and tougher. All the way up past the border.

How do you know it's tougher?

I've read about it. Heard about it.

I have heard we should not believe everything we read or hear.

He smiles. Yeah, I've heard and read that too.

She gestures at a lone buzzard gliding high over the open flats. Look at that stupid thing. Searching for something dead to eat in a place where almost nothing lives and so there's almost nothing to become dead.

Maybe he's keeping an eye on us, Eddie says.

Ho ho, that is so very funny.

It is past noon when they follow a curve around a rocky hill and see a beat-up Plymouth station wagon blocking the road ahead. Two men in caps and sunglasses are standing to either side of the raised hood.

Eddie stops twenty feet shy of the wagon, unable to go around it because of the rock wall to the right and a stony slope to the left. He doesn't see anybody in the wagon but that doesn't mean there isn't anyone in it. For a second he considers putting the truck in reverse and backing up fast around the bend until he has enough room to turn the truck about and scoot the other way. But then what? Go back to the last junction and take a different road? Hell with that.

One of the men lifts a hand in greeting and starts toward them, showing very white teeth. The other one moves up beside the station wagon's passenger-side window.

As he lowers his window, Eddie withdraws the cocked MAC from under the shirt on the seat, keeping it out of the men's view. He places it on his lap and fingers the safety off.

Miranda holds the Glock between her knees and says, Are they—?

Watch the other one, Eddie says. If he shows a gun, shoot him.

"Hola, amigos!" the smiling man says, coming up to within a few feet of the truck, taking off his glasses and hooking them on the neck of his shirt. We have a loose electric connection, but I can fix it if I had pliers. Do you maybe—

You're in luck, Eddie says. I have some in the back. I'll get them.

The man's grin widens. Very good, my friend. Damn good luck for us that you have come.

Still holding the MAC out of the man's sight, Eddie opens the door and steps out. The man tugs at his shirtfront and says, What heat, eh? And reaches behind him with his other hand as if to tug the back of his shirt too.

Eddie brings the MAC up to the door window and tells him to freeze. The man does, his hand behind his back, his expression that of someone who has just set eyes on an ugly blind date.

"Cuidado!" Miranda yells.

The other man has snatched a double-barreled shotgun from the wagon—and in the course of the next three seconds a load of buckshot converts a section of the right side of the truck's windshield to a pale web of fractured safety glass centered on a hole the size of a grapefruit and Miranda feels a spatter of glass bits on the side of her face and fires four times into the shotgunner's chest and the other man starts to bring a revolver from behind his back and Eddie shoots him with a jet of bullets that knocks him backward off his feet.

Miranda continues to lean out the window and point the Glock at the awkward heap of the shotgunner as Eddie goes over to the man he shot and regards his bloody chest, the stillness of him. He picks up the revolver and gives it a look and lobs it down the slope. Then goes to the shotgunner and rolls him onto his back with his foot. The man's sunglasses cling to one ear. He tells Miranda this one's dead too and she gets out of the truck.

He sets the MAC's safety and hands the weapon to her and tells her to bring the shotgun. Then drags the shotgunner by the feet to the edge of the slope and pushes him over and the man tumbles down about midway before getting snagged on a clutch of prickly pear cactus.

You said they couldn't cover these back roads, she says. She is staring at the man on the slope.

What?

You said there are too many back roads for them to guard.

You think . . . ? Hey, girl, these guys aren't *Sinas*. You ever seen Company guys with shitty weapons like these? A car like *that*? These are local hicks who thought they were Pancho Villa.

Bandits? Out here?

Like everywhere else, yeah.

He flings the shotgun whirling and it strikes the rocks below and breaks in two between breech and stock.

That's crazy. Who is there to rob out here?

Whoever comes along. They probably watch this road every day, praying somebody'll come by with more than a few pesos in their pocket.

Like us.

Yeah . . . except unarmed. He glances back toward the road bend and then hastens to the other man and drags him over to the slope.

You're *sure* they're not Sinas? she says.

Maybe in their dreams.

He gives the man a shove and he goes flailing all the way to the bottom and comes to a halt on his back with his ankles crossed and one hand behind his head and the other on his chest.

Look at that, she says. He looks so at ease. A minute ago he was complaining about the heat.

Let's hurry it up, Eddie says.

Oh yes, let's hurry before somebody comes along any day now.

They find nothing of interest in the Plymouth wagon. She says maybe they should take it. It will be less noticeable than a truck with a shotgun hole in the windshield. He says no. The bandits may have come from someplace up ahead and the wagon might be recognized.

He puts the transmission in neutral and releases the brake and they push the wagon over the slope. It bounces and sways all the way to the bottom, then veers and crashes over onto its side in a swell of dust.

They get back in the truck and move on. He has her count the cartridges left in the Glock's magazine. Five. Plus one in the chamber. The MAC is down to seven.

A few miles farther on, peering in the side mirror, he says, Look back there. It's amazing how fast they get the word.

She looks in her side mirror and sees a convergence of buz-zards spiraling down toward the road bend.

Jesus, she says. This fucking country.

20

Martillo and Pico

Over a late breakfast in a rear corner booth of Chucho's, a small café in Nogales, they once more review the lean packet of in-formation about the Porter kid. A single sheet of basic data. A single photograph. A summary account of his known actions since Friday night. A set of police reports about the fight in the sugar field. An inventory form listing everything recovered at that scene.

Pico scoops the last of his huevos rancheros into his mouth with a fold of flour tortilla and goes over the data sheet on the kid. Martillo permits the waitress to refill his cup, then returns his attention to the reports.

It's interesting, Pico says, that one so young was able to dis-pose of two Sinas and two cops by himself. A simple rancho guard.

He may not be so simple or have been by himself, Martillo says. The girl may have been with him. She may still be with him. Martillo is one for factual exactness whenever possible.

If she was with him, Pico says, do you think she killed any of them?

I cannot know that.

Because if she was with him and did not kill any of them, then it's even more interesting that he killed all four.

Martillo and Pico have known each other since boyhood, have fought side by side against other street gangs and trained together in the army special forces and worked as a team for

the Zetas before breaking away on their own—and yet Martillo
is still prone to irritation with Pico's propensity for perplexing
assertions. He knows, however, that to ask him to clarify some
puzzling remark is to risk a lengthy and convoluted explication
that may be even more baffling than whatever he said in the first
place. He therefore holds his tongue and keeps his focus on the
document before him.

And a minute later says, Hey.

Pico looks at him.

That special bunch of Sinas pistol men, Luna Negra, they
all carry phones issued to them by the organization. Best money
can buy. Batteries that can light up Hermosillo for a week.

So I've heard. What about it?

The list of items the cops found at the scene includes a cell
phone. Found it on one of the Sinas.

Martillo says no more, affecting to study the inventory sheet.
Pico knows he's waiting for a prompt to continue. It's how Martillo has always been. Big dramatizer. He once said that if he had
to choose another profession he would like to be a movie actor.
He believes he could play roles like those of the famous Emilio
Fernandez—known to all Mexican moviegoers as "El Indio"—
whom he strongly resembles. He sometimes amuses himself by reciting some of El Indio's lines as General Mapache in *The Wild Bunch*.

So? Pico says.

So there's only one phone on this list.

Pico drums his fingers on the tabletop. *So?*

I have to wonder if anybody's looked at this list besides the
cop who put it together. Wouldn't any Sina who looked at this be
a little curious why the other guy didn't have a phone on him?

What's there to be curious about? Maybe the guy didn't
take it with him because they didn't need two phones. Maybe

he forgot it somewhere. Left it home, at his girlfriend's, some cantina. Maybe lost it in the cane field. What's the big mystery?

Martillo makes no response, keeping his eyes on the papers in front of him.

Pico smiles and cocks his head. You think the kid took it.

Without looking up, Martillo purses his lips.

Makes no sense, man, Pico says. According to this report, he didn't take the segundo's phone. Probably knows Sinas phones are wired, at least suspects it, so why take the chance? You can buy a throwaway anywhere.

Very true, Martillo says. But, my little friend, are you aware that all Luna Negra phones have a homing device in them? A tracker?

How do you know that?

Martillo puts the fingertips of one hand to his forehead and closes his eyes and says in the sage tone of a stage magician, I know many things unknown to the minds of mortal men. I have cosmic mental powers that—

How the fuck you know?

A captain of Luna Negra told me, and he is not one to lie for simple pleasure.

Pico smiles. The kid didn't want the *phone*. He wanted the tracker.

The device is not on the phone's menu, but genius is not required to find out if it has one. The kid maybe knew how to look for it.

And he wants a tracker because . . . ?

You're running for your life. Your only chance is to get across the line. You're from way the hell the other side of the country and don't know anything about the desert except it can kill you quick. You're going to have to cross with a bunch of peons and a guide who might desert you at the first sign of trouble. Everybody knows the stories. But if you have a tracker . . .

Of course, Pico says. If you get lost or in trouble you turn it on and hope like hell somebody picks up the signal and finds you before you cook. Even if it's the Border Patrol, at least you're alive.

Exactly, Martillo says. However, the tracker in these phones is a very interesting kind. The Sinas get them from South Africa or Israel or some damn place. Its signal can't be picked up except by a pair of connected receivers that have to be tuned according to the kind of phone the tracker is in. Not very complicated, actually, and the weather can interfere with it the same as with any other electrical gadget. But it's one of the best for avoiding interception of its signal.

And you know this because . . . the Luna captain?

He was very informative and highly appreciative that I was paying for all our drinks.

But Porter doesn't know the kind of tracker he has or he wouldn't have taken it. The only ones who know how to pick up its signal are the people after him.

Your quickness of understanding is admirable, Martillo says with a benign smile.

And this Luna captain told you how to tune to the signal.

No. He said the Luna phones are programmed by a communications crew before they're issued. But I'll bet the technicians at Azteca can provide that information. They know everything in the world about such devices.

You are a wise and clever man.

Martillo's wide grin exposes a row of four gold teeth. That is why they pay me so well, he says. My wisdom and cleverness.

And me? Why do they pay me so well?

Because you are with me, of course.

Ah yes, of course.

Listen, if the Sinas had bothered to give some careful attention to this inventory, they would know all of this too. And this very minute they could have receivers set up along the border and ready to find him the minute he turns the thing on.

But they don't know. And we do. And we are not going to tell them. Fuck them. We deserve the Boss's reward.

You are very eloquent and persuasive and have convinced me entirely.

But, Pico says. What if he doesn't turn the thing on? He might not have to.

That is sadly true. Actually, the odds favor that either the Sinas will get him or he'll make it over the line and to the pickup point. In either case, he won't be turning it on.

Actually, for all we know, the other Sina didn't even have a fucking phone.

Martillo makes a wry face. That too is possible. Actually.

So if the kid doesn't have it, or has it but doesn't turn it on, we got no more chance of finding him than anybody else. All we can do is wander along the border with our thumbs up our ass, looking for crossers and hoping he's in some bunch we run into. What are the odds of finding him that way?

On the other hand, Martillo says, if he does have the thing, and if he does have to use it, it won't be until he's on the other side. Assuming, of course, he gets past the Sinas. All things considered, we ought to wait for him on the other side and hope he gets across and has some reason to turn the thing on.

Pico drums his fingers. That's a lot to hope for, he says.

Yes. But even if he doesn't have it or turn it on, if he gets to the other side he'll still be in the desert, and we just have to find him before he makes it to the pickup point. And if he *does* turn it on . . .

He's ours, Pico says. Assuming of course he gets past the Sinas.

He's smart. He might do it.

Think he will?

Martillo shrugs. What is life but constant hope?

Pico sighs. Glances around. Leans forward on his elbows and says, I think maybe we should call the Azteca people and tell them what we need and what we need to know. Just in case.

I think that's a very fine idea.

Glad you like it.

21

Eddie and Miranda

They go through another village and then have to halt while two young boys drive a raucous herd of goats across the road. One of the boys stares hard at the windshield, then points at it and calls something to Eddie.

He rolls down his window. What?

The kid points again and says, Who shot you?

Eddie tells him they were hunting rabbits but one of the rabbits had a gun and shot back.

The boy finds this hilarious and shows his white teeth in laughter. He goes to the other boy and points at the truck as he speaks to him, and the other boy laughs too.

A few miles farther down the road, Eddie stops the truck and gets out. He searches the ground, picks up a large rock and tests its grip and heft, tosses it aside, then finds one shaped roughly like an oversize house brick and affording a solid grip on one side. He tells Miranda to get out of the truck and then starts smashing out the windshield. It is no simple task to break apart its laminated safety glass and he is drenched with sweat when he knocks out the last clung-together shards into the cab. He scrapes off the remaining glass ridges from the windshield frame and they sweep the glass out of the truck with their hands.

Then drive on, the inward flow of hot air woven with weak threads of coolness from the air conditioner ducts.

The sun is more than halfway down the sky when they crest a rise and see quadrate green fields in the distance ahead, and past them the indistinct form of Caborca. But they are well acquainted now with the illusory effects of desert expanse and they know the town is farther than it looks.

They come to a dirt road of smooth grade and the countryside transforms. They drive past fields of cotton, fields of corn. Low green vineyards. Long rows of irrigation furrows and white sprinkler pipes. The air gains vapor and is much less hot. It smells of wet earth and feels wonderful on their gritty faces.

How incredible this is, she says. All these good things growing. Think how much water must be under this ground. This is like a great big what-do-you-call-it, what you see in desert movies, where there are palms and pools of water.

Oasis, Eddie says.

While Miranda continues to study the passing countryside, he considers his plan—and now sees the folly of it. He has of course been expecting the Company to have lookouts at Sasabe and

Sonoyta, but only now does he truly appreciate what that means. Both places will be *packed* with lookouts. They'll be on every street corner. They'll have descriptions, probably pictures. The Company will certainly have posted a bounty. What's the chance in either place of finding a coyote who isn't in the service of the Company one way or another? Or even an independent who won't turn him in for the reward? To look for a guide in either place is more than just risky—it's enormously stupid.

What had he been thinking? He berates himself for a dunce.

The wiser thing to do, he now reasons, is arrive at the border in hiding among a group of crossers. Under the eye of an independent coyote who will naturally want to avoid attracting attention. Hook up with an independent in Caborca and go with him to the border. *That's* the ticket. At the border, the coyote or somebody who works for him takes you over the line. And there you are.

Except nobody really needs a guide to cross the border in the desert. What you need is somebody to get your ass *out* of the desert once you're over the line. That's what you're really paying for. But what if after he takes you across, the guide lights out? Been known to happen. Plenty of stories.

What you need, he tells himself, is a backup plan. And you've known it all along. It's why you bought those phones, why you took the tracker. So quit the bullshit and make the call. Tell them where you are, what you got.

Nope. No way. They'll tell me go fuck myself. That's what I told them, that's what they'll tell me.

Maybe, maybe not. But even if they do, so what? Even if they say fuck you, you're no worse off than now. Nothing to lose by asking.

Hell there isn't. I won't give any of them the satisfaction of telling me no.

Well, you better be damn sure that's how you want it. You've had a good look at that map. That desert's one big dead zone. Forget finding a cell connection out there. Shoulda bought a satellite in Hermosillo.

Yeah. Shoulda coulda woulda.

So? No backup plan?

Yeah there is, Eddie thinks. Stick close to the guide. He cuts out, cut out with him. He objects, put the gun in his face. That's the backup. Simple's always best. Basic rule.

All right then. Find a coyote in Caborca. Bus station's a sure place. Of course, it's also a sure place for lookouts. But they're not likely to give this heap a very close look. Or make Miranda for a woman. Just a couple of guys clunking along in a work truck, if they take a look at all.

"Oye," Eddie says.

She turns to him from the window and he tells her what he has in mind.

Whatever you think best, she says. You're the one who says he knows all about smuggling.

If they connect with a coyote in Caborca, they'll abandon the truck there. But because you never know, he takes the precaution of filling the truck's tank at a Pemex just south of town. In a little café beside the gas station, they buy chicken empanadas and cold bottles of orange soda and eat their food at a stand-up counter, fending off flies all the while, then wash up at the sink in the grimy restroom. She inspects his wound, which has scabbed nicely and shows no sign of infection, then reseals the bandage. They get directions to the bus station from the woman at the register. In the truck he withdraws five thousand dollars from the money belt and puts two grand in one front pocket of his pants and three in the other. And they head into Caborca.

It's a small town but a busy one this late Sunday afternoon. Dusty and spare of trees. Its chief shade the shadows of buildings against the low sun. The traffic heavy and slow. Nobody seems curious about their lack of a windshield. Eddie finds the 6 de Abril Plaza, and a few blocks past it the bus station.

The street fronting the depot is chockablock with honking, racketing vehicles, the sidewalks crowded. The stop-and-go pace of the traffic is an advantage, affording Eddie a careful look around.

The truck is almost abreast of the station's entrance when he feels a sudden hollowness in his belly. Over there, he says, and juts his chin toward the front doors, where people are streaming in and out. The two in the cowboy hats.

She leans forward to look past him. The men stand to either side of the doors, giving the eye to everyone entering. Their hats white, their clothes denim, necklaced sunglasses dangling on their chests, open jackets bulging slightly under one arm.

"Sinas? Estás seguro?"

He nods. And bound to be more of them inside, he says.

She shrinks down in her seat and he tells her to sit up. Look hot and bored.

The hot part is easy, she says.

They follow the creeping traffic past a taxi stand where people are cramming themselves into a dilapidated green cab expelling a blue cloud of exhaust smoke. Up ahead and near the corner, a bus pulls up, "Caborca" in the destination window above its windshield.

A stocky man in a long-billed fisherman's cap bobs out of the sidewalk crowd and begins addressing himself to the men filing out of the bus—at the same time casting nervous glances toward the station doors, craning his head to see through the crowd. It's clear to Eddie that the man is aware of the Sinas and is fearful of them. An independent poaching on their turf, reason enough for his nervousness. But the man is adept at using the sidewalk traffic to screen himself from their view, and Eddie admires his daring. The Sinas seem unaware of him.

Most of the men the stocky guy speaks to shake their heads or ignore him, but now three of them stop and nod, and the man points them over to the wall, where they go and wait while he turns his attention to the last of the men coming off the bus, a guy in a short-brimmed Panama, and gets him too to join his group.

The one in the fishing cap, Eddie says. That's our guy.

Miranda regards him as they creep past. He's a coyote?

A hook. He sends crossers to the coyote.

Eddie takes a left at the corner and finds a curbside parking spot near the end of the street and leaves the engine idling. He slips the Taurus into his pants under his shirt and uses the side mirror to watch the corner behind them.

Before long the stocky man comes into view with the four men and says something to them as he points down the street. A couple of them make grateful gestures and they all hurry away.

Eddie waits until the stocky man has gone back around the corner and the four men have passed by on the other side of the street, then gets out of the truck and puts Miranda's tote into his backpack for greater bulk and slips the pack on over his shoulders. He tells her to slide behind the wheel and keep the motor running.

He goes back to the street fronting the bus depot and sees the stocky man standing near the sidewalk wall, again shifting his attention between the Sinas at the doors and oncoming pedestrians who might be migrants seeking help to get to el norte. Assuming the look of an apprehensive stranger, Eddie starts toward him. The man sees him coming—a hopeful migrant with his worldly possessions on his back—and sidles out to intercept him, smiling.

Hey there, my friend, he says just loud enough for Eddie to hear him, "Viajes al norte?"

Eddie's wide grin abets his squint to better hide the blue of his eyes in the waning daylight.

A few minutes later, the man—who'd said his name was Ernesto—takes Eddie around the corner and points the way toward the address he has given him, where the coyote can be found with his assembled crossers. Eddie has told him he is Pedro Mendoza from Mazatlán and will be accompanied by his sister, Rima, who is waiting for him at a little taco place down the street. Ernesto said that was nice to hear, that a family should always try to stay together. Eddie thanks him again and starts away.

At the end of the block, he looks back, sees that the man has gone, then jogs across the street to Miranda and the truck.

Eddie's timing is very lucky, Ernesto had told him, because there's a group leaving for the border this very evening. The entire crossing will be very simple, the man assured him, an easy walk of a few hours to a back road where they will be met by a transport van, then taken to Tucson, a nice town with many Mexican compatriots. From there he can choose to go his own way, or, if he prefers and is willing to pay a little extra, he can be transported to someplace else, someplace bigger, with more opportunities for employment. To Phoenix or Los Angeles or Chicago, wherever he wishes. For still a bit more money, he can even be assured of having a job when he gets there. What's more, he did not have to give money to anyone except Mister Canales, the man Ernesto was sending him to, at the Hotel Pájaro, four blocks from the station and on the street to the left. And the cost for going to Tucson? A bargain, Ernesto told him. He stated the price and Eddie mentally converted the peso amount to $650. A bargain for sure. It confirms his suspicion that the coyote Ernesto works for is an independent. Even along the lower Rio Grande, prices have been jumping since last year, and no big gang would charge so little as $650.

Eddie parks the truck a block past the hotel's street and switches off the engine. He has told Miranda they are now brother and sister, Pedro and Rima Mendoza, and don't forget her name. She says she's never heard of anybody named Rima and he says she has now. It's a great relief to her to dispense with the bandanna binding her breasts, and as she starts to rebutton her shirt he reaches into it and fondles her. She smiles and says that it seems like weeks since they have made love. Months, he says, a hundred years. He fingers a nipple and she slaps his hand away, telling him it is no way to touch a sister.

He takes out the two thousand dollars and counts out seven hundred and puts it in a shirt pocket and returns the remainder to his pants. Then extracts the M-16 in its two parts from the backpack and slips the rifle under the front seat. Whoever steals the truck is going to get a nice bonus. Though the MAC has only seven rounds in its magazine, he leaves it in the backpack, then takes out her tote and is about to hand it to her but then pauses.

Tell them but don't ask.

The thought comes to him like a whisper and he smiles at his mental image of a lightbulb shining above his head.

If you don't ask for help, he thinks, they can't turn you down. Give them the information and nothing more. Don't even give it to them directly. Relay it to them. They'll know what to do with it if they want to. And if they choose to do nothing, so what? They can't say they refused you. None of them can. Because you're not *asking* for a damn thing. They're anyway a backup at best. Odds are you won't need them. Won't even have cause to turn the thing on.

What's wrong? she says. He takes the three phones from the tote and hands her the bag and puts the Sinas phone and one of the prepaids in his pack. She slings the bag onto her shoulder, ready to go. It holds a few clothes, the first-aid supplies, packs of cigarettes, and the Glock. The switchblade's in her pocket with her Mexican cash.

For a moment he can't remember the number he wants to call, a number he has called many times before but not in the past six months. Then it comes to him and he quickly presses the buttons.

She watches him intently.

He's ready to hear surprise at the sound of his voice, is set to deflect questions and say he must keep the call very short and then quickly give her the information. But the phone is answered by a default recording that informs him no one is available to take his call and to please leave a message, and he smiles at his good luck.

"Hey, Little Momma, it's Edward." He's the only one who calls Catalina by that name or would ever dare to, and she has never objected. Continuing in English, he tells her he's sorry he hasn't time to explain but he has to hurry. He will be crossing the border into Arizona sometime tonight. He asks her to tell Rudy and Frank that he has a Buddha and tells her the make of cell phone he has. He says that if Rudy and Frank don't know what a Buddha is, to ask Aunt Laurel. "Tell them I said they can do whatever they want to with the information. Be sure to tell them that, Little Momma." He pauses, then ends the call with, "I hope you're well."

Who was that? Miranda says. Did you call somebody to help us?

Help? You think we need help? I'd say we're doing pretty good on our own. A few minutes ago we were close enough to spit on the bastards and they didn't spot us.

Did you ask for help?

Sort of. But don't count on getting it.

Why not? Who was it?

Somebody on the other gulf.

She shakes her head. Nobody that far away can help.

I don't think so, either. But like I said, we're doing okay on our own.

He opens the door and drops the used phone next to the curb, then starts up the truck and backs up, crushing the phone under the tire. He shuts off the motor and leaves the key in the ignition. They get out and he puts on his backpack and touches the pistol under his shirt. And they head up the street.

22

Eddie and Miranda

Twilight. Streetlights coming on. Bats swooping over a weedy vacant lot. The air smells of dust and fried peppers.

The hotel stands midway down the street. A small white-washed structure of two stories fronted by a scrubby yard and a lighted sign that reads "El Pájaro." It is flanked by a small grocery on one side and on the other by a cantina from whose open door issues radio music. The jumpy polka strains of a conjunto band.

Cool and alert, Edward, cool and alert, Eddie tells himself as he leads Miranda up the walkway toward the front porch, where three men are sitting in the weak glow of an amber bulb above the door. He pauses at the bottom step and sees now that they are two men and a boy, one of the men tall and mustached and wearing a light white coat despite the heat, the other clean-shaved and crew-cut, in worn denim pants and work shirt. The boy is about fourteen, also in work clothes. Eddie introduces himself and Miranda as Pedro and Rima Mendoza and says they are from Santa Rosalba, a village a little west of Hermosillo. He says Ernesto has sent them to see Mister Canales, who can arrange for them to cross into the north tonight.

The tall one rises from his chair and comes to the top of the steps. "Yo soy Canales," he says. You have been told the cost of the service?

Eddie says he has, but he can pay only in American money and hopes that's acceptable.

Canales smiles. How did you come by so much in American money?

From our brother, Eddie says. He has been in the north for two years and has sent us money almost every month. We can't wait to join him.

Of course, Canales says. Family is of first importance. And where is this brother?

Las Vegas. He says we can get work there.

Ah, Las Vegas, Canales says, and grins and pretends to shake dice in his fist and roll them. A very exciting place, I am told. Tell me, young man, do you speak English?

No sir, but my brother does. We will learn from him.

Never let them know how much you know. Basic rule.

Without the least alteration in his tone or affable aspect, Canales says, "I would dearly love to fuck your sister in the ass and then make her suck my cock."

But Eddie is on high alert and isn't caught off guard by this old trick for testing someone's knowledge of a language by insulting him under the mask of a smile. Charlie Fortune had taught him about the tactic. He affects a puzzled look. "Cómo, señor?"

Forgive me, Canales says. I was showing off my own English. I simply said that with such determination, you will go far. He gestures at the other man. Give the money to Beto.

Eddie takes the thirteen hundred dollars from his pocket and hands it to the Beto guy, who gets up and goes into the lighted foyer and closes the door behind him. Eddie assumes he's counting it. Maybe checking somehow to make sure it's not counterfeit. Oh man, he thinks, what if it is?

I see you are traveling light, Canales says. Very smart. But be sure you have food and water to last you until tomorrow. You can buy what you need at the little store over there.

Beto comes back out and says, "Todo bien," and gives the money to Canales.

Eddie and Miranda go to the store and buy bottles of water, small packs of raisins, and beef jerky. When they get back to the apartment house only Beto is still on the porch. He ushers them inside and down the dim first-floor hallway to a rear apartment and into a small living room where eight other migrants are already waiting, seated on various pieces of dingy furniture, clutching their backpacks, totes, plastic bags. The boy is there too, but not Canales, whom they will not see again. Beto sits down next to a window overlooking the driveway.

Though its windows are open, the room is hot and smells of body odors. All but one of the migrants are men and most of them return Eddie's nod of greeting. He recognizes the four he saw Ernesto solicit at the bus station. The men all stare at Miranda but are too shy to meet her eyes, except for the guy in the Panama hat, and she looks away from him. The other member of the group is a woman traveling with one of the men.

While they wait for their transport they listen to the cantina music coming through the windows. Miranda lights a cigarette and uses a cardboard coffee cup as an ashtray. No one else lights up but nobody seems to mind her smoking. The migrants chat quietly and Eddie soon comes to know that the couple are married and named Martínez. They are bound for Phoenix, where the woman's brother has been working at a plant nursery for almost a year. A man named Sando and his teenage nephew are from a village in Nayarit and going to a big farm near Albuquerque to work alongside the brother of the man and father of the boy. Three of the men Eddie saw recruited by Ernesto are relatives named Fonseca, two lean brothers and a short fat cousin, who are headed to Denver for jobs in a packinghouse. One of the brothers inquires politely about Eddie's plans, and they are all impressed to learn that Pedro and Rima Mendoza are going to Las Vegas, that glittering symbol of American fortune, to work with a brother at a grand hotel, Rima in the kitchen, Pedro with the grounds crew.

The man in the Panama looks bored by the talk. He is of compact build and has a constant squint. When the elder Sando asks him his name, he says Benito Juárez. Sando misses the sarcasm and says, Truly? Like the great hero? The man laughs without humor, and Sando looks in confusion at the Fonsecas, who look away. The Panama guy tugs his hat brim lower and leans back against the wall with his arms and ankles crossed. Eddie pegs him for some smalltimer on the run.

∽∾

The windows are dark when the group hears a vehicle come up the driveway. Beto says, "Síguenme," and they quickly take up their things and trail from the room after him.

They exit the building by its back door, next to the end of the driveway, where an idling Chevy Suburban equipped with oversize rough-country tires and three bench seats awaits them. The driver is wearing a reversed baseball cap and smoking a cigarette.

Eddie holds Miranda back as Beto herds the others into the second and third rows of seats. The Panama guy gets in ahead of Martínez and his wife, and Eddie smiles when Martínez catches on to the man's ploy and draws her back and gets in ahead of her, putting himself between her and the Panama. As Eddie had anticipated, the others and their baggage fill up the second and third seats, and Beto takes him and Miranda around to the double rear doors and they get in and sit facing each other on the floor behind the third seat, the backpack and tote between them. It's where Eddie prefers to be. At the rear exit. Just in case.

Beto slams the back doors shut and then goes around and gets in the shotgun seat, the boy seated between him and the driver, and says, "Vámonos."

23

Catalina

For years now, it has been the maids' practice for one or the other of them to stand outside the bathroom door whenever Doña Catalina takes a bath and listen carefully for any sound of distress, to be ready to rush in and give assistance should she need it. Though they believe this ritual to be a secret from her, Catalina has in fact been aware of it since its inception, her hearing and intuitive perception of someone's near presence still more acute than the maids can imagine. Yet she has never let them know of her awareness. Because if some accident should befall her—a knock on the head from a fall or a faint, an inadvertent slip in the shower or submergence in the tub, any of the not uncommon bathroom mishaps the aged are subject to—far better the ignominy of being rescued by her maids than to die because she was too proud to let them keep furtive vigilance over her. The simple fact of the matter is that she has no desire for life to end, never mind that she has had a greater share of it than the measureless majority of those who have ever lived. She recently read a persuasive argument that pride, long established as the deadliest of the seven great sins, has been supplanted by greed. She had to admit it was so in her case, though at times she's no longer sure there is very much distinction between the two. She has often heard it said that the worst thing in life is to grow old and have to depend on others. Long ago she would have agreed. Now she knows how much worse it must be to grow old and have no one to depend on.

Once she's out of the tub she begins singing softly, as is her habit, so that whichever maid has an ear to the door will know she has survived one more bath without bad luck. She emerges in her robe to a deserted hallway and goes to the kitchen, where both maids sit at the little table, having coffee and cinnamon rolls. A kettle of water for her evening tea is simmering atop the stove. A saucer holds a small pot of honey and a slice of lemon, and in her favorite mug is a ready tea ball, its little chain dangling over the rim. Rosario gets up and pours hot water into the mug, and while the tea steeps they all bemoan this summer's heat, which seems to them to be worse than usual. The older maid, Lidia, says she has prayed to the Holy Mother to please let it rain tonight, though the weather report says there is only a small chance of it.

Catalina takes the tea into her bedroom and sets it next to her phone on the table beside her reading chair. And sees the red gleam of the little phone's message light.

24

Rudy and Frank

It's been a long Sunday.

Félix García and two of his guys, Tacho and Roberto, had been waiting for us last night when the Beechcraft set down at a private field a few miles north of El Paso. He greeted us as Rudolf and Francis, the way Aunt Cat calls us. We got into a black Grand Cherokee with Félix at the wheel, and with the other two following us in a gray Ram pickup we drove up I-10 to Las Cruces and stopped for supper at a Mex place Félix is partial to.

Félix is our cousin and our elder by twenty years, an underboss of an organization that controls most of the wetback traffic between El Paso and Ojinaga. We'd met him only once before, about three years ago, when he made a rare trip to Brownsville for a special meeting with Charlie Fortune and some other people and a brief visit with Aunt Cat. His grandmother, Angelica Wolfe Garcia, was Aunt Cat's sister-in-law and Frank and my great-grandaunt. Ever since she married into the García clan and went to live in El Paso, the Garcías and Wolfes have often been of help to each other professionally.

Aunt Cat had informed Félix about Eddie's situation. Over a supper of roast kid and rice and bottles of Bohemia, he said Eddie had to be pretty stupid to get crosswise with the Sinas.

"He's not stupid," Frank said. "Rash at times. He's a kid."

"Whatever," Félix said. "You know how big the Sinas are?"

"We read a newspaper now and then," I said.

Félix didn't think the kid had a chance in hell of making it to the border. Even if by some "wild-ass miracle" he did, the odds were one in a million he'd get any farther, since the Sinas have people all along the line between Nogales and California. And even if by some even greater miracle he did make it over the line, he'd still have to cross the worst part of the Sonoran Desert—la tierra del diablo, the locals call it. The sad fact, Felix said, was that the Sinas had probably already nailed him and there was no way we'd ever know for sure.

I'd been thinking the same thing and it saddened me in a mode I wasn't used to. I could tell the thought had crossed Frank's mind too.

"No disrespect to Doña Catalina," Félix said, "but she's got you on a fool's mission. Me too. Anybody but her asked me to do this, I'da laughed in their face."

He told us he's familiar with Nogales and knows a place there called Casa de Gallos, which bills itself in English as a "gentlemen's club" but is in fact a very fine whorehouse with beautiful girls. And just down the street from it is an excellent cantina with pool tables. He proposed we check into a hotel in that neighborhood and spend the next couple of days sporting with the girls, shooting a little pool, putting down a few beers. Then we call Catalina and say we're very sorry but we found no sign of Eddie. "She's happy we tried and we all go home," he said.

He caught the look that passed between me and Frank. "I know," he said. "You want to keep your word to the old girl. Me too." Which was why, he said, he'd brought Tacho and Roberto. He told us they're of Yaqui descent and know the Sonora border very well, they can speak three languages and can go without sleep for days at a time. He would send one of them to Sasabe and the other to Sonoyta. They'd keep their eyes and ears open and if they got any wind of Eddie they'd give us a call on a satellite and we'd haul ass out there.

"How's that for a plan?" Félix said. "You won't be lying when you tell her you tried."

Frank looked at Tacho and Roberto, assaying them in some private way. They hadn't said a word throughout the meal. Then he looked at me.

"Okay with me if it's okay with you," I said.

We didn't get to Nogales until after midnight, Frank and I managing to get a little sleep on the drive. The town dwarfs the American one of the same name directly across the border, so that only when you speak of the American Nogales do you have to specify which one you mean. We checked into a hotel, and while Félix went off to make a landline call from a phone at the rear of the lobby we had a drink with Tacho and Roberto at the bar. We'd left our weapons with a pal of Félix's on the U.S. side because the Mexican authorities can be very harsh indeed with somebody who tries to slip a

gun into the country. Such stringent gun-control laws are pretty
funny when you consider the kind of firepower steadily shipping
in to the cartels, some of it from us Wolfes, I admit. But Félix had
a connection in Nogales, a guy named Trejo, who could fix us up.
When he got back from making the call he said that sometime
before dawn a dark green Trailblazer would be parked next to the
Cherokee in the far corner of the hotel lot and the keys to it left
for us at the front desk. In the Trailblazer would be a large tool chest
containing five Beretta nines and a pair of M-4 carbines, plus extra
loaded magazines for each weapon. While it was unlikely we would
need the guns, it was better to have them and not need them than
need them and not have them. Longtime rule.

Frank and I slept late and then joined Félix in the hotel patio for
brunch. He told us Roberto and Tacho had departed before sunrise, one in the Trailblazer, the other in the Ram. They'd slipped a
note under his door and left the keys to the Cherokee at the desk.
The note said, Todo exacto. Félix had gone out to the Cherokee
and found the tool chest with the weapons in it, minus two pistols
that Roberto and Tacho took, but with the nice surprise of scopes
on the M-4s. Trejo would charge a bit extra for that amenity but
had been wise to include it. In such open country the lack of a
scope could be a serious deficiency. Tacho and Roberto knew
what Eddie looked like because Félix had given them a copy of a
picture of him taken at Aunt Cat's birthday party six months ago.
He'd received the picture yesterday afternoon in El Paso via e-mail
from Jessica, sent at Catalina's instruction. I wouldn't think Aunt
Cat had explained to Jessie why she sent it or that Jessie asked.

   We lingered over coffee till past noon and then Félix took
us for a leisurely drive around Nogales so we could have a look at

it. He had his sat phone at hand in case Roberto or Tacho called.
We all had Berettas under our belts.

There's no discounting the difference between the heat here
and what we're used to. On the Texas coast, midsummer's as humid
as dog breath and the sky's full of bright clouds that can swiftly
blacken and tower into thunderheads. You sweat plenty. Here your
sweat evaporates as fast as it forms and the air is so drily hot it can
make your nose bleed. The sky is huge and cloudless and the pale
blue of a gas flame. The sun's a white smear. There hasn't been a
wisp of cloud all day, but the TV said there was a chance of rain
tonight. I thought it was a joke but Félix said it could happen. He
said the only thing you can truly predict about a desert summer
is that it will be dry and scorching except for rare times when it
isn't, and those exceptions sometimes give notice they're coming
and sometimes don't.

He drove us all around, showing us this and that, including
the fence—made mostly of old sheet metal panels—separating
the gringo and the Mexican Nogales. The fence runs for a few
miles through the hills east and west of the towns, but doesn't
do much to slow the wetback traffic, as the coyotes simply take
their chickens to crossing points beyond the ends of the fence.
Félix said there are parts of the border with only a single strand
of wire to step over or duck under, and in some places there's no
fence at all, not for miles. Only a sign here and there to denote
the boundary line.

A few blocks past the city bullring Félix pointed at a gigan-
tic warehouse on our right that covered almost the entire block,
its sign identifying it as Azteca Construcción y Electrónica, SA.
He said it was the central warehouse of a construction supplies
business, which also happens to traffic in black market goods,
mainly explosives, arms, and electronic gear, though it could get

you almost anything you might want—an SUV, say, with plates registered to a dead person. Its biggest customer was said to be the Sinas. Félix keeps an open account with Azteca because its inventory is larger and its delivery quicker than those of any supplier in El Paso. His Nogales connection, the Trejo guy, is a managing partner and the one who arranged for last night's delivery of the Trailblazer and guns. According to Félix, the cops have raided the place only once in the past three years—about five months ago, acting on a tip to an uncrooked cop chief. But a cop on the Sinas payroll alerted the warehouse and the raiders found no scrap of evidence. It didn't take long for Trejo and his partners to learn that the tipster was a guy who'd once bought some guns from them and later traded the information to the police to get out from under an armed robbery rap. Trejo gave the guy's name to the Sinas, and the next evening when the tipster's wife got home from work she found his head in the refrigerator. Minus a tongue. They stashed the rest of the guy in pieces all over the house but were careful not to leave a drop of blood anywhere on the floor, as if they didn't want to make it easy to find the pieces. The cops found all of him except for the tongue and one foot. A few days later a stink led the missus to look under the washing machine in the utility room and there was the foot. A few days after that as she was making herself breakfast she found the tongue in a jar of jelly.

"I tell you, I gotta hand it to those guys," Félix said. "They've got a real sense of, ah ... "

"Theater," I say.

"Exactly."

We were in the left lane and slowing for a red light at the intersection past the warehouse when an orange Land Rover gunned across in front of us from the right lane over into the left-turn lane. It would have cleared us by a couple of feet even if we didn't hit the brakes, but Félix reflexively stomped them, sending me hard against the dashboard and Frank banging against the back of my seat. A sedan behind us screeched its tires too to keep from ramming us.

"Stupid bastard!" Félix yelled.

The Rover was at the head of the turn lane, waiting for the light to change, and we pulled up alongside it. On its door was a logo showing a jagged black mountain range with "Gila Geological Inc." under it in red lettering and "Tucson, AZ" under that in smaller print. The two guys in it wore dark glasses. The one in the shotgun seat was skinny and had a short thatch on a bullet-shaped head. The driver was a bear-size mestizo with a thin mustache and thick shiny hair combed straight back. He reminded me of somebody, some badass character actor in the movies, but I couldn't place him. If they were aware they'd nearly caused an accident, they gave no sign of it.

Félix rolled down his window and yelled, "Hey! Hey fuck-heads!" He flapped his arm out the window. "Hey!"

The bullethead turned and stared at him.

You stupid cocksuckers! Félix said. Learn to drive!

The bullethead grinned and cupped a hand to his ear. The driver didn't even glance our way.

Can you can hear this, asshole? Félix said, and gave him the finger.

The bullethead grinned wider and brought his hand up shaped like a pistol and pointed his forefinger and clicked his thumb at each of us in quick succession, then put the tip of the finger near his mouth and blew on it.

Hey, go fuck your *mother*! Félix yelled.

The bullethead read his lips on that one. He lost his grin and started to open his door, but the big guy snatched him by the arm and I grabbed the back of Félix's shirt to hold him back too—and then the turn light turned green and the Rover gunned away in a tight left.

Félix stuck his head out the window and yelled, Fuck your mother in the *ass*, dickhead!

"Take it easy, old cuz," Frank said. "You scared them off already."

"Who's that shithead think he is?" Félix said. "And where'd that other one learn to drive? El Paso?"

Our light turned green and we got rolling, but Félix kept on muttering about "dickheads" and "shiteaters" and "ratfuckers" until Frank and I busted out laughing. He demanded to know what was so fucking funny, which only made us laugh harder. He stared ahead for the duration of another block before he started laughing too. Then a minute later he said, "I don't know about you guys, but I'm ready to go get laid."

We had a fine time at the Casa de Gallos, where the girls were fairly good-looking, if not quite the sublime beauties Félix had described, then ate supper at a steakhouse, then repaired to the Cuervo Loco Cantina for a few beers and some eight-ball, where Félix proved to be a shark and took us for twenty bucks apiece. When we got back to the hotel, the sun was down and a hot breeze was swaying the trees and sailing trash paper down the streets.

Now, at the end of this long Sunday, we're bellied up to the hotel bar, having a nightcap. The bartender says the evening forecast is a seventy percent chance of rain, though it likely won't be more than a shower. Roberto and Tacho each phoned Félix during the afternoon and once again just a few minutes ago, and they gave him identical reports both times. Sasabe and Sonoyta was crawling with Sinas but there was no sign or word of Eddie.

"Like I told you," Félix says, "they probably took him down already."

We call it a night and I go up to my room and hit the shower. When I come out my prepaid is tweedling on the dresser top.

It's Frank. "Check your phone mail and then get over here."

There's a message from Aunt Cat, saying Eddie called her and left his own message for us. She recites it in a carefully measured tone, then adds, "I presume this information is something that can help you to find him. Do it."

There's a pause, as if she's about to say something more . . . but she doesn't.

When I get to Frank's room he's just getting off the phone with Aunt Laurel. She was irked at being awakened at this hour—it's close to midnight in Brownsville—but when he said he had an urgent need for whatever information she could give him about a device called a Buddha, her tone changed and she asked why he wanted to know about that. He told her it had to do with a project we were working on and that was all he could say for now. She explained what the thing is and how it works. She said any pair of receivers would do, and that it was a good thing he knew the kind of phone the Buddha was in, but she had to go out to Delta to look up the tuning code for it. Frank gave her his cell number and she said she'd call him from the shop.

While Frank checks the local directory for a nearby electronics store and gives it a call, I phone Félix and tell him something's come up and for him to get over here.

The first place Frank tries has the receivers we need and is open till midnight. Then Félix shows up and I repeat La Gata's message for him.

"He *made* it to the border? And he's gonna cross *tonight*?" Félix says. It peeves him that Eddie didn't tell Aunt Catalina where he was calling from. "It'd be pretty fucking helpful to know that. Is this kid slow in the head or what?"

"I told you he isn't," Frank says in a tone that makes it clear he's had enough of Felix bad-mouthing Eddie. It's one thing for us to do it, something else for him to. Félix holds Frank's stare long enough to convey he isn't intimidated, and they both let it drop.

But I can see Frank's as irked as I am by Eddie's remark that we can do whatever we want with the information. Not too subtle in letting us know he's not asking for our help, even though he obviously wants it and damn well needs it. Stupid kid. There oughta be a rule against underage pride, at least until you learn how to keep it in check with regard to your own family. Then again, I have to admit our family's not always a model of tribal harmony.

While we wait for Aunt Laurel's call it occurs to me it would be useful to have a topographical map of the area. Félix says he can take care of that and seems glad of the chance to be of help. He makes a call and fifteen minutes later a guy shows up at the door with an excellent topo.

25

Eddie and Miranda

With its load of crossers the Suburban heads out on the main highway under a clear moonless sky of gathering stars. The traffic sparse. Envisioning the road map he has consulted many times in the past two days, Eddie recalls that the highway through Caborca runs northwestward all the way to Sonoyta. They are going the other way. Toward a small town called Altar twenty to twenty-five miles east of town, where a dirt road branches north to Sasabe.

They pass a road sign reading "Altar 5 km" and pull over at an isolate wayside café. There are only two vehicles parked in front, and Beto directs the driver, whom he calls Cisco, around to the rear of the building. Waiting there is a dark Ford Excursion. They stop alongside it, and by the light over the café's back door they can see that it is packed with people. A man gets out of it and Beto gets out too and they walk off behind the vehicles to talk.

Who are they? somebody asks in low voice.

More of you, Cisco says.

Eddie sees the other man give Beto something that he puts in his pocket—money, no doubt. The man then taps a number into a cell phone, says something into it, and passes the phone to Beto. Beto speaks, listens for a while, then says something more and returns the phone. The two men return to their vehicles and Beto gets in and says, Let's go.

They pull out onto the highway, the Excursion following.

How many more? Cisco says.

Nine, Beto says.

What's the report on—

"Lingo, man," Beto says, jerking his head rearward. "Little chickens got big ears."

"What's the scout word on the gate?" Cisco says.

Eddie smiles at their switch to English. He knows "gate" means a crossing point, but the guides obviously want to keep the chickens from knowing what they're talking about. It's why Canales tested his knowledge of the language—probably tested all of them. Beto and Cisco's facility with the language and their Texas accents make him wonder if they might be American-born.

"The Border Patrol got extra guys all over the number one gate tonight," Beto says. "Our scout can run decoys in there but he don't reckon they'll draw off enough of the Greenies to help us get by, not with all that backup they got."

"What about farther out? Number two gate?"

"Same thing. We gotta go to three."

"Oh man, that's in mule road country," Cisco says. "The big dicks been going at each other over who owns it."

"It's nobody's yet," Beto says. "We'll be okay."

Cisco mutters something more but doesn't argue.

Beto turns around to face the migrants and says, Listen, my friends. They say it might rain tonight. Let's hope so. The Border Patrol hates working in the rain, even in a little drizzle. Bunch of pussies.

Nervous laughter from the chickens.

At Altar they cut north on the dirt road, but only a few miles later they turn off onto a narrower road, hardly more than a trail, that takes them west a short way before curving back northward. It's slower going here than on the Sasabe road, but Eddie figures they assume there's less chance of running into any of the big gangs' smugglers. They're anyway probably headed for a crossing somewhere west of Sasabe.

Now the night is entirely black but for the forward reach of the headlights and the lustrous mass of stars. Even in the flatlands of south Texas Eddie has never before seen such starlight. But on this moonless night the sky will get no brighter. Behind them the Excursion has switched off its lights and is almost invisible in the darkness and the Suburban's trailing dust. Most smuggler vehicles along the lower Rio have a cutoff switch for brake lights and taillights, and Eddie would bet these do too.

The darkness inhibits conversation. The main sounds in the Suburban are of its rumbling wheels and the assorted creaks of its chassis. In the side glow of the headlights, passing saguaros look otherworldly. Occasionally there appear distant headlights off to their right, bearing south on the Sasabe road, and then they're gone. At times they see the feeble lights of a village. A breeze has kicked up and tumbleweeds skitter across the road. Eddie can hardly make out Miranda's form in front of him. He strokes her ankle and she puts her foot to his crotch and presses lightly. He cannot see her face but knows she's grinning. Some girl.

They've been driving more than an hour when Beto says, There it is. All Eddie sees that Beto could be referring to is the derelict remains of an overturned minivan on the roadside ahead. As they come abreast of it Cisco turns left into scrub brush that slaps and scratches against the Suburban as it pitches and yaws like a boat on a restless sea. They proceed like this for a time before the ground smoothes out and they're on one of the multitude of backcountry trails in this region.

Beto turns and says, Only a few minutes more, my friends, and you will be crossing into the promised land.

Much excited whispering.

Then for a startling instant the Suburban is flooded with light as the Excursion flicks its headlamps on and off.

What's he want? Cisco says, glancing at the rearview.

All they can see is the dark shape of the Excursion close behind them. And then the road bends and they can see the distant headlights behind the Excursion and advancing on it.

Oh fuck, Cisco says.

"No cop lights," Beto says, reverting to English. "Not yet anyway."

The chickens in alarmed chatter. What is it? What's happening?

Be quiet, all of you, Beto says.

"Better cops than big dicks," Cisco says. "We run for it or what?"

"Can't outrun that thing. Look how it's coming. Hold your speed. Maybe they're not after us. Maybe they'll pass us."

"Yeah, right," Cisco says. "Maybe they'll give us a friendly little beep as they go by." He nods to their right. "There's the gate."

"Keep going. Nice and steady."

The headlights come at furious speed, growing harshly brighter. They vanish when the Suburban goes over a rising curve, but then the headlights clear the rise too and come faster yet. They are closing so swiftly that Eddie is sure they're going to ram the rear of the Excursion. Then the lights swing out from behind it and a dark SUV goes roaring by in a swirl of dust and cuts in front of the Suburban, its brake lights flashing intermittently as the driver taps the brakes. And all three vehicles slow to a stop.

The breeze clears the dust, and a Lincoln Navigator stands ten yards forward of them in the Suburban's lights, its rear window impenetrable, its own headlight beams bright on the trail before it. Now a rear door opens and a man steps out with a pistol in his hand and motions for the Suburban driver to roll down his window.

Cisco does it, and the man orders him to turn off the motor and switch to his parking lights, and Cisco does that too.

The Navigator is now but a dark form against the forward cast of its own headlights. All its doors open and more men materialize.

"Oh man, are we fucked," Cisco says.

"Maybe not," Beto says. "Maybe they'll settle for taking the bunch."

Eddie hopes their assumption is correct, that the interlopers are wetback smugglers pissed off at independents for cutting in on their trade. Better that than Sinas. He has the Taurus in his hand and hears the zipper of Miranda's tote as she goes for the Glock. He puts a foot against her leg and she places a hand on it and squeezes.

The men spread out but stay forward of the Suburban, giving themselves an angle of fire at the vehicles from both sides without risk of hitting one another. Eddie counts six of them, for sure, maybe two more, hard to tell. A flashlight abruptly shines on the Excursion and then two others play over the Suburban.

Someone orders, Go see.

Miranda's hold tightens on his foot as one of the lights comes over to Beto's window and he rolls it down. The light moves from Beto's face to the boy's to Cisco's.

And Eddie knows.

Sinas. Looking for him.

The man at the window begins to pan the light slowly over others, pausing briefly on each face.

Somebody ratted. Ernesto or Canales, probably both. The Sinas at the Caborca station spotted Ernesto and grabbed him, gave him some pain, questioned him, showed him pictures, went to Canales. Had to be that way. Or some other way. Or simple goddamn luck. However it was, here they are. Nothing to do now but play it as it comes.

The Martínez woman turns her face from the light's dazzle and the man says, Look over here, cunt! And next shines it on the Panama guy and tells him to take off his hat.

Now the light fixes on Eddie and holds on him and he squints against it. He waits for the man to tell him to remove his cap, but then the light shifts to Miranda and holds on her. And seeing her so starkly lighted in her orange-and-black baseball cap, Eddie thinks, The caps! Ernesto and Canales would have mentioned them.

The light comes back to him and he can almost hear the smile in the man's voice as he says, You two back there, get out.

But then various of the Sinas start yelling and the flashlight flicks away from Eddie to join the other two lights aiming up the curve behind the Excursion. There's a rising rumbling of engines and a vehicle comes bounding over the rise with another one behind it, all headlights blazing.

They come down the road and fishtail to a stop behind the Excursion in billows of dust. A dozen or more men rush out of the vehicles and spread out in a line of shadowy figures to either side, and one man steps up close to a headlight that reveals the machine pistol in his hand. He says something Eddie doesn't hear clearly, and another man says "Sí, jefe," and heads toward the Excursion. All the Sinas but one are sidestepping out of the headlight glare.

The Sina standing fast shouts, Who the hell are *you* assholes?

We told you chicken-runners to stay off our roads, says the one by the headlight.

Chicken-runners? the Sina says. Fuck you, prick! You don't know who you're—

A crackling burst from the machine pistol staggers the Sina backward in an antic dance, and at the same time the man at the Excursion opens fire into its windows with an automatic weapon at point-blank range.

And then they're all shooting—the darkness detonating in a flaring rage of gunfire and screams. The chickens duck below the windows and Eddie yanks Miranda down beside him as stray rounds punch the Suburban and pop through its glass and Beto yells, *Go!*

The motor cranks up and revs wildly and the wheels spin under them for a second before gaining traction and the Suburban springs forward. Eddie peeks over the seat and sees Cisco hunched low at the wheel and veering around the Navigator just as a man with both hands against his stomach lurches into his path and is batted into the blackness.

They speed away with headlights off, churning a haze of dust between themselves and the Navigator's headlights and the flashings of the gunfight.

And then the trail curves and clears a rise and the lights behind them disappear.

26

Eddie and Miranda

The trail is only vaguely visible in the meager reach of the parking lights and they skid off it on the tighter turns, the Suburban each time shuddering, rocks banging the underside, Eddie fearing for the oil pan. A sharp curve along an embankment tilts them so steeply they almost capsize.

Beto tells Cisco to take it easy, slow down, nobody's chasing them, they're too busy killing each other, it's a turf fight between big dicks.

The Suburban slows. They're still running without taillights. Eddie can see nothing behind them but darkness.

Beto says they can use the headlights now and Cisco turns them on and heaves a long breath. God *damn,* he says.

Those others, the Martínez woman says. My God . . . those poor people!

"Cállate, mujer!" her husband says, and she goes silent.

They're all scared, naturally, but Eddie has a hunch gunfire is not an entirely new experience for any of them. He sets the safety on the Taurus and slips the pistol back into his pants and feels Miranda tug at her tote bag, replacing the Glock.

Where to? says Cisco.

"Keep going," Beto says in English.

"I *know* keep going. Where *to*?"

"There's another gate. Farther up. Keep going till I tell you."

"You still gonna cross? Hell, man, why not wait till—"

"I got good money coming for delivery of this bunch by morning."

Beto turns to the chickens and says, Listen to me, all of you. It's terrible about the others, but thanks be to God *we're* all right. Those lunatics aren't coming after us and in a few minutes we'll be at the crossing point. We're all right now. We're safe.

The chickens make low sounds of relief.

"Fuckers were looking for somebody," Cisco says. "That first bunch."

"Seemed that way," Beto says. Hey you, Mendoza. Why'd he tell you and your sister to get out?

Eddie's been waiting for it. He raises his hands in a gesture of profound incomprehension and puts a strain in his voice. The hell if *I* know! Maybe he thought I was somebody else. Man, all I could think was *why me*? Christ, I nearly shit my pants! I'm not ashamed to admit it.

He prompts a few chuckles.

I damn sure know why he wanted your sister to get out, Cisco says.

Hey man, Eddie says.

Yeah, yeah, Cisco says. Don't scare me, tough guy.

c∞ɔ

The rush of adrenaline has blunted Eddie's perception of time,
and when Beto tells Cisco to stop and they come to a halt at
the end of a wide bend under the star-bright sky, he has no
clear idea how long it's been since they fled the gunfight. Ten
minutes? Forty?

Back up, Beto says.

Cisco slowly negotiates the long curve in reverse, backing
up about fifteen yards and onto a downward incline before Beto
says, Stop.

The headlights shine on a trio of saguaro cactuses at the top
of the rise, the rightmost cactus leaning against the center one.
Close behind them stand a few fence posts.

"That's it, Francisco old buddy, that's the marker," Beto says
in English. "Kill the lights." Cisco switches off the headlights and
the world goes dark but for the vast spangle of stars against which
the three saguaros are visible. "Be right back," Beto says.

He gets out and they watch him scrabble up the incline and
then lose sight of him. He's gone only a minute or two before he
slides back into the vehicle and points off to the right.

"The Aguila Mountains are over there, all by theirselves,
maybe five miles off. A low little range but I can make them
out okay against the lower stars." He is speaking as if reciting a
lesson well-learned. "I keep those mountains hard on my right
and a couple of miles up alongside them I come to a pass. Fairly
narrow and runs a mile or so. From the other end of it I'll see
a little bigger set of mountains to the east about another five
miles. That's the Viudas. I cut around the lower end of them and
another two miles farther on I'll hit the Sells road just a little
south of a good pickup point. Maybe fifteen, sixteen miles all

told. Rough but mostly flat ground. Strong bunch like this can walk it in five, six hours tops."

"Seem awful sure about that for never crossing here before," Cisco says. "How you know so much about it?"

"Been told by guys who know. Listen, you get over to So-noyta and call the pickup people on a landline and tell them the change in pickup spots. About six to eight miles down the Sells road, tell them. Where the road cuts through a rock rise. They'll know where you mean." There's a soft blue light from Beto's watch as he checks the time. "I figure we got maybe eight hours before first light. Tell them the spotter can start making passes an hour before dawn."

"Shoulda brought a compass, man," Cisco says. "It's a new gate, no moon, supposed to rain."

"Day I need a compass you can shoot me for a worthless sack."

His disdain for a compass is familiar to Eddie. Every guide he's met on the lower Rio Grande feels the same way. It's a point of pride among them to make their way by expert reading of the land's lay. And forget cell phones. They're for pussies and anyway useless in all the dead zones of the deserts. Besides which, if the Border Patrol catches you with one they'll make you for a guide, and the law's much rougher on a guide than on a chicken. That's why you dress like them and if you're caught you talk like them and play dumb as them. Instead of jail you're booted back to Mexico and can get right back to work.

All right, friends, Beto says, here's the door to the north! The land of plenty! Everybody out. And no smoking. We can't make even the smallest light.

Possessions in hand, they tumble out the doors in a low excited babble, laughing softly. They bend and stretch in the wonderful feel of the light wind after the cramped ride, their recent terror overcome by the thrill of arriving at the border. The boy is coming too. Apprenticing the trade is Eddie's guess.

Beto tells Cisco, "Watch out for anybody coming your way. Fuckers mighta called for help." He shuts the door and slaps the Suburban's roof. Cisco drives off around the curve and is gone. In a whisper Eddie tells Miranda to hold on to his backpack strap and then eases over next to Beto, holding to his plan to stick close to the guide and if he cuts out, cut out with him. If he objects, produce the gun.

The crossers are but shadowy forms to each other as they follow Beto up the stony incline to the saguaros and a fence of two sagging wires. Beto holds one wire down with his foot and raises the other with his hand and they all pass through and into the United States.

Miranda tugs at Eddie's backpack and he half-turns to her mouth at his ear, and she whispers, We made it!

27

The Boss

Two of the gunmen yet alive. One drags himself into the glare of headlights and there affixes a belt tourniquet to his bloody leg and then one to the maimed arm of his ambulatory comrade whose lower jaw and tongue have been shot off, blood running off the gaping wound and sopping his chest. This one then fetches a satellite phone from the Navigator and brings it to the sitting man.

An hour later the scene stands cleared of vehicles, armament, the dead. The bodies of the Sinas, including the two who bled to death while awaiting the arrival of their fellows, go to graves. Those of the other bunch—who are identified as members of Los Espantos, an enforcement unit of the Baja organization—are taken to a Tijuana roadside and left there in an orderly and headless row. A note attached to one by a steak knife in the sternum reads, The stupid need no head.

Tomorrow evening the heads will be returned to their employer in a pair of sacks flung smashing through the front window of the exclusive Tijuana club where the Bajas' leader will be dining in a private back room and in the company of a police captain, a flock of pretty women, and a dozen bodyguards. At about the same time, the Espantos chief will be dancing with a girl of fifteen in an Ensenada nightclub and whispering something into her ear that makes her laugh just as a pair of Sinas less than ten feet away open fire on them with submachine guns and as other Sinas begin shooting the Espantos at a table and at the bar. The gunfire will last almost fifteen seconds and the Sinas will vanish from the premises in less time, not a man of them hurt. In addition to the chieftain and the girl and the seven other Espantos present, six bystanders will be killed by the gunfire, seven others will be wounded, and many others badly hurt in the panicked stampede for the doors.

Four days later an American Border Patrol agent cutting for signs of crossers along the weathered fence line will call his headquarters to report a stationary vehicle he glassed a half mile south of the border that morning and which was still there in the afternoon. Mexican authorities will be informed of it and the next day dispatch a pair of policemen to that region where they rarely venture. They will discover a Chevrolet Suburban with its left-side tires flat and bullet holes in the left door and a dead man at the wheel. He will have wounds in his left side and one in the left temple encircled by a powder burn. His remains will eventually be identified as those of Francisco Soto Esquivél, whose criminal record is lengthy but unimpressive.

The Boss receives a report of the gunfight at the border even as the crew that cleaned up the scene is on its way back to Nogales. He is told the fight may have been started by some misunderstanding about a large SUV full of chickens who were all killed and that nobody among the dead fit the description of Porter or the girl. He is both angry and relieved. Angry that the kid is still out there on the loose and might yet get away. Relieved that Martillo might yet capture him and bring him to Culiacán alive.

28

Eddie and Miranda

It is rocky ground thick with scrub brush and cactus, but as Beto said, they're a strong group and can move at a quick pace. Heading east-northeast by Eddie's reading of the polestar. They weave around rocky rises and traverse arroyos—dry sandy streambeds more commonly called washes in Arizona, some narrow and shallow, some as wide as highways and several feet deep. To the west a distant range of mountains stands in low silhouette against the stars.

Eddie keeps close enough to Beto and the kid to hear bits of their low-voice exchanges. It is clear that they are related and that the boy is recently arrived from some other part of the country. He seems familiar with night-sky navigation but Beto has been tutoring him in the deceptive effects of desert darkness and distance.

❦

After a time they arrive at the low Aguila range. Eddie reckons they've been walking nearly two hours. They hold close to its left flank, watching for the pass that should soon present itself. The breeze has grown to a light wind and Beto tells the boy it's a lucky thing because it covers their tracks. If Border Patrol sign cutters should come along later they won't find any mark of their passage. Even a Papago couldn't find our tracks tomorrow, he tells the boy.

What's a Papago? the boy asks.

A kind of Indian. This is Papago country.

I thought we were in the United States.

Beto laughs low and says, We are. I'll explain it later.

Now he stops and points and says, "Hay está el paso."

The boy says he sees it.

Eddie does too. Their night vision by this time keenly honed and able to distinguish the deeper darkness of the pass a short way ahead. He gauges its breadth at the base at about fifteen yards, but it's hard to say in this gloom.

The wind has begun to gust. The Panama guy curses as his hat whips off his head and into the night. Eddie and Miranda take off their caps and stuff them into the tote.

"Mira, tío," the boy says, looking west.

A horizontal band of insuperable blackness is rising very fast along the lower western sky and has obliterated the mountain horizon.

It's the rain they said we would get, the boy says. But it looks harder than they said. Look how dark. At least there's no lightning.

Or thunder, Eddie thinks. Or even the smell of rain.

The others have stopped to look back at the ominous black cloud that is growing with astonishing speed, rising like a titanic ocean wave and extinguishing the stars as it comes. The wind ahead of it blowing harder now and flinging sand.

"Ay qué chingada," Beto says. "No es lluvia."

Eddie too knows what it is. He has seen such storms in Texas but never the size of this.

Beto shouts for them to run for the pass, and they scramble up the scree slope after him.

What is it? one of them yells. What?

With Miranda holding to Eddie's backpack, they lag behind Beto and the kid but still outdistance the rest of the group as they head into the pass and the even greater darkness between the high rock walls they cannot see.

And then the wind comes roaring after them into the pass and the colossal cloud of dust swallows the mountain. . . .

29

Martillo and Pico

That afternoon they cross into Arizona at the Lukeville port of entry. The inspector says "How you fellas doin?" and glances at the topographical maps lying on the console, the surveying instrument cases in the back, the two large plastic coolers. He examines their Arizona driver's licenses identifying them as Nicolas Caldera and David Harris. They are prepared to present American passports, to show him mineral samples and the clearance documents for them, but he asks to see nothing else. He hands back the licenses and gives the Land Rover an admiring look and says he'd sure like to have one of these babies someday but it ain't about to happen. On his salary he couldn't even afford the gas. Martillo says he can't afford one either but at least he gets to tool around in the company's. "Lucky guy," the inspector says, and waves them through.

Provisioned with food and drink in the coolers, Martillo and Pico meander to and fro over the desolate expanse a few miles above the border and between Sonoyta and Sasabe, their unit of paired receivers in constant search of a signal from the kid's tracker. The receivers are small enough to be tucked under the front seats if need be. The single screen is eight square inches and shows a topographical map—a nicety installed at the excellent suggestion of the Azteca technician who coordinated and tuned the receivers. The map's view can be adjusted from a scale of half a mile per inch to twenty miles per inch. At present the view is set to a range of sixty miles in every direction from the Rover. Back in Nogales an associate named Gómez is monitoring a satellite connection with a Sinas communications staffer and will relay to them any reports about Porter.

They drive over haphazard trails, over ground so malformed it would stop most vehicles in their tracks. They take turns at the wheel and in panning the desert with binoculars. They have retrieved their handguns from behind the door panels—Colt Anaconda .44 Magnums with six-inch barrels, now tucked beside them on each side of the console. In the rear, in long cases bearing the Gila Geological emblem and labeled "Transit/Tripod," are Pico's Remington 700 police rifle and Martillo's Sako sniper model, both with Leupold scopes.

Shortly before dark they spy an SUV they at first take for the Border Patrol. They are ready to explain that they will be in the area for the next few days and nights searching for various types of minerals that glow under ultraviolet light, that Gila Geological has been commissioned by the Arizona Department of Mines and Mineral Resources to find and map the areas of highest concentration of such minerals throughout Pima County. But as the vehicle draws nearer they see it's the Indian police. When the Indians are close enough to read the logo on the Rover door, they wave a hand and drive away.

Amazing, isn't it, Martillo says, the way nobody interferes with geologists? It's as if we're a natural part of the environment. Like one of the gringos' protected species.

Those Indians, they were Papago, right?

Yes, but now they call themselves Tohoho Ododom or something. They even got the gringos to call them that instead of Papago.

Stupid gringos, Pico says. Letting Indians tell them what to call them in English. The gringos say "Mexican," not "Mexicano," right? They say "Spanish," not "Español," don't they? So why let the Indians tell them to call them Toohohoo Odohoo or whatever the fuck instead of Papago. They're still Papago in Mexico. Try telling us to stop calling them that. The gringos should've told them to mind their own business or they might start calling them Fuckheads instead of Papagos.

My goodness, Martillo says with feigned shock. I had no idea you had such strong opinion about the sovereignty of language.

I am a man of strong opinion on many subjects and you are one who has no idea about many things. It has always been so.

Now, now, my skinny friend. No need to be testy with me because the gringos disappoint you.

∽≫◦

A wind comes up. Sheets of sand undulate over the ground like live things. The scrub brush bobbing. The sun goes down and the night rises. They leave the Rover's lights off and put on night vision goggles.

Time passes and the wind builds. They get a call from Gómez, who says Sinas operatives in Caborca have reported that a young couple fitting the general description of Porter and the girl left that town a few hours ago with a group of chickens headed for a crossing point not too far west of Sasabe. Both were wearing Hermosillo baseball caps.

So far so good, Pico says. If he can get by the ones at the border it'll be just him and us.

They reduce their patrol to a range of twenty miles east of Sasabe and adjust the topo map on the receiver screen to a radius of the same distance.

The wind is gusting harder yet when they get another call from Gómez. But now the transmission crackles and hisses with weather interference and it is with great difficulty that they come to understand there's been a gunfight between Sinas and Espantos crews on the border somewhere near the midway point between Sasabe and Sonoyta. Martillo must ask again and again if the fight had anything to do with Porter before Gómez comprehends the question and then he in turn must once again repeat himself a number of times to make clear that he doesn't know if the fight involved chickens but it is certain that the kid is still at large.

Martillo shuts off the phone and tosses it onto the seat behind them. Piece of shit, he says.

No it's not, Pico says, weaving the Rover through a cluster of saguaros. It's this crazy wind, something weird with the weather.

Martillo studies the topo map on the screen and points to a spot approximately where Gómez said the fight occurred. If the kid's group was there, he says, it was almost certainly where they were planning to cross. A lot of gates around there. And if they had to run for it, they'd go west, away from Sasabe, wouldn't they? He studies the screen and then circles his fingertip over a small section of it and says, To somewhere around in here, that's where I'd cross. From here they have a fairly clear line back to the Sells road up . . . here, where I'll bet you they were headed in the first place. The guide probably has a pickup point a little south of town.

Pico stops the Rover and regards the screen map. What about these mountains here? he says. The Aguilas. They have to go around them. He moves his finger on the screen and says, Unless . . . is this a pass?

Very good, my sharp-eyed little friend. I wondered if you'd see it. What they'll do is cut through that main pass and come out right here. From there they can bear around the south end of this next little range—what is it? the Viudas—and from there it's a straight run up this way to the Sells road.

You could have been a great coyote, Humberto. The best of them.

I could have been a great president of Mexico as well. But where is the fulfillment in occupations like that?

But what if they start from somewhere closer to either end of the Aguilas? Pico says. It might be shorter for them to go around the mountains than through the pass. If we position ourselves somewhere in here—he indicates the open ground between the Aguila and Viuda ranges—we can watch the pass and also have a clear view to both ends of the range. Whichever way they come, even if the fucker doesn't turn on the tracker, we'll spot them.

That is a truly excellent proposal.

It is, isn't it?

They are circling around the Aguila range when Pico gestures westward and says, Look there.

The starlit horizon appears to be elevating.

Looks like a hard rain coming, Pico says. Big help that's gonna be.

But as the swelling cloud looms closer they see it's not rain. And minutes afterward are forced to a stop, arrested under the tidal wave of dust. . . .

30

Rudy and Frank

It seems a lot longer than the thirty-three minutes it takes Aunt Laurel to get back to us with the calibration code. Frank writes it down and thanks her and is about to cut off when she says something else.

"I'm sorry, tía," he says, "it's really all I can tell you for now. Thanks again. We gotta go."

He thumbs off the phone and looks at me. "She knows it's about Eddie. She didn't say so but I could tell."

We decide he and I will take the Cherokee, get the receivers and a satellite phone, and head out to start patrolling for Eddie's signal. Félix will stay at the hotel and if Tacho or Roberto calls him with more information he'll let us know.

An hour later we're bouncing over a narrow stony trail winding westward, me at the wheel. We've got plenty of water and a big sack of sandwiches, a pair of high-power binoculars, the Berettas, and the M-4s. Our receiver hookup's tuned and looking for the Buddha's signal.

The wind's really blowing when we get to Sasabe, which turns out to be a ragged-ass little place of dirt streets lined with cantinas and a few ramshackle hotels and motels serving mostly as holding pens or so-called "safe houses" for groups of chickens waiting to be taken across. The main street is full of late-model pickups and SUVs, a lot of them without license plates.

"Gee, I wonder what kinda business the owners of all these fancy wheels might be in?" Frank says as we slowly roll through.

"Think he might be here?"

"No. If he's smart enough to get this far he's smart enough to know every town along this stretch is bound to be overrun with Sinas people looking for him. Little bitty burg like this, he'd be made right off. My money says he hooked up down south with some independent who's crossing his bunch farther out in the big nowhere."

Now we're past the town. The sky ahead has turned solid black.

"What the hell *is* that?" Frank says.

Then we're hit by the biggest bastard dust storm we've ever seen. The Cherokee's rocking and the dust is so thick we're blinded by the reflection of our own headlights. I cut down to the parking lights and we can scarcely make out the shape of the trail a few feet in front of us. There's nothing to do but turn around and creep our way back to Sasabe.

"Christ damn," Frank says. "If he's out there he's gonna drown in dirt."

The main street's now empty of traffic but the street sides are lined with vehicles parked every which way and the dust is so thick it's all I can do to keep from hitting any of them as I make my way along. Near the neon haze of a cantina, I make out a spot between two big SUVs and pull into it. We're not about to leave the Cherokee unattended with the stuff we've got in it, so Frank gets out—admitting a charge of dust that whirls through the Cherokee—and goes into the cantina. A few minutes later he's back with a couple of cold ones, admitting another dust flurry when he gets in. Then we sit there and sip beer and watch the dust roll by.

And keep an eye on the receiver screen.

MONDAY

31

Eddie and Miranda

The dust pounds through the pass, the wind in frenzied swirls. Eddie cannot see farther than the end of his outstretched arm. He hears muted yellings through the wind. Then the nearer cry of Miranda as she falters and falls. Her sudden release of his backpack upsets his balance as he starts to turn toward her and he loses his footing and falls on his ass. The dust drives into his face, chokes him, burns his eyes. He tries to get up but cannot, and for a terrifying second thinks he might be partly paralyzed, then realizes the pack is snagged on something. A rock, a scrub root. He writhes rearward and comes free of the restraint, then gets up, coughing, covering his nose and mouth with one hand, squinting against the dust.

She's calling, Chacho! Chacho! and sounds no more than a few feet away, but the crazily whirling wind makes it difficult to fix on the location of her voice. Here! he shouts. I'm here! He hollers for her to stay in one place and keep yelling, don't stop yelling. He moves carefully over the uncertain ground, now a little to his right, now to his left, hollering, I'm here! I'm right here!

From his left she calls, "Aquí 'stoy, Chacho! *Aquí!*"

He puts out his arm and waves it slowly from side to side as he sidesteps toward her voice. Then sees her vague form and finds her arm and draws her to him.

She unzips the tote and takes out bandannas and they tie them across their lower face bandit-style to defend against the dust. They hear the hackings of others, muffled cries. Eddie tells her to hold tight to his pack strap again and don't let go even if she falls. They move together through the darkness and dust, yelling, Here! We're over here! And soon reunite with a Fonseca brother and his fat cousin and the Panama guy, clinging to each other and all three also with bandannas over their mouths and noses. They next find the Martínez couple, coughing like consumptives, their hats lost to the wind. Miranda gives them her last two bandannas. Eddie flinches when Beto yells, Where are you? from right behind him. He turns and Beto and the kid appear before him like phantoms.

They hold close to one another in a chain of joined hands and shuffle about in search of the other three, yelling, We're over here! This way! In a few minutes they find the Sando uncle and nephew. It takes a while longer to find the last of them, the other Fonseca brother, whose cries are of pain. He's on the ground, his ankle broken in a misstep.

Beto says there's nothing to do but leave him with water and food. They have to keep going, he says, even in the dust, or they'll be too late for the pickup at dawn and the Border Patrol will easily find them in daylight. The dust will anyway stop very soon, it always does. When they meet with the pickup people, he'll send someone out to retrieve this hurt man.

The other two Fonsecas are distressed by the idea of abandoning their kinsman, but the injured one says not to worry, he'll be all right with enough to eat and drink until someone comes back for him. His brother and cousin give him most of their food and water, and the cousin jokes, You will get fat as me if you eat it all. His brother gently eases the shoe off the foot with the fractured ankle so he might be more comfortable, and he promises to return with whoever is sent to get him. I'll see you soon, the injured one says. Damn right, the brother and cousin say, and each hugs him good-bye.

All right, Beto says, let's get over to the wall. We'll follow it all the way out and that way we won't get lost from each other.

Which wall? the Panama guy says. We've been turning all around in this fucking pass. I got no idea which way we were going.

I do, Beto says. I turned only once, and this one with the broken foot was behind everybody else and I'm still facing the way I came to him. So we turn around and go that way. Now let's get over to the wall and stay close together.

Eddie senses that the group is reassured by Beto's confidence—the man does seem to know his stuff. With Miranda again clutching his pack strap, he once more positions himself directly behind Beto and the boy. Feeling their way along the rock wall, the group presses on through the darkness, catching each other in stumbles, breathing dust, coughing and cursing.

Mules

Seven nights from now, after a week of daily high temperatures of not less than 105 degrees, a crew of drug carriers bearing heavy

backpacks will come through this pass under the bright beam
of a quarter moon and find Alberto Fonseca lying crippled in
an open patch of moonlight amid empty water bottles, prattling
in hoarse unintelligible whispers like some becrazed wilderness
prophet. Absent all pity for yet another fool come to this, they
will pass him by without pause. All but the last mule in the line,
who will stop and regard him for a moment. And then, in merciful
impulse, reach down to him and cut his throat.

32

Eddie and Miranda

As the darkness ahead becomes less dense, they know they have
come to the end of the pass. Yet the torrent of dust persists, and
even after emerging from the pass they are still but ambiguous
shapes to each other. They pause to rest, gulp water, spit mud,
blow their noses with their fingers.

But there's something odd. Eddie feels it. Then someone
behind him says it. The wind has changed direction.

Beto says that's so. It is sometimes the way of these crazy
storms, he says. It's a good sign. It means the dust will soon end.

They tell each other how much they hope so. Dear God, if
only this damned dust would stop!

Eddie overhears Beto telling the boy that the mouth of the
pass is facing east, and although they can't see them in this dust,
the Viuda mountains are no more than two hours ahead. They have
to go around the south end of them. If the sky was clear enough
to see the mountains against the stars, they would go straight
toward the end of the range and from there head northeastward
and would strike the road near the pickup point. But in this dust,

if they try to estimate where the south end is and then miss it,
they might go too far southward and not know it until too late
and miss the pickup. The thing to do is head a little to their left
and be sure they don't miss the mountains altogether. They will
then have to sidetrack to get around them and that will add to
their walking distance, but they still have enough time to make
it to the road in time to get picked up.

If you had a compass, tonto, Eddie thinks, you wouldn't
have this problem.

All right, let's go, let's go, Beto says. Very soon we'll be on a
nice comfortable ride to Tucson!

They follow him into the dusty blackness. Over the stony
ground of scrub and cactus. Across sandy dry washes large and
small. But feeling strong for being closer to the end of their
journey.

They move on through the relentless haze of a world without
form or measure of time. And then as suddenly as if by the turn
of some cosmic switch the wind is free of dust and they can see
each other more distinctly. Eddie guesses it's been two hours since
they went through the pass, maybe three. They must be very close
to the Viuda range by now.

They remove their bandannas and revel in the pleasure of
deep breaths. They dig into their food supplies and feed ravenously.
Only the Panama guy is without rations, and he asks the Fonsecas
if they can spare him something. We were all supposed to provide
for ourselves, the fat one says, but gives him a candy bar anyway.
The man takes it without thanks and tears into it.

As Eddie and Miranda share a bottle of water and some of
the jerky, she whispers that she's been thinking that if the Border

Patrol catches them, he is the only one who won't get sent back. He is an American, he's already home. In case I do not have the chance later, she says, I want to say I am very grateful to you for helping me get this far.

I've been thinking about that, he whispers back. Listen and remember this. If we run into any kind of cops I'm a gringo reporter doing a story on illegal border crossers. You're my Mexican wife and came along to help my cover. They want proof of any of that, I can get it.

You can? How?

Never mind. I just can.

And you would tell the Border Patrol a . . . you would say that for me?

Don't worry, you're not going back. By next week you'll have a Texas birth certificate.

She hugs his arm and presses her face to his shoulder.

The sky remains solid black and the wind is still gusting, but Beto tells the group the clouds will soon break and they'll be able to make out the mountains ahead. They are probably within a stone's throw of them already. You are my best bunch ever, he says. Not even a dust storm could stop you. Come on, let's get going. No time to lose.

But the cloud ceiling does not break. And then the wind assumes an unmistakable scent and they hear the first rumble of thunder.

Oh wonderful, Beto says. *Now* the rain.

In the distance the sky abruptly brightens in an incandescent web of lightning and then goes black again and a prolonged roll of thunder follows.

Shit, Beto says. They said it was going to be a light one.

In another ten minutes bright jagged forks of lightning are coming one after the other, and each crackling thunderclap is louder than the one before and follows more closely on the heels of the lightning. Rain begins to pelt them in fat drops—and then comes crashing on them like a cataract, saturating them, rapping on their heads.

At least it will wash this damn dirt off us, the fat Fonseca says loudly, prompting a few dull snickers.

The lightning illuminates a ragged line of mesquites up ahead, and when they get there they see that the trees mark the bank of a wash thirty feet wide and five feet deep, its bed with a slight upward incline to their left. At the moment only a thin sheet of water is rushing over the sandy bottom but they all know what's coming.

Beto and the boy jump into the wash, and Beto yells up at the group, Quick! Hurry! Before it hits.

He sends the boy running to the opposite side to help the others out when they get there. As the chickens descend into the wash, Beto yells for them to go, go, shoving them past him.

In the glimmers of lightning Eddie and Miranda run splashing across the shallow current and Eddie boosts her up to the boy on the bank, who takes her hands and pulls her out. As Eddie scoots up beside them he feels the Taurus slip from his waistband and he tries to catch it but misses. He has an impulse to go down and get it, but the boy is already assisting the two Fonseca men to climb out, and he thinks the hell with it, they've made it to the States and are anyway still armed. Now the Fonsecas are out and helping the Martínez couple to get up the bank.

But the Sando uncle has fallen midway across the wash, his bag of goods whisked away on the stream. Beto was right behind him and stops to pull him to his feet, and the nephew runs back to help.

They half-drag the uncle to the bank and they're pushing him up to helping hands when Eddie feels the ground begin to quiver. And then, as the nephew starts to climb out, the flash flood erupts from the darkness roaring down the wash like a train, and snatches him and Beto away in a black blink.

On all fours at the edge of the bank, the boy yells, "Beto!" and leans out to try to see him—and the bank rim gives way under his hands and he plunges headfirst into the churning flood and is gone too.

They stand huddled close under the driving rain and stroboscopic lightning, nearly shouting to make themselves understood above the thunder and the booming of the current in the wash. All but the Sando uncle, who sits at a distance with his face in his hands.

They are agreed that all three are surely drowned. No one could survive a current like that. And who knows how far the water might carry their bodies? For miles. The Martínez woman says it's terrible that they can't bury them, and her husband agrees, but he agrees too with the lean Fonseca who says there's nothing they can do now but go on.

Go on where? the Panama guy says. We got no idea where the fuck we are.

We go due east, Eddie says. We'll come to—

East? the Panama guy says. Which way's *that*?

The way we were heading, straight across the wash, Eddie says. We keep going that way and we'll come to another low range. It can't be much farther. We go around it to our right and then follow a straight line a little to our left and we'll come to the road. I think we can still get there in time to get picked up.

How you know all that? the Panama guy says.

I heard the guide say it.

Yeah? Well I'm not so sure *he* knew what he was talking about. We could be heading into fucking nowhere. Listen, where I come from, a gully this size usually runs past some farms. I say we follow it to one and get some kind of ride from there.

A farm? Miranda says. Out here?

Nobody asked you, bitch.

Nobody asked you either, asshole.

What?

You heard me.

Eddie steps between them. You go whatever way you want, he says to the man, but I'm going the way I said. Anybody who wants to can come with me.

The man fumbles at his clothes and in the next blue radiance of lightning he is pointing a small semiautomatic pistol at Eddie.

They're all going with you, the man says. But the food and water goes with me. Now empty your bags. Everybody! *Now!* You, he says to the fat Fonseca, put it all in one.

They crouch to empty their bags on the muddy ground. Eddie takes off the backpack and unbuckles it and slips his hand inside and fingers the safety off the MAC and brings the gun up and in a single blazing burst fires its seven remaining rounds into the man's center mass, prompting shrieks from the Martínez woman and one of the men.

Under the shimmer of ghostly light the man lies supine and unmoving. The chickens hunched low. Eddie goes to him and picks up the gun—a .25-caliber—and chucks it away. He kneels and seeks a pulse in the man's neck but isn't sure he feels one or if it's only a shudder of the earth, the tremor of his own hand.

Miranda comes up beside him. Alive? she says.

I don't know.

Move, she says. He stands and steps aside and she points the Glock and shoots the man through the forehead, the yellow gun blast prompting another small cry from the Martínez woman.

Now we know, she says.

The others stay hunkered, too frightened to move. Lacking ammunition for the MAC, Eddie hurls it into the racing flood of the wash. The chickens are relieved to see him do it. And to see the girl put the pistol in her bag. Eddie again tells them they can come with him if they wish.

Who *are* you? the lean Fonseca says.

A guy who wants to get the hell out of here, same as you.

The Martínez man says something to his wife and she begins gathering the food and water they dumped out. We'll go with you, Martínez says. The Fonsecas say they will too, that it's best they all stick together, and they hasten to recover their meager supplies.

But the Sando uncle is gone. No one saw him leave. They shout for him between crashes of thunder. Did he run off in fear of the shooting? Go downstream to search for his nephew's body?

We can't go looking for him, Eddie says.

The Fonsecas agree. They have to keep going. They must get to the road in time to meet the pickup vehicle. Their cousin Alberto is waiting for them to return for him.

Miranda looks off toward the surging wash and says, You think maybe he . . .

I don't know, Eddie says.

"Ay Dios," the Martínez woman says, and makes a sign of the cross.

Eddie drags the Panama guy to the wash and rolls him into the torrent and the body is gone. Then he returns to his pack and picks it up. And pauses. And thinks, What if we don't find the road? What if the Panama guy was right and Beto wasn't sure where they were? What if they do find the road but don't get picked up? What if . . . ?

Do it, he thinks.

He sets the pack down again and hunches over it and slides his hand under the flap and feels around for the Sinas phone. He brings it up to the edge of the flap and opens it and is glad to see the screen light come on. It's reputed to be weatherproof and its battery to be a dynamo but he has no idea how much of its power has been drained since its last charge. He taps a short sequence of numbers.

There. You can't say you didn't try. They'll pick up the signal or they won't. Maybe try to help, maybe won't. Maybe can't.

If any of the others are curious about his action, none of them says so. He reseals the flap and slips the pack over his shoulders and starts walking. Miranda at his side, the others following.

They shortly come to a fence of sagging wire and the fat Fonseca wonders aloud what kind of ranch anyone could ever have tried to have in this wasteland. A goat ranch, maybe? the Martínez man says. "Un rancho de babosos," the lean Fonseca says, eliciting chuckles at the image of a fenced ranch of drooling idiots.

33

Martillo and Pico

They listen to CDs of the marimba-laden Jarocho music they are partial to and tell stories they've told each other many times before. They figure the kid's group is waiting out the dust storm, either in the pass or hunched down behind rock cover near one end of the range or the other.

When at length the dust ceases, they crank up the Rover and put the night goggles back on and drive until they can make out the east end of the pass that cuts through the Aguila Mountains. They park on a rise with a clear line of sight toward the pass mouth and over the open flats to the north and south, and there wait for the group to emerge from the pass or present itself at either end of the Aguila range.

I wish there was a moon, Pico says. We wouldn't have to wear these damn goggles.

If you're going to wish for what's not, why not for floodlights every quarter mile?

Hey, if I was going to wish for something that can't be, I'd wish for Penelope Cruz to be here to help pass the time. And for you, oh, Salma Hayek. How's that?

Martillo lifts his goggles to look at him, suspecting a gibe. He has always believed that his former wife bore a striking resemblance to the actress Salma Hayek, but never said so to anyone except to her. If Pico noted the likeness he never remarked on it, and Pico's mien at the moment as he scans the darkness suggests that the mention of the actress was a simple coincidence.

The horizon comes aglow on crooked legs of lightning. The darkness issues a long low snarl of thunder.

Do you believe *this*? says Pico.

We'll be able to see them more easily with the lightning, Martillo says. If it keeps up.

And if doesn't hit us, says Pico.

34

Rudy and Frank

We've been taking turns catnapping and watching the screen when the dust all of a sudden quits. The wind's still blowing but at least we can start patrolling for the Buddha's signal. We can both use some coffee before we set out, so I hustle down about three blocks to an all-night café to get some to go.

The place is jammed with guys who'd waited out the dust like us, and by the time I get back to the Cherokee with a couple of coffees and a dozen cinnamon churros, the sky's full of thunder and lightning. A double whammy of weird weather. Frank's as incredulous and as pissed as I am. We no sooner get the lids off our coffee and start up the Cherokee than the rain hits—coming at us on the wind like a sidewise waterfall.

There's even less chance of picking up Eddie's signal in this storm than there was in the dust. The smart thing to do would be to stay put and wait out the worst of this one too. But we're fed up with being stuck here, so the hell with the smart thing. Better to poke along at ten miles an hour in a thunderstorm and with no chance of getting the Buddha's signal than sit here another minute.

35

Eddie and Miranda

They walk and walk through the incessant storm. The night endless. They encounter other washes but luckily none so wide or deep as the one that took Sando, Beto, and the boy. But the currents are yet strong enough to knock you down should you make a faulty step, and they can drown you quick in less than three feet of water. They traverse some of the wider washes by way of large rocks, hopping from one to another in the tricky flickers of lightning, clutching briefly to each rock before hopping to the next. They cross some of the shallower washes by forming a chain of tightly linked hands and straining to keep their balance against the current's hard tug at their knees as they slowly sidestep across. At one ford Mrs. Martínez slips from her husband's grasp and only the fat Fonseca's tenacious grip on her wrist keeps her from being whisked away. He pulls her back to them and with Martínez's help gets her back on her feet. But the Martínez provisions are lost.

None among them has a watch. By Eddie's reckoning they should have come to the Viuda range by now, even with the slow crossings at the washes. Could they have strayed off course and missed the Aguilas altogether? Not very probable, he tells himself. It's just the storm confusing his sense of time, making it seem longer than it's actually been. The others are likely to be thinking the same thing. They walk on. The thunder and lightning lessen. The wind drops, and the rain dwindles to a drizzle. The blackness begins yielding to gray.

36

Martillo and Pico

Only by their watches do they know when the day has dawned. The black sky gives no indication of it. The storm now playing out but for light rain and lingering wind.

Pico lowers the night vision binoculars and says, I think maybe they went by some other way.

Maybe so, Martillo says, irked at the interruption of his reverie. He was thinking about his former wife, how she used to love thunderstorms, especially at night. She would run out into them and dance and come back to him sopping. The smell of her then. And when she woke beside him in the mornings. And after she finished a hard ride on her stallion or lay beside him on the beach at Acapulco while the sun dried the seawater on her skin. . . .

"Mira!" Pico says.

On the topographic receiver screen is the little red dot of the tracker signal. But now it's gone. And now it's back. Weak and wavering.

Fucker turned it on, Pico says.

I have eyes, Martillo says.

Jesus Christ, look where they are. Below the border. What the hell they doing *there*?

The dot disappears. Martillo gives the receiver a little slap.

Weather's still playing hell, Pico says.

The dot returns. Martillo adjusts the receiver map for a closer view of the topography.

Why turn it on down there? Pico says. What's going on?

Be quiet a minute.

They watch the screen.

Going south, Pico says. The fucking Sinas got him. That's why he turned it on.

Martillo shakes his head. If the Sinas had him, that tracker wouldn't still be on and moving at walking speed. All right, listen . . . we don't know how long ago he turned the thing on, how long before we could pick up the signal. But we know they had enough time to get to the Aguilas before the dust hit. Let's say they got there. If you're in a pass when the dust blows in and you're blind, what would you do? Besides curse God for a motherfucker?

Feel my way out along the wall. Like we were taught.

Naturally. So would any coyote who's any good. But look. If they started following the wall before they were past here—this narrow branching passage on the right. See?—they'd follow it, wouldn't they? Thinking they were still in the main pass.

Not if they followed the left side of the wall.

But if they had done that . . .

Yes, of course, they would have come out of the pass and we would have seen them. They went into the branch. Which would bring them around like this—Pico moves his finger along the screen—and they'd come out . . . down here. Facing back the way they came.

More southerly, actually.

But they think they're still going east. Toward the Viudas.

And will continue to think so until the sky clears up enough for them to realize where they are. By that time they're going to be even farther south.

So if they don't know they're lost, why'd he turn the thing on?

You can ask him.

Pico laughs. Let's go.

We can't go straight at them, Martillo says. Not over that terrain. The big washes will be running like white rivers. We have to circle around on the higher ground.

If we go down this way. Pico says—again running his finger over the screen—and cut west through here . . . it'll put us due south of them. If we get there before the sun shows, they'll come straight to us. And if before they get to us they realize they've fucked up and turn back, we just come up behind them.

A commendable plan.

Glad you like it, Pico says, and starts up the Rover.

37

Rudy and Frank

We have a couple of close calls crossing washes, neither of them very deep but both packing unbelievable force, Frank driving both times. The first one's so strong it nearly overturns us before we make the opposite bank, and the second picks us up—you know how much a Cherokee *weighs?*—and twirls us completely around as it carries us partway downstream before we luckily hit a shallow and the wheels grab and Frank's able to gun the Cherokee up the opposite bank. Hell of a driver, Frank. I'm pretty good too but I'm not sure I could've got us out of that one.

We keep at it for the rest of the night, chugging back and forth through the storm, which starts petering out shortly after dawn. Pretty soon it's down to a drizzle and a few last gusts of wind, but the sky's still black for a while longer before graduating to a bleak gray.

I'm doing a turn at the wheel when a red blip shows up on the screen. I stop the Cherokee and we watch the blip fade, disappear for a few seconds, then come back. Then we realize where he is. According to La Gata's message he'd said he was crossing last night, but the directional and distance readings have him 19.2 miles from us, to south-southwest as the crow flies—and still in Mexico. We watch the blip a while to see if he's moving.

He is. South.

"Maybe the chasers cut him off and it's the only way he can run," I say.

Frank spreads open the topo map and has me hold a flashlight on it while he uses a toothpick from his shirt pocket to make a scale according to the one on the map. In a minute he's got Eddie's present position at almost nine miles below the border.

He lays out a route that weaves us around the longest escarpments and the widest washes. Then says, "Let's go get his dumb ass."

I think about calling Tacho and Roberto to come give us a hand, then reject the idea. You don't ask a friend to risk his ass in your personal fight. Kin, yes, but not friends.

Frank probably had the same thoughts, but he didn't say anything. Why should he? He knows the rule.

38

Eddie and Miranda

The storm at last desists.

They're sure the hour is well past sunrise but the cloud layer is still so dense they can see no hint of the sun's location. In this gray light a mountain range takes form in the distance ahead.

"Al fin," the lean Fonseca says. There it is.

It's a low range but much longer than Eddie expected from Beto's description—and obviously a hell of a lot farther from the Aguilas than Beto had thought. But at least its southern end is almost straight ahead. The sight of it quickens their stride.

We'll never get to the pickup place in time, Martínez says.

Maybe we will, Eddie says. Maybe Beto was wrong about how long they would wait for us.

Wouldn't be the first thing he was wrong about, the fat Fonseca says.

The clouds thinning.

∽≫∼

They have just come over a low rise and started to head around a high outcrop when Mrs. Martínez says, Look!

They turn and see her pointing to their rearward left at the pale glow of sun through the waning overcast above a distant range.

They halt and look at it.

It's in the wrong place, Martínez says. His tone chiding, as if the sun were somehow confused.

I don't believe this, the lean Fonseca says.

Neither does Eddie. But disbelief isn't much of an argument against obvious proof.

It should be there, Mr. Martínez says, pointing in the direction they've been moving.

We're going the wrong way, the fat Fonseca says. We've *been* going the wrong way.

That stupid Beto son of a mangy bitch! his cousin says.

Eddie wonders how the guide could have been so wrong about the pass facing east. How they might have veered so far off course. How the sun could be so high already. The cloud cover is dispersing quickly, the sky brightening.

That fence we crossed, the lean Fonseca says. Hours ago. That wasn't no ranch fence.

Dear God, says Mrs. Martínez. Where are we?

I think back in Mexico, her husband says.

We're *miles* back in Mexico, says the lean Fonseca. Look how high that sun is! Oh, that goddamn bastard Beto!

What do we do? the Martínez woman says.

I don't know, her husband says. He looks around at the others.

There's nothing to do but go back to the border, Eddie says, and hope somebody comes along on one of those trails.

And if nobody comes along? the fat one says. We'll be fucked.

We'll follow the border to Sasabe, Eddie says, thinking he's the one who'll be truly fucked if it should be Sinas who find them. And in case we have to walk it all the way, he says, we better go easy with the water that's left.

Walk to Sasabe? the fat Fonseca says. How far is *that*? We'll fry to death.

I don't know, Eddie says. What would you prefer to do? Sit here and wait for God to send a helicopter?

My brother's waiting for me back in that pass, the other Fonseca says. I have to go back for my brother.

As soon as somebody finds us, we'll call the Border Patrol and they'll get your brother, Eddie says. Hell, maybe the Border Patrol will spot us before anybody else.

The clouds now scattering. Sunlight flooding the stark world. The heat rising fast.

We were going to Phoenix, Martínez says softly. We have work waiting for us in Phoenix.

Next time, Eddie says.

I have to rest for a minute, for only a minute, the Martínez woman says. She steps down into a wide wash along the foot of the outcrop, the wash bed already drained of the water that ran through it in the storm, and sits down with her back against the rock wall. Her husband kneels beside her and gives her a small drink of their last bottle of water.

Miranda squints up at the sun and then goes to the arroyo and crouches and opens her tote, takes out the Glock and slips it under her shirt into the front of her waistband, then rummages in the bag and finds her cap. She insists that the Martínez woman take it. It's going to be very hot, Miranda tells her. You'll need it more than I will. The woman protests but the husband accepts for her and thanks Miranda very much.

The Fonsecas are ranting about all the ways they would kill that whoreson Beto if he was still alive when the lean one says, Look! Out there, look!

Eddie turns and sees the black speck of a faraway vehicle coming from the north. His hand goes to his waistband before he remembers having lost the Taurus. The speck dips out of sight and then rises into view again as it advances over the contorted landscape.

The others come out of the arroyo to have a look. The fat Fonseca waves his arms over his head and yells, "Aquí! Estamos aquí!"

The lean one calls him an idiot. You think they can hear you? They can't even *see* us yet.

The vehicle again goes out of view behind the near rise flanking them. And then—with a sound none of them has ever heard before—much of Mrs. Martínez's head disintegrates in a red spray an instant before they hear the rifle shot.

39

Martillo and Pico

They are behind rock cover on a ledge near the base of the mountain's north slope. Through the binoculars they can see the tiny figures of the chickens coming toward them from north-northeast under the gray sky. Six of them.

They have decided to take him alive if they can. It's worth the large bonus and out here it shouldn't be hard to do. A crippling shot but make sure he doesn't bleed to death. Get him to Nogales and ship him to the big chief of the Sinas by way of a sub-boss. First take a picture of him with the day's newspaper to prove they had him alive—in case something happens to the kid en route to Culiacán. But even if they have to kill him, they can still collect a bonus for his head. The rest of the chickens of course they will kill.

They could hit them from here but the group is still too far away and the light too weak to let them distinguish—even through the scopes—which one is Porter, never mind be sure of a nonfatal hit. So they wait and watch the group draw nearer as the clouds thin out.

The chickens come over a low rise and descend it and stop. Four men, two women—one very shorthaired but with obvious tits. Watching them through binoculars, Martillo and Pico see that only now has the group become aware of the sun's position. They grin at the chickens' gesticulations, their great surprise at realizing where they are. The things they must be saying.

The clouds are beginning to give way to the heat of the sun, the daylight brightening fast. At four hundred yards the chickens look almost close enough in the scopes to hit with a hard-thrown rock but their features are not distinct. One man clearly too old to be the kid, one obviously too fat. They are fairly sure which of the other two is Porter, but fairly is not sure enough, so they will not kill either of the two from here. Cripple both, then go see. They decide which of the possible Porters each of them will shoot. Martillo will then kill the rightmost other two chickens, Pico the other pair.

But now the women and the older man go out of view behind an outcrop, and Pico curses. They would prefer to have all of them in sight and put them down before anyone can even think to take cover. But what the hell, it doesn't really matter. The two possible Porters are among the three men out in the open. When those three go down, the most likely reaction of the three behind the outcrop will be to come out into the open in stunned incredulity and look around. Then it's pow-pow-pow for them.

Martillo bends to his scope. Set?

"Oye," Pico says. And points north.

A tiny dark dot of a vehicle. Heading toward them but yet miles away. Its speed checked by the rough ground.

Sinas, I'll bet, Pico says. They must've found out the kid's got the tracker and homed on him. One car, though. Can't be a half dozen of them at the most.

Most likely just two or three, Martillo says. Fewer who get him, the fewer to share the reward.

We drop them? Their chief might not like it.

Affecting a tone of self-justification, Martillo says, We had no choice, Mr. Bossman. How could we know they were Sinas? They came driving up like federals, didn't say who they were, didn't say shit, just started shooting. We responded in self-defense, as you would have. I guess they wanted the reward all for themselves.

Pico laughs. You know, you're such a good liar even I believe you. You could write novels, Humberto. Maybe even movies.

Certainly I could. But where's the satisfaction in that kind of life? He looks out at the distant vehicle. They'll be another twenty minutes getting there, maybe more. We'll do the chickens, then deal with these.

They put their eyes to the scopes and see that the chickens have spied the vehicle too and all of them are now out in the open. Very cooperative, Pico says.

Hey now, Martillo says. The black-and-orange cap. It's what they were wearing. The bitch and the kid.

And still together, Pico says. Must be love.

Martillo makes a sound of disgust and says, I'll pop her first, they freeze, you drop the left Porter and the two beside him, I drop the right two. Set?

Set.

Martillo shoots and then Pico—and with the smoothness of swift machines they work the bolts and each shoots twice more and in five seconds all in the group are down.

40

Eddie and Miranda

The abrupt destruction of Mrs. Martínez's head arrests them where they stand—and even as the woman is falling, the lean Fonseca's leg jerks oddly and he cries out and then Eddie's leg is knocked from under him and he falls and strikes his head hard.

When he opens his eyes he senses having been unconscious but cannot guess for how long. A few seconds? Minutes? He is on his back, looking at the white sky. His head throbs. Someone close by is whimpering. Eddie tries to sit up and falls back with a cry at the surge of pain in his left leg.

His next awareness is of being on his side with his cheek in his own sandy vomit. He was out again, and again without an inkling of how long. He can see now a jagged segment of his left shinbone jutting from the bloody wound. The nearby whimpering persists.

A hand closes on his shoulder from behind and he is yanked onto his back and cannot stifle another cry at the jounce of his leg.

A rifle muzzle inches from his face. A thin figure in a hat looms blackly over him against the brightness of the sky.

"Este's el!" the figure calls. Then squats and pats Eddie down and strips the money belt off him and peeks into it. My goodness, the man says, what a very well-to-do chicken we have here. He drapes the money belt over his shoulder and removes the belt from Eddie's pants, and Eddie cries out again as the man binds it in a tourniquet directly above the wound. The man grins at him and says, When you run for it, kid, it's best to know north from south.

The thin man looks over at the whimpering man, the lean Fonseca, then rises and walks over to him, the rifle dangling from his hand like an outsize pistol.

Help me, Fonseca says. Please.

Certainly, the thin man says. And shoots him dead-center in the forehead.

The fat Fonseca lies a few feet from his cousin, arms and legs flung wide. Farther off, Mr. Martínez is sprawled half-sitting against a thick creosote shrub, his head at an awkward tilt on a neck nearly severed by the Magnum round, a wide stripe of blood down his shirtfront.

Miranda?

Eddie turns his head the other way and sees her not six feet from him. On her stomach, face toward him but mostly obscured by her arm, one eye visible and closed. The ground beneath her dark with blood. He cannot tell if she's breathing.

He hears voices and turns to see the thin man now atop the outcrop and standing next to a large man crouched behind a pair of boulders, peering out between them. They are looking off in the direction of the coming vehicle.

"Chacho." Her timbre thin. . . .

Martillo and Pico

They hear her weak call and look over and see her on her stomach, one arm stretched out toward the kid. Who starts crawling toward her.

So! *She's* the bitch, Pico says.

Excellent shooting, Joselito.

She moved, man.

Then this time put the muzzle against her head. In case she moves. I'll take care of these guys.

Martillo returns his attention to the scope. The vehicle is now about 250 yards away. An SUV with two men in it. It's on slightly more level ground and isn't swaying so much now but its route is still winding. He lets them draw closer, sighting on the driver.

As Pico comes off the rise, Martillo shoots—and says "Chingado!" as he works the bolt and fires again.

Pico hoots and says, Oh dear, did somebody miss?

They dipped just as I fired.

Yes! That's what *she* did! She dipped. "Pues?"

Hit the driver. Maybe got a piece of the other. They're in an arroyo. I can see the roof.

Martillo detaches the Sako's box magazine though it still holds two rounds and replaces it with a full seven-round box and works the bolt, then glances at his watch and again peers though the scope. Bastards aren't going anywhere, he says. Show me just part of a head and they lose it. We'll give them ten minutes. They don't come out, we'll drive down and finish them.

Whatever you say, my large friend, Pico says. Then turns to watch Porter crawling toward the girl, who says, Chacho, I can't . . . I *can't.*

Bet you a thousand pesos he doesn't reach her inside the next minute, Pico says, and checks his watch.

Just shut her up, Martillo says.

41

Rudy and Frank

The tracker signal hasn't moved in a while and we're wondering what the hell's happening. The signal's coming from less than a quarter mile ahead and on the other side of a low rise, and we're snaking our slow way there. I keep shifting from the receiver screen to the binocs, scanning the little rise but seeing no sign of anybody.

We're little more than two hundred yards from the tracker and I glimpse something on the crest of an outcrop behind the rise—a light reflection? At the same moment, the left front wheel hits a rut and the Cherokee dips to the left as a hole pops through the windshield and we hear the shot. Frank grunts and his right arm jerks off the wheel and he one-hands the Cherokee to the left and a second round smacks through the glass and takes off the top of the gearshift lever.

Frank bounces us down into a wide gully and brakes hard. The windows are below ground level and I'm pretty sure we're out of the shooter's line of sight, but he might still see our roof.

I snatch up a carbine and lower my window, then reach over and cut off the engine and listen hard for the sound of a coming vehicle. But all I hear is a raven squall twice and then nothing but our own breathing. The tracker signal on the screen hasn't moved.

Frank's leaning forward, holding his bloody shoulder and breathing through his teeth. There's a big smear of blood on his seat back and a bullet hole in it. I ask if he can work the arm. He does so with a snarl of pain, then says he'd rather not do it again. But if he can work it, it's not that bad. I set the carbine against the door and tell him to let me see. He flinches when I wipe at the blood and see the humerus. Half an inch over and the shoulder joint would've been blown apart. "Mostly tissue damage but mighta chipped bone," I say. "Bleeding's slow."

He takes out the Beretta with his left hand and flicks off the safety, and I get out my pocketknife and cut off his shirtsleeve and tell him to man up. He grits his teeth and growls like a pissed-off dog while I quickly bind the shoulder with the sleeve.

"That'll hold it."

He nods and blows a couple of long breaths, sweat streaming off his face.

No telling how many they are, but he agrees with my hunch that it's not more than two or they'd have hit us with a volley instead of just two shots. For sure they're waiting for us to peek out. The nearest outside cover is about ten yards away, a thick growth of prickly pear cactus stretching fifteen feet or so along the edge of the bank. If I can find a peephole through it and spot them before they spot me. . . . But they've got the edge. We don't know where they are on that rock but they know exactly where we are and know the cactus patch is our only cover. They're going to be fixed on it and ready to shoot at the first sign of movement behind it.

But you make do with what you got. I open the door and slip out with the M-4, hoping they don't have enough angle to see the top of the door and know at least one of us is on the move.

I hustle over to the cactus in a crouch and find a gap in it much like a rifle port in some old garrison—more than a foot wide and almost as deep. Gives me enough latitude to scan their ridge and prop my barrel on the bank without it sticking out of the cactus and giving me away. I set the selector on three-round and settle myself and start panning through the scope . . . slow left, slow right. . . .

42

Eddie and Miranda

He crawls on his side to keep the jutting shinbone from snagging on the ground, but every movement jostles the wound and evokes a small cry he isn't even aware of. He is almost to her hand now. Staring hard at him, she says, Chacho . . . I can't . . . *do* it. Her eyes bright with pain but telling him something more.

He crawls up to her until his face is almost to hers.

Damn you, kid, the thin man says behind him. You just cost me a thousand pesos.

Eddie looks over his shoulder and sees him a few feet away, regarding them with a small smile and again holding the rifle like a pistol. Pointing it at them.

Better move your head, boy, he tells Eddie. I haven't been shooting real good today.

Please, she says. Let him . . . kiss me. . . . Please.

Kiss you? Pico says. Jesus, girl, you in a *movie* or what?

Ah, man, Eddie gasps.

Pico lowers the muzzle and grins. I am *such* a fool for romance, he says. Do it quick. Too bad you can't make it a last fuck. Be more fun to watch.

Eddie pulls himself closer to her and rises on his elbows and she partly turns her face up to his with a whimper. He puts his left hand to her cheek and kisses her gently. His back blocks Pico's view of his right hand sliding under her, feeling the heat of her blood. She groans.

"Ya, basta," Pico says. Move your head, kid.

Eddie ends the kiss and gingerly starts to shift himself out of the line of fire—then whips out the Glock she lacked the strength to withdraw and shoots Pico three times in the span of a second, the first bullet hitting him just above the heart, the second in the junction of the collarbone, the third passing through an eye and removing a portion of the back of his head. As he falls, Pico reflexively triggers a round that ricochets off the stony earth a foot from Eddie's head.

On the outcrop the big man jumps up with an expression of shocked rage. Eddie fires at him and part of the man's left ear vanishes—and the pistol's slide locks back, all bullets spent. The man starts to raise his rifle and then makes a jerky sidestep to the distant chirp of an automatic rifle and he drops out of Eddie's sight.

Be dead, be dead, Eddie thinks.

The man yells, Mother . . . *fuckers!*

Eddie cannot think what to do. There is no cover he can crawl to. The man is wounded but maybe still capable of getting up and shooting him from up there. He's got me, Eddie thinks. And waits.

Then comes the sound of an engine starting up on the other side of the outcrop and then a vehicle rumbling away.

43

Rudy and Frank

I've made only a couple of scans through the scope when I hear a distant rush of handgun poppings and a single rifle crack from somewhere ahead. I catch a movement of something at the rim of the outcrop as the scope passes over it and I cut back to it as the handgun pops again and I see the top half of a large figure silhouetted against the sky and I squeeze off a three-rounder....

44

Eddie

He manages to get up and hops on one foot over to the thin man's Remington police rifle, oblivious of his own outcries at the pain of his maimed shin. When he stoops to pick up the weapon he loses his balance and screams when he falls on the wound. Then he's up again and hopping over to the outcrop, shrieking like a berserker. He flings the rifle up to the crest and then climbs the slope on both hands and one foot.

He sees the orange Land Rover winding away through the broken badland, angling around toward the border. Then looks northward and is puzzled not to see the vehicle that had been coming. And then it backs out of an arroyo, a dark SUV he would guess at two hundred yards, and it starts coming again.

He spots the Rover guy's rifle lying on the ground. A Sako. He hops over to it, whimpering, and carefully lowers himself to pick it up. He'll do what he can against the ones coming, but if they're going to kill him he can at least see to it right now that the one in the Rover doesn't get away from them either.

He eases himself to a prone position, yowling with his pain, then takes up the Sako and chambers a round and braces the barrel on a rock to steady his sighting. He peers into the scope but his vision is hazed and he wipes away the pain tears and puts his eye to the scope again.

He's certain the Rover has bulletproof glass and so concentrates on the tires. He fires and the left rear of the Rover abruptly sags. Yes! He chambers a round and wipes his eyes again and resights and with the next shot flattens the right-side back tire. The Rover presses on but its progress is perceptibly slowed, its weaving course more ungainly. He watches it in the scope and waits till it alters course enough to give him a sight line on a front tire. And with the next shot blows out the left one.

Still the thing drives on. Not gonna get too far on three flats, bubba, Eddie thinks, working the bolt. Then again, who knows? Better get that last one. But as he waits for a clear sight on the right front tire his focus begins to blur.

Don't fade, he tells himself, don't. . . .

His head slumps off the rifle stock and into the dirt.

45

Martillo

Oh, those cocksuckers! Those eaters of shit! Sons of mangy bitch whores!

A three-round burst, he'd heard it distinctly. M-4. Two hits. One in the left ass cheek which hurts plenty but the one through his lower ribs is the one he's worried about. Kidney's probably fucked. He's known worse pain and the wound's not a gusher, but it's red enough it could be a nicked artery. Need a doc fairly soon. Otherwise he'd circle back right now and put all those cocksuckers—

Bam! The left rear tire collapses. Jesus. That's gotta be Porter, the Sinas can't be there yet. Fucking kid! Busted leg and kills Pico and still gets up there and—

Bam! The Rover's right rear sags. Oh, you little bastard! You little rat cunt. Oh, you . . . He feels something on the side of his neck and puts his fingers to it and they come away bloody, then explores his left ear and learns a segment of it is missing. That little shit!

He would pay any price for the opportunity to teach Porter something about pain. But what chance of that? Those Sinas closing in will have the kid's head in Culiacán before the sun sets.

Well, no matter, Martillo thinks. He'll find out who they are, those bastards who shot him. Find them and at least get the satisfaction of giving them pain they've never even imagined.

Bam! The left front dips.

His fury is of some avail against the agony in his side as he wrestles the crippled Rover over the uncertain ground. But now the shredded tires have come off their rims one after another and he thinks this must be what it feels like to drive a very shitty tank. Not even a Rover's going to get very far on three rims over ground like this. He calls Gómez on the satellite phone and the man makes him repeat himself several times even though the connection sounds clear enough to Martillo. He tells Gómez the coordinates of the border location where he can meet him, Gómez again making him repeat himself before finally saying he's on his way.

Gómez will get him to a Sinas doctor in Nogales and that'll be that. A little healing, then start hunting for the fuckers who shot him.

He's driving over a series of rocky rises, from the crests of which he can now see the border fence just fifty, sixty yards ahead. The horizon already quivering with ground heat. Then he hits soft sand at the bottom of a rise and the Rover mires.

God *damn* it! Now he's got to walk to the fence and wait in the sun for Gómez. He manages to get his door open but when he starts to step out the world tilts and he falls headlong.

What the hell? It takes all his effort to sit up. His hat. He needs his hat from the front seat. And his pistol. Hat and pistol and he'll be set. Fucking desert sun. Ni modo. Another fifty yards and there you are. Fence. Border. He tries to stand and falls over. . . .

It's a labor to open his eyes. The lids gummy. His right cheek burning in the sand. He can't make sense of the black shape he's seeing in front of him. Then recognizes it as the horizontal form of a huge raven standing very close to his face, black feathers gleaming. And now another beside it. He hears the raucous calls of still others close by. The two ravens step closer, black eyes bright, bills parted. One of them croaks and Martillo would swear it said, "Cuato." Then the other bobs its head at him and Martillo's left eye goes black.

He gasps in shock and tries to lift his head but is unable. Can shift it only somewhat to better see with the remaining eye as the other raven pecks into the left socket too and he sees the red slime extracted on its beak. He wants to scream at them. Frighten them away. But he cannot summon the breath. . . .

Gómez will not find any sign of Martillo at the coordinates he was given. But he will have in mind that there was great pain in Martillo's voice and perhaps the man was not very clear in the head. So he will drive on, slowly, keeping a sharp eye, and after a time will see at a distance the low swirl of buzzards. He will finally arrive at a spot on the fence about fifty yards south of a high sandy rise, behind which the buzzards are alighting and where ravens are hopping about. He will consider the situation for a minute or two, then turn his car around and head back for Nogales. And all the way back he will be looking forward to his wife getting home from her job at the maquiladora and to kissing her and taking great pleasure in whatever she will cook for their supper.

Seventeen days will pass before anyone discovers the Rover. A trio of Papago scavengers on one of their regular truck searches along the most isolate areas of the border will happen upon it. You never know what you might find jettisoned by border crossers in these badlands, or, sometimes better still, in the packs and pockets of the dead. The Rover will be their largest bonanza in years. The vehicle in excellent condition but for the lack of three tires. A pair of Magnum revolvers. Two tracker receivers. Four binoculars, two of them infrared. A satellite phone. A Rolex wristwatch and excellent boots and a fine suit needing only a thorough cleansing to rid it of the various stains imposed on it by the half-withered corpse. Nearly five thousand pesos and more than seven hundred dollars in its pockets. Four gold teeth in the dead man's mouth. After stripping the body they will bury it, but on their return from Tucson with the tires and a generator pump to inflate them they will find that the corpse has been exhumed by coyotes and reduced to a ragged thing of bones hung with a few scraps of black flesh. Even the skull largely flensed. They will not reinter these remains, which a few hours later are all that will be left behind in the fiery light of the setting sun.

46

Rudy and Frank

We find six of them behind the rise, all shot, five of them dead—
four men, one woman. The ants already busy at eyes and mouths.
The dead woman missing half her head. Man, those Magnums.
The other woman's still breathing but hit bad and unconscious.
Younger than the dead one. Maybe the one he was running with.

There's a Glock lying there and I pick it up and tuck it in
my belt. The only other weapon in sight is a Remington cop rifle
in a guy's hand. Frank stands over him and says, "Look familiar?"

The dead man's missing an eye and it takes me a second to
recognize the bullethead Félix almost got into it with in Nogales.
World's smaller all the time. There's a money belt beside him
and I pick it up and see it's holding a bunch of hundred-dollar
bills, then fasten it around my waist.

Frank finds the tracker phone in a backpack we assume is
Eddie's.

But no Eddie.

Not till we go up on the outcrop and find him belly-down
and unconscious, with a belt tourniquet above a shinbone that's
badly shot but still in one piece. His pulse strong, though, respira-
tion good. A Sako rifle next to him, a pair of binoculars.

I scan with the glasses and spot an orange vehicle slowly
moving northward. "It's that Rover from Nogales," I say. "Big
fucker was driving, remember?"

"Yeah. Well, he's the big fucker who gets away," Frank says.

"Must've been him I shot. I know I hit him."

"Well, there's hitting and there's hitting."

I give him a look he ignores.

Eddie moans as I haul him upright, doing my best to keep his weight off the bad leg. Frank does what he can to help get him up on my shoulder. The kid's solid and heavier than he looks. I hear him puke and feel it sop the back of my shirt at the waist.

I ease my way down the slope and then carry him over to the Cherokee and lay him on the back seat. He says something too slurred to catch, then his eyes open, red and glassy with pain. "Miranda," he says. And passes out again.

Frank brings the Sako and the Remington and gets on the satellite to Félix, telling him as much as he can without getting too specific, in case of intercepts. But Félix is an old hand at improvised phone code and gets the picture pretty quick. He says he's sure his man "T" can make the necessary arrangements and says he'll get back to us quick as he can.

Now there's only the girl. We go over to her and I tell Frank her name's Miranda. If it's her. Breathing shallow and raspy. Pulse weak. The round hit her in the back and punched out a hole under her left tit big enough to fit your fist in. God's own wonder she's still among the quick.

"Nothing to do," I say.

Frank gives me a look of a sort I don't often get from him.

"She's lung-shot, Frankie. She won't even make it to the car and you know it."

"It's probably her," he says. "Tell me we should leave her while she's still ticking. Let me hear you say that."

I take all the care I can getting her into my arms, but she gives a deep groan, even as out as she is.

I'm almost to the Cherokee, her blood soaking warm through my clothes, when the feel of her changes. I stand there holding her while Frank searches her throat for a pulse. Then I set her down and go through her pockets. A switchblade and some Mex money but nothing in the way of ID.

The best we can do is cover her over with big rocks.

The others we leave to the scavengers.

I take off my shirt and toss it away. The dead guy nearest to being my size is the bullethead, so I strip him of his shirt and put it on. It smells like coal smoke.

We're swaying and jarring eastward when Eddie says, "Hey?"

Frank turns in the shotgun seat and I crane my head to look at Eddie in the rearview.

"Miranda?" he says.

"I'm sorry, kid," Frank says.

Eddie closes his eyes.

Eddie

He feels the reverberant earth passing under him, growling through the floor of the Cherokee like some badland spirit in a tremoring rage to get at him. He wants to weep. Howl. Wants to shoot something. But only lies there closed-eyed and tight-jawed in his red pain.

He considers yelling for them to stop, turn around, go back for her, take her with them. Bury her at sea. In the Gulf she would have loved.

So that her spirit won't feel like it's holding its breath until it can get back to where it belongs.

Then thinks how goddamn stupid he is. There isn't any her anymore or even any spirit of her except in his head. And she'll either stay there or she won't.

And thinks how even stupider it is to believe there's any possibility she might not stay there until there's no more him either.

47

The Boss and Tiburón

In the company of El Tiburón, Flores, and a trio of bodyguards, the Boss exits his Culiacán headquarters through its double section of foyers and its triple sets of barred, electronically controlled doors with armed guards at each set. The five-story building bears a large sign identifying it as Relámpago Finanzas, SA and its network of security cameras is monitored round the clock by a crew in a room on the mezzanine.

The Boss has many things on his mind at present, among them the chafing lack of any word from Martillo about his search for Porter. Would it be such an inconvenience for the bastard to take a minute to call and say how the thing is going? If he has a lead on the kid? If he's crossed into the north in pursuit of him? He's not obligated to submit reports, no, but couldn't he do it as a favor, a sign of respect, one man to another? Not that arrogant son of a bitch. Martillo may be the best at what he does, but the Boss has very nearly decided that he will not deal with the smug prick again.

They descend the wide stone steps from the building entrance to the cars waiting at the curb, the Boss's car parked between the two bodyguard SUVs. A front-foyer guard pokes his head out the door and calls down to Tiburón that there's a phone call for him from Mexico City that claims to be urgent. Does he want to come take it or have the security guys transfer it to his phone?

Tiburón pats his coat pockets and says to the Boss, Shit, I left it on my desk. I'll meet you at the Cocina. He jogs back up the steps and into the building.

The lead SUV pulls out, the Boss's Town Car behind it and followed closely by the rear guard vehicle. Almost every day the Boss has lunch in a private, well-guarded room at the Yaqui Cocina restaurant, a place in his old neighborhood and across the street from a police station whose every man is on the Sinas payroll. Each time they go there, his driver proceeds by a different one of a dozen routes, depending on which one Tiburón has told him to follow.

Tiburón prefers to take the call on his own phone and waits in the lobby for the security man to come down with it. Then he walks off a short way for privacy before saying, "Bueno."

He expects it to be an underling assigned the job of making this call to detach him from the Boss's party, but instead hears the familiar voice of the rabidly ambitious young man named Jaime Montón Delacruz, better known as El Chubasco. During recent weeks Tiburón has had a half dozen clandestine meetings and a number of phone talks with him, the upshot of which has been El Chubasco's assurance of Tiburón's imminent chieftainship of all Sinas operations between the border and Ciudad Obregón.

Today's route is as you said? Chubasco asks.

Of course.

Good. I was certain it would be.

There are several seconds of silence and then Tiburón says, Is there something more?

Ah, you wonder why I've called. Well, simply to share the moment.

Share the moment?

Listen.

More seconds pass.

And then Tiburón hears it. Half the city hears it.

But no one can ever know if the Boss and those in the car with him as it made a turn at an intersection heard anything more than the tap against the windshield in the millisecond before the rocket-propelled grenade blasted the car into flaming fragments....

Not a minute later, as Tiburón and the building guards stand on the sidewalk, gazing toward the rising black smoke in the distance—Tiburón thinking, You should have given me what I deserved, you should have—three vehicles abruptly pull up directly in front of them and Tiburón sees the smiling face of El Chubasco behind a passenger window as men jump out of the far-side doors and raise automatic weapons above the car roofs.

In that last second of his life, like a man proud of his excellent health who suddenly learns he has a metastasized cancer, El Tiburón, who regards himself as a man of sage practicality, is profoundly saddened by the knowledge that he is dying of a stupid greed.

48

Rudy and Frank

It's a small hospital at the edge of town, owned on paper by a highly reputable medical association, Félix tells us. In fact it's an Azteca property. Félix had spoken to Trejo, who then spoke to some people, and by the time we arrived in Nogales both Frank and Eddie were already registered admissions under false names. Trejo had also arranged for guards to be posted both inside and out, some in medical dress, some clothed as janitors or groundskeepers.

Frank gets patched up in less than an hour—wound debrided and stitched, shoulder bandaged, arm in a sling. He's lucky. The bone was only nicked, like I'd thought. The docs don't expect any complication from it. Trejo's guys bring us fresh clothes and we clean up in a bathroom.

Eddie's in surgery for two hours. Afterward the doctor explains the process but all I really catch is that the shin was set with a plate and screws. The great danger is of bone infection but the doc says he's certain they've precluded that possibility.

When Eddie's rolled into a room, we go in to see him but he's still sleeping off the anesthesia. His leg's in a blue plastic cast from foot to just below the knee.

"His color's good," Frank says. It's what our grandmother used to say in favorable judgment of somebody's medical condition or recuperative progress. And I feel myself grin for the first time in a while.

The whole thing was going to cost us a pretty penny, but we've had time enough to arrange everything before we come back to Eddie's room at dusk. He's sitting up and cleaning off the last of his supper plate. A little glassy-eyed with pain and meds, but ravenous, a good sign. Frank asks how he's doing and Eddie says okay.

We'd already decided to let him take the conversational lead, give us an idea of the lay of his psychic land, but he only looks back at us without expression, now at me, now at Frank. I think he really doesn't know what to say. He looks down at his hand and works it open and closed, like he's just learned how to do it.

"I think the word you might be looking for is thanks," Frank says.

"Yeah," he says, still looking at his hand. "Thanks."

"Hell, kid, don't mention it," Frank says. He tells Eddie the doc says he can travel in a couple of days.

"I can travel now."

"You gotta be hurting," I say. "Probably best not to push it."

"I'm ready," he says. "Let's go."

It's what we were hoping to hear.

Félix pulls up at the front door in the Cherokee, and we hustle out to it, Eddie wheelchaired out by one of the Trejo guards. We set him on the back seat and I sit behind him. The Trailblazer follows us with Roberto at the wheel and Tacho riding shotgun. Another half hour and we're through the Nogales port of entry and heading for Texas.

Frank and I haven't informed anyone that Eddie's okay, and I ask him if he'd like us to call his folks or maybe Aunt Cat, let them know he's headed home.

He says no. He'll do the notifying when he gets there.

He keeps trying to nap, but even though he's pumped to the gills with painkiller he obviously can't sleep, and he finally sits up and stares out the window, face pinched with pain.

"Hey?" Frank says. "Who'd you kill to get them on your ass like that?"

Eddie leans back on the seat and closes his eyes, like he didn't even hear the question. But then says, "Guy who hit her."

We're well into New Mexico before Eddie speaks again.

"I'm going back to school."

We wait for more but that's it.

Then again, what more is there?

It's nearly eleven o'clock when we take off from the same field north of El Paso in the same Beechcraft that landed me and Frank there two nights ago.

It's been hours since Eddie's last pill. He keeps shifting in his seat and groaning low, like he's trying to find some position that will accommodate the pain. I offer him another OxyContin but he shakes his head, then sits slumped with his forehead against the window and stares out at the blackness.

We're across the aisle from him, Frank with a ratty paperback of *Winner Take Nothing,* which he's read God know how many times, me with a book of crossword puzzles I picked up at the hospital.

About a half hour into the flight Eddie says, "Hey?"

We look at him. He's still facing out the window.

"How come you did it?"

"What?" I say.

"You know. . . . Come for me."

We just look at him.

He turns to us. "It a rule or what? I never heard it said is why I'm asking."

We stare at him another few seconds before Frank says, "Yeah, well. There's some you don't hear said a lot."

Eddie cuts his eyes from one of us to the other. And nods. Then turns back to the window.

Frank regards him a moment longer, eyes narrow. Assessing. Then turns to me and winks and gets back to his book.

A minute later Eddie leans back in his seat and closes his eyes, grimacing and grunting low as he shifts this way and that before sighing in a way that has nothing to do with having found comfort, and settles himself.

EPILOGUE

Catalina

She wakes in deep darkness. And knows he's alive. In pain but alive. And on his way home. Knows these things without knowing how she knows.

Her open windows show no stars and the earlier sliver of moon has long since set. A light wind rustles the palm fronds and ebony leaves. As always in this dark hour she can smell the river on its way to the sea. And smells too the coming rain. It did not rain as predicted last night, or today, but she can smell it on the air now and knows it is nearing swiftly. A relief from the swelter of recent days.

Ah, the days. They come and they come until they no longer do, but for some uncommon few such as herself they have come beyond all equitable allotment. She once told the boy that if he lived long enough he would find the years passing more swiftly than he could believe. He had smiled at her with youth's amused condescension toward the old. In her own childhood—so distant now it seems a myth—she no doubt showed the same smile when her Grandmother Gloria alleged that each year was now nothing more than Friday and Christmas.

She slips her hand under the pillow to feel the comfort of the bone-handled Apache knife with which at sixteen she killed two men and which in her will she has bequeathed to the boy. The weapon was a gift from her great-grandfather Edward Little on the celebration of her quinceañera. He whom she called Buelito. Who taught her much about the turns of the world and who loved no one but her just as she loved none other than him. Until this one named after them both and who from the moment she first saw him as a babe has reminded her of Buelito. Who can say why these things are?

She rises and puts on her robe and goes to a chair by a window and sits looking out into the darkness. Then the first drops are ticking into the trees and she breathes deep the earthy aroma of the closing rain.